He was moving toward her, closing the space between them. She took one step back, then another, until she was pressed to the wall with nowhere to run.

"You're afraid," Sammy stated. "What are you afraid of, Rachel?"

"Nothing."

"Tell me the truth. Your're afraid of me, aren't you? I've seen it in your face before, I can see it in your face now. Sometimes you look up from that notebook of yours and catch me staring. And I can tell it bothers you. Why does it bother you, Rachel?"

When she didn't answer, he asked, "Do you ever wonder what I'm thinking when I'm watching you?"

She swallowed.

"Want to know?"

She shook her head.

"No? But you're a shrink. You're supposed to want to hear my deepest, darkest secrets. Isn't that right? My deepest, darkest desires."

His voice was rough, threatening . . . and heaven help her, sensual.

She brought up her hand. Fingers splayed, she pressed against his chest, trying to hold him back, but he didn't move. . . .

FOREVER

FOREVER
Theresa Weir

BANTAM BOOKS
NEW YORK • TORONTO • LONDON • SYDNEY • AUCKLAND

To Carrie Feron, editor extraordinaire.

Thanks for opening the doors and inviting me in.

It's just too bad you couldn't stay for the party.

This edition contains the complete text
of the original hardcover edition.
NOT ONE WORD HAS BEEN OMITTED.

FOREVER

A Bantam Fanfare Book

PRINTING HISTORY

Doubleday edition published September 1991
Bantam edition / November 1991

ISBN 0-553-29380-X

Published simultaneously in the United States and Canada

Printed in the United States of America

RAD   0 9 8 7 6 5 4 3 2 1

ONE

HE WASN'T DEAD.

His head hurt too much for him to be dead.

When the pain peaked to a point where he couldn't stand it anymore, Sammy cried out. Then a nurse came and jabbed a needle into his thigh, and off he went, back to never-never land.

Gradually the periods between the peaks of pain lengthened, and little by little he became groggily aware of his surroundings, enough for him to sometimes realize that he was in a hospital.

He noted the passing of time, of whole days and nights, of rough hands turning him and jabbing him.

As the pain became less severe, it was replaced by all sorts of unpleasant sensory perceptions, the most ceaseless being a high-frequency sound, like a radio tuned to nothing. There were other sounds, sounds worse than the constant whine of the radio.

Voices.

Unfamiliar voices. Moaning voices, seeming to echo through a long, corrugated tunnel. He hoped they'd stay at the other end of that tunnel.

Sammy tried to ignore the sounds. Sometimes he could. But the smells were another story. They permeated the air, made him want to breathe through his mouth instead of his nose. Smells of greasy food, unwashed bodies, and pine disinfectant.

Not home.

Definitely not home. And not summer camp. Definitely not summer camp.

Wherever he was, Sammy didn't like it, so he tried to stay hidden.

That's the ticket. Keep your head down. Never sit with your back to the door. Never give 'em more than your name, rank, and serial number. And blood type. It was a good idea to know your blood type. Sammy's was A. Not rare, but not as common as, say O positive.

Blood type . . . blood type . . . Gotta be a joke there somewhere. A joke could be found in everything.

Okay. He had it.

GI walks up to a girl in a bar. Says, "Hello, sweetheart." She reads his dog tags. "A," she says. "Not my type."

Corny-joke drum roll. Da-*dum*.

Guy goes up—

Pain shot through Sammy's head.

Reality check.

Molly. Where was his sister Molly?

He struggled to open his eyes, finally succeeding.

A ceiling light, the shade littered with dead bugs, tilted above his head. Green, hazy walls swirled around him. The pain in his head grew worse. But he had to be quiet. Those moans . . . he didn't like those moans. They brought the nurse. And he didn't like the nurse.

Maybe if Molly came and read to him the way she had when he'd gotten his tonsils out, he'd feel better, he'd forget about the sounds and the pain in his head.

His lips were dry, but he finally managed to press them together to form his sister's name. "Molly!" he croaked, his voice echoing weakly down the the long, corrugated tunnel.

Louder.

Had to be louder, and then maybe she would be able to hear him.

"Molly!"

Shouting made his head hurt more. Still, he shouted again. And again.

But it wasn't Molly who came. It was the nurse with the mustache. A thin, dark, villainous-looking mustache. Her face loomed above him, going in and out of focus.

He'd seen her before, smelled her before. She was part of the routine. And she reeked of stale body odor and staler cigarette breath.

Suddenly, seemingly from out of nowhere, the cold metal end of a glass thermometer was forced between his lips and jabbed halfway down his throat. Then his jaw was clamped shut by a pair of onion-skin hands.

He gagged and recoiled into the pillow under his head. He spat, the thermometer shooting out of his mouth.

"Oh, no, you don't," a raspy voice said.

Jab.

The metal point was shoved against the base of his tongue. He tried to work it out again, but she was ready for him this time with her viselike hands.

"There's more than one way to take a person's temperature," the nurse warned, daring him to spit the thermometer out again.

He stopped fighting. No way was she taking his temperature that way.

She reminded him of an army nurse he'd once had somewhere. Where . . . ?

The army.

Army? He'd never been in the army.

But in his mind he could visualize himself lying on a muddy, blood-stained gurney, a big nurse bent over him. She was stitching up the gash in his leg. Her hands were bloody from the last guy she'd worked on. And the guy before that, and the guy before that.

Her actions were robotic, as though she'd worked in a factory most of her life, sewing seams all day long. To her, Sammy was just another seam.

She jabbed the needle in and he let out an unholy scream, just to let her know she was killing him. She didn't even look up.

There must not have been any novocaine available, he thought, giving her the benefit of the doubt.

He didn't think she was sadistic. He figured she'd just desensitized herself to everything to get through it all.

With both hands he gripped his leg. "A guy could die of shock here," he gasped through gritted teeth. "You've got a screwed bedside manner. Why'd you ever become a nurse?"

Her hands stilled and she looked up at him with hard eyes. "I don't remember."

Another jab and another scream.

Her face blurred, became that of the other nurse, the one with the major B.O. and cigarette breath. She removed the thermometer, leaned over the bed, and said something.

He struggled, trying hard to focus on the present, on what she was saying.

She loomed nearer.

He tried to shrink away from her, but he was trapped by the bed beneath him and the incredible heaviness of his own body.

"Are you having much discomfort?" she asked.

Discomfort.

Nurse talk for pain. For extreme agony.

If he said yes, she'd send him back into oblivion. Oblivion was nice, but he knew if he spent too much time there, he might never come back, he might never get out of this place.

He shook his head.

Her eyebrows went up and her mustache twitched. He didn't know if she suspected his lie, or if she was simply surprised that he'd responded.

"Do you remember crashing your car?"

He swallowed. "No," he finally managed to answer through dry lips.

"Do you know where you are?"

Hell. He had to be in hell.

"Do you know your name?" she asked.

Puddin' Tane. Ask me again, and I'll tell you the same.

He was getting tired of this. It was hard to think. It made his head pound.

"What's your name?" she repeated, louder this time, her stale breath gusting in his face.

"Sam-my," he croaked.

That seemed to please her. "Sammy who? What's your last name?"

"Sam-my . . ." He had a hard time curling his tongue against the back of his upper teeth. "Thoreau. Sam-my Thoreau." It sounded more like "throw," but she got the picture.

"That's good. Very good. Now, tell me, Sammy, where do you live?"

Sammy's a bum. He lives out of a suitcase.

Where the hell had that come from?

"Where do you live?" she repeated.

Why was she doing this? What was the point? But at least she wasn't cramming pointed objects down his throat. Like a student eager to escape a thrashing, he forced himself to play the game.

"I-o-wa," he said. Easier to say than Thoreau.

From somewhere in the distance, from that place he

didn't want to go, came the annoying tinny sound of a TV game show.

"Close enough. How old are you?"

"What?"

"How old are you?"

"Eighteen." Was that right? No.

She frowned and clicked her tongue. "Now, think, Sammy. How old?" she asked again.

"Nineteen." *I think.*

"Are you sure?"

He nodded, not sure at all. Not sure of anything.

"Wrong. You're thirty-eight, Sammy."

Thirty-eight!

Beep. Sorry, contestant. Thirty-eight is the wrong answer. How much money did you bet? All of it? Too bad.

"Thirty-eight," the nurse repeated.

Sammy could feel his heart thumping in his chest like some poor, scared rabbit's. She was lying. Why was she lying? "*Nine-teen,*" he insisted.

"*Thirty-eight.*"

Where was this place? Where was Molly? What the hell was going on here? "Get away from me, you crazy bitch."

The nurse's eyes narrowed. Hickory-switch time.

"You're the one who's crazy," she said, spitting the words out one at a time. "You want to know where you are? I'll tell you where you are. You're in a mental ward at the Prophetstown Veterans Hospital."

Mental ward?

Crazy, crazy, or just plain lazy?

"You're . . . lying."

She lifted one corner of the bedsheet and shoved it in front of his face. "Can you read, Mr. Samuel Thoreau?"

He struggled to focus on the stamped letters. PSYCH WARD.

Sammy's world slanted and he felt himself falling off.

He didn't consciously think about what he was doing. A guy's got to protect himself. He had to get the crazy woman away.

He lifted his arm and shoved, almost knocking her to the floor, his strength surprising him. But there was a price to pay. The effort caused razors of pain to cut through his skull. A reprimand from Above.

Oh, my God, I'm heartily sorry. . . .

His head fell back against the pillow and he squeezed his eyes shut. You weren't supposed to hit girls. But did she count? She had a mustache.

Deep in his private agony, he heard frantic scrambling, heard a door bang, heard the nurse's deep voice echo down a long hallway.

"Orderly!" she bellowed. "Orderly! Patient out of control!"

Sammy was trying to sit up, when suddenly several pairs of hands were on him, shoving him down, restraining him. He fought and struggled while the pain continued to knife through his head. But the hands held him fast.

"You just bought yourself a ticket to the quiet room," a male voice said.

"Better up his dosage of vitamin H," another voice said.

They all laughed.

Da-dum.

Sammy didn't get it. What was the joke?

"Yeah, pump him full and knock him out. Then pack him off to seclusion."

Take the key and lock him up, lock him up, lock him up . . .

"Increase his dosage of Haldol," the male voice said.

"Got it right here."

He opened his eyes a crack to see the nurse coming at

him, a long hypo in her hand. The scene had all the weirdness of an LSD public-scare flick.

"No!" He struggled against the hands.

"You're only making it worse," a faceless voice told him.

But Sammy didn't quit. He couldn't go down without a fight. The smell of rancid sweat stung his nostrils. A sharp jab pierced his leg as the army nurse took another stitch.

"Enjoy the trip."

More laughter.

The bed began moving. Out a doorway, down a hall. He saw strange, passive faces. Strange, leering faces. *Crazy* faces.

Faster and faster the bed moved. Feetfirst, he sped down the long, corrugated hallway, toward the faroff voices, toward the other end of the tunnel. Stainless-steel double doors opened, then closed after him.

TWO

MOLLY FOLLOWED THE NURSE DOWN THE HALLWAY of the hospital, the delicate clicking of her heels a contrast to the nurse's lumbering strides.

The place didn't look like any hospital Molly had ever seen. She could tell that the floor tiles had once been black and white. But now, after years of being shuffled on by slippered feet, the colors had blended together. The windows, covered with what looked like heavy chicken wire, were so high, nobody could possibly see out. What light managed to filter through the layers of grime was feeble and gray.

"We've been trying to get ahold of you for the past two weeks," the nurse said over her shoulder, her gravelly voice heavy with censure.

"We were out of town," Molly murmured, feeling terribly guilty for not being here when her brother needed her. But apparently no one had tried very hard to find them. Molly had left a phone number and address with her daughter, Amy.

The nurse stopped next to an open door. "He's lucky to be alive," she said, crossing her arms over her chest, the pose reminding Molly of a prison guard. "They said he was doing a hundred when his car left the road." Again, that censure. But Molly was used to censure where her brother was concerned.

"His physical injuries weren't all that bad. It's the aftereffects that are causing problems."

Afraid of what she was going to find, Molly stepped just inside the small, poorly lit room . . . and saw a man lying on his back, his face turned toward the ceiling, a white bandage wrapped around his head.

Oh, God.

Sammy.

Since the phone call early that morning, a blessed numbness had seeped into Molly's brain and taken over her limbs. Now the full impact of Sammy's injury hit her like a shock wave.

He was so still. . . . Sammy was never still.

Her vision blurred and her throat tightened. It wasn't fair. Not Sammy.

"He might not be very responsive," the nurse said. "He's been displaying signs of extreme agitation and violence, so we're keeping him under sedation." She shrugged her broad shoulders. "We didn't want him to hurt himself or anybody else."

"Sammy can be—" Molly searched her mind for the right words. *Stubborn* and *irreverent* were adjectives often used in reference to her brother, but to Molly the description had always seemed unfair and extreme. "He can be a bit high-spirited," she said. "But Sammy would never be violent."

"Head injuries change people."

Your brother might be a stranger to you, the doctor had told her. Something too unthinkable for Molly to face.

Molly hadn't liked the doctor, and she didn't like Sammy's nurse. The woman's white uniform was no longer white, but gray. The front made Molly think of a grill cook's apron. And now that she was standing so near, Molly realized that some of the unclean smell permeating the psychiatric ward was coming from this woman.

Sammy shouldn't have a nurse like her. And he most certainly didn't belong in this depressing place. In a place where the walls were the color of split-pea soup. A place where there was hardly any light.

Molly approached the bed.

Carefully, so as not to startle him, she touched the back of his limp hand. There was no reaction.

In the two weeks he'd been there, he'd lost a great deal of weight. They said if he didn't start eating more, they would have to tube him.

She leaned closer. "Sammy . . ." she whispered. "It's me. Molly."

It seemed as if her voice coaxed him away from some burdensome place. Some weary place. Sammy's gaunt face slowly turned until his glazed eyes found hers.

"Molly . . . ?"

His once-vibrant voice was a weak whisper. And his beautiful dark eyes were empty.

Oh, God. She couldn't stand it. Not her teasing, laughing, irrepressible Sammy. Not Sammy, whose soul had burned brighter than anyone else's.

No one had bothered to shave him. And it seemed to her that by their neglect they had already relegated him to the status of nonperson. Like the blank faces she had passed on the way to his room.

Sammy didn't belong here.

But his face looked like the others. Blank and empty.

No! A world without Sammy was unthinkable.

She felt despair rising in her—a frightening sensation. Before, whenever she was upset, whenever she needed someone to talk to, she'd turned to Sammy. He'd always made her laugh. He'd always been her champion. Now . . .

She tried to tell herself that Sammy's spirit was still in his body somewhere, that it was just dormant. Like spring during the cold Iowa winter. Warm weather would come. He would get well. He had to. For her.

Even though she was six years older than Sammy, she'd always leaned on him. Now it was her turn to be strong.

"I want a razor," she told the nurse.

"We don't allow razors here."

"He needs a shave."

Normally Molly would have been intimidated by a woman who could probably throw a grown man across the room, but this was for Sammy.

Seeing that Molly intended to hold her ground, the nurse huffed off and returned with a rusty battery-operated shaver. She thrust it at Molly. "I don't know why you bother. He doesn't care."

"How do you know?"

The nurse let out a snort and left Molly alone with her brother.

While Molly shaved him, Sammy lay there, docile and unmoving.

Her eyes stung. Childhood memories tumbled in her mind.

They were total opposites. Sammy was outgoing; she was painfully shy, terrified of the world.

"I'm such a coward," she'd once told him, ashamed of her many fears.

"Wrong," he had replied, his eyes unusually serious. "You're the bravest person I know. Life is easy for somebody who isn't afraid. But every day, instead of hiding, you face your fears."

As a child, Sammy used to whistle. It was such a sweet, joyful sound that it sometimes made Molly cry just to hear it. But then, after Vietnam, Sammy didn't whistle anymore. And he didn't make her smile quite as often.

She had prayed that he would adjust and learn to leave

the past and all of its bad memories behind. Deep in her heart she had always hoped he would whistle again. . . .

"I have to go now," she said when his face was clean-shaven. She didn't know if he looked better. Now the hollows in his cheeks were more apparent. "Austin is waiting for me outside. You know how impatient he is."

Sammy had always called Molly's husband his stressed-out brother-in-law. He was being nice. He could have called him a lot more things.

Molly bent and kissed his cheek. "Good-bye, Sammy."

He blinked. Then, with words that seemed to take all of his energy, he whispered, "Bye . . . Molly-o."

A childhood name. She leaned closer, touched his arm. "Is there anything you want? Anything I can get you?"

". . . Want . . . out . . . of . . . here . . ."

Winter sunlight glinted dully off the fender of the silver Mercedes as it snaked down the smoothly paved lane that led away from the veterans' hospital.

Sitting in the passenger seat, Molly could feel her straight brown hair hanging in tired strands around her face, having escaped the clasp at the back of her neck. No matter how she tried, she could never seem to get it all together. Not like Austin, who was dressed impeccably in a gray suit that was color-coordinated with his car. Her husband liked to tell her that she could make the most expensive outfit look like a rag.

But Austin's scorn didn't hurt her. He'd lost the power to hurt her long ago. Seeing Sammy, *that* had hurt her.

How was she going to convince her husband that

Sammy couldn't be left in that awful place with its dingy walls and terrible smell?

She looked at the digital clock set in the bird's-eye-maple dash. Four o'clock and it was almost dark. In two hours they would be back in La Grange. But the house would be empty.

An empty nest.

All those nights she'd spent lying awake, worrying about her daughter, about Amy's asthma, about whether or not dental X rays were really necessary, about food additives, about nuclear plants and chemical warfare and the flame retardant used in little Amy's nightgown.

Now Amy was grown up and gone. Married. But Molly still worried.

Eighteen was too young to get married, Molly had tried to tell her. Getting married meant selling your soul, your individuality, but Amy hadn't listened.

During the wedding Molly had wanted to scream at them to stop. She'd wanted to tell her daughter to hang on to her freedom, to be a child awhile longer.

But she'd managed to keep her hands clasped tightly in her lap, keep her lips pressed firmly together.

Sammy had been there, lending support and strength. He'd sat beside her, his wild, dark hair slicked and tamed. To keep Austin happy, he'd rented a suit and tie. But always one to thumb his nose at convention, he'd completed the outfit with a pair of hightop sneakers.

And just when Molly thought she couldn't stand it anymore, just when she thought she would have to get up and run out of the church, Sammy had reached over and squeezed her hand. When she'd looked up, his dark eyes had been full of empathy and understanding.

"Your brother got what he deserved," Austin said, easing the car away from a stop sign. "He always drove like a maniac."

To Austin, there was no such thing as plain bad luck.

Everybody got what he deserved in life. People were born guilty.

Sammy. I can't leave you in that awful place.

"I never could figure him out," Austin said, executing a turn with an open palm on the wheel. "He could have done anything, been anybody."

"You mean he could have been clearing six figures and driving an expensive car?"

"Yeah," Austin agreed, her sarcasm lost on him. "Instead, what does he do? He lives out of a suitcase half the time."

Sammy had always said a person shouldn't own more than he could fit in his car. And yet there had been things he couldn't seem to let go of, and those things had managed to wind up in cardboard boxes in Molly and Austin's attic.

"He hasn't had a steady job his entire life," Austin continued.

"Vietnam changed him. You know that." But Austin didn't understand grief. To understand grief, a person had to be able to love, and love deeply.

"Vietnam's just an excuse. Anybody else would have gotten his act together by now. And you know damn well Sammy would never have ended up over there if he hadn't gotten himself kicked out of college. Face it, Molly. Your brother's a bum." He shook his head in disgust. "Ever since I've known him, he's been on the road to nowhere."

"He was looking for something. And you talk as if Sammy's some sort of vagrant. He's good at what he does."

"What's so hard about putting a few words down on paper? And the only time he does any writing is when the phone company shuts off his service or the bank is getting ready to repossess his car. The only thing your brother ever did that amounted to anything was that stint as an army reporter. And he almost managed to get himself kicked out of that assignment too."

"For telling the truth."

"He just wanted to stir things up, the way he always stirs things up. Just like he's doing now."

Why had she stayed with Austin for so long, so many years? Molly wondered distantly.

Habit. Life with Austin was a habit. At first she had stayed because of Amy, but later, after Amy had grown up and moved away, she stayed because she was tired. And old. Forty-four wasn't *old* old. But if a person was as old as she felt, then Molly was old. Very old.

They pulled up to a stoplight. To her right, in the next lane, was a woman in a faded green car with rusty fenders. A cigarette dangled from her lips; her eyes were squinted against the smoke. Hanging in the back window, in a plastic dry cleaning bag, was a black sequined dress. Molly wondered where the woman planned to wear that dress. Then she wondered what the woman's house looked like. Was she married? Divorced? Single?

Sometimes—a lot of times—Molly would see a stranger and wish she could be that person. Not just take her place, but actually *be* her. And whenever she caught a glimpse of a silver jet winging across the sky, she would imagine herself inside it, going someplace, anyplace. It didn't even have to be first class.

The light turned green. They continued straight. The woman beside them turned right.

Sammy.

She had to pull herself together. For Sammy. She couldn't leave him there.

There was nothing she hated more than a confrontation with Austin. He had a way of turning everything around, making her feel foolish and stupid. But this time she wouldn't back down. This time she wouldn't retreat. She couldn't.

She took a deep breath. "I think Sammy should have another opinion. I think he should be transferred—"

"Transferred!" Austin's reaction was instantaneous and totally predictable.

"Are you out of your mind? He doesn't have any insurance. If he wasn't a veteran, we'd have a helluva problem on our hands."

"Maybe a research hospital like the one in La Grange. That way, he'd be nearby."

"Who's going to pay? I sure as hell won't foot the bill. Leave him where he is, Molly. He's damn lucky to be there."

Why did everyone keep saying how lucky Sammy was? They were trivializing his problem, his life, *him*. Her brother knew more about living than any of them ever would.

"You might be his closest relative, but that doesn't mean you owe him. Sammy is thirty-eight years old. He isn't your responsibility and he sure as hell isn't mine."

"He's my brother."

"And what did brother Sammy ever do for you besides stir up trouble? Tell me that. *You're* the one who took care of *him* after your mother died. But what did Sammy ever do for you in return?"

Austin and his business mind. I give you two years; you give me two years.

She knew he wouldn't understand, but she decided to say it anyway. "Sammy made me laugh." *And he loved me.*

"Made you laugh!" Austin snorted. "I hated having to go anywhere with him. There was never any telling what he might do next. He was always embarrassing the hell out of me."

Public image was so important to Austin. He would never understand. It wasn't in him to understand. He was too self-absorbed to have ever noticed Sammy's light.

"Come on, honey."

The false endearment made her wince.

Austin reached over and gave her leg an awkward pat. "You're just going through a rough time right now. You know what the doctors said. It could take years for his condition to improve, if he improves at all. I hate to be so blunt, but once you face the facts, things will be easier for you. He doesn't have the money to be transferred. It would be financial suicide."

But Molly had money from the sale of her roses. Money she'd been stashing away for years. Money nobody knew about, not even the government.

She had always thought that someday, when the notion hit her, when she wasn't tired and when the sun was shining, she would pack a suitcase—just one. Then, without telling anybody, she'd leave for Florida. Once there, she would check into a hotel and register under an exotic name. Something like Jasmine or Camille. She would spend her days lying on the beach, letting the sun soak life back into her. It could take years, so she had saved a lot of money.

But deep down she had always known that she would never go. It was just a dream that kept her moving from one day to the next.

She would use her secret money to get Sammy transferred. Austin would never have to know.

was too self-absorbed to have ever noticed Sabrina's habit.

"Come on, honey."

The Electrohome made her wa...

THREE

FIRST-YEAR-RESIDENT MARK ELLIOT TUCKED THE PA-
tient file under his arm and strode down the hall to Dr.
Rachel Collins's office, the soles of his sneakers squeak-
ing on the polished linoleum.

Her door was open. He could see Dr. Collins sitting
at her desk, blond head bent over some paperwork. Even
though she was at least five years older than Mark, she
looked as though she belonged in high school, not a
university hospital. She was small, no bigger than his
kid sister. And her haircut, which had a Joan of Arc look
to it, along with a pair of wire-rimmed glasses, helped
complete the impression of youth. But her looks were
deceptive. She had a stamina that amazed him. She held
up under pressure. And she possessed something only a
small percentage of the psychiatrists and psychologists
he'd run into did—the capability to truly listen to
patients, then use that information to help them.

And she never hassled him about the way he dressed.
He appreciated that.

He rapped his knuckles on the door frame. She looked
up, welcoming him with a smile.

"Come in, Mark. I was just going over some lab
reports."

He stepped in, hitched up his lab coat, and perched

himself on a corner of her desk. "Your new head-injury patient has just been admitted." He slid the file from under his arm. "Delivered fresh from the vegetation administration."

"Mark."

He recognized it for what it was, a token chastisement, one given with good nature. She was his superior. It was part of her job to keep him in line.

He opened the file and flipped through the forms. "Guess who the attending physician was?"

"Macintosh?"

"None other than the lobotomy king himself. How'd you know?"

"I wonder how you managed to make it through med school with that disrespectful attitude."

"I excelled in other areas, so they put up with me."

She smiled again.

She had a nice smile. A little on the sad side, but nice. Mark liked to coax those little smiles from her. It bothered him to know that she lived alone and never went out. She never even attended any of the staff parties. She worked too hard, too long. Sure, doctors were notorious workaholics, but this was more than that. With her, work was an escape.

He glanced at his digital watch—9:55. "Gotta run." It made him nervous to sit still for very long. He jumped off the desk. "Some premeds are coming at ten."

"Why don't you have mercy on them this time and skip the tour of the morgue?"

"I might. It all depends on whether there are any good-looking girls in the group."

"You won't impress anybody by showing them cadavers floating in formaldehyde."

He made his eyebrows jump up and down. "Yeah, but when the girls faint, I get to catch them." With that, he left, the tails of his lab coat disappearing around the doorway.

Mark had some rough edges, Rachel had to admit as she watched him go, but she liked him. And more important, the patients liked him. He had a wonderful, relaxed bedside manner that Rachel hoped he'd never lose.

She picked up the new patient file and flipped it open.

Patient: Samuel Thoreau. Male Caucasian.

Age: 38

Height: 6'

Weight: 180

Marital status: single

Reason for admission: Patient sustained irreparable damage to the association cortex of the cerebrum.

Prognosis: Chronically debilitated

She made an irritated sound. According to the dates, he'd been at the VA hospital just over three weeks. How on earth could they make such a serious prognosis in so short a time? How could they write a patient off so easily?

There was a brief profile attached. She saw that before his accident Mr. Thoreau had been a freelance writer for magazines like *Rolling Stone,* plus other publications she'd never heard of.

She turned to Dr. Macintosh's letter of admittance.

Patient responds violently to outside stimuli. Is confused and incoherent. Communication is limited to physical violence and profanity. Patient requires restraints and solitary confinement. Surgical sedation is advised in order to restore patient to effective citizenship.

Effective citizenship! Surgical sedation! Archaic. Lobotomies had gone out with Moniz, the twentieth-century charlatan who had actually won a Nobel Prize in Medicine for his crude and horrifying work in psycho-surgery.

She flipped through the papers. There was nothing about CAT scans or EEGs. No neurological studies whatsoever.

She did see that the patient had been given Haldol regularly—in amounts most people wouldn't be able to tolerate.

It had to be a misprint.

But on the bottom of the chart was another note: Patient requires abnormally high dosage of Haldol in order to be kept under control.

He was courting addiction. It was going to take a while to get his system cleaned out.

She picked up the phone and ordered several tests. Then she took the stairs from the fifth floor to the psychiatric ward on third to meet Mr. Samuel Thoreau.

The majority of Rachel's cases were outpatients. A few were sometimes hospitalized for short stays, but it had been over three years since she'd taken on anyone who might require long-term, intensive therapy, the kind that could be so emotionally draining. She hoped she was ready for it.

When she reached Samuel Thoreau's room, Rachel's first reaction was indignation.

He was lying on his back on the bed. Even though he appeared to be totally sedated, his wrists were secured to the side rails and he was wearing a green hospital gown that had the word *psycho* stenciled across the front in three-inch black letters. The labeling was the VA's way of dealing with what they kindly referred to as mental escapees.

"He arrived like this," the floor nurse whispered. "I

got his blood pressure, but when I tried to take his temperature his teeth clamped down so hard on the thermometer I was afraid it might break off in his mouth. I wasn't sure what to do with him. . . ."

"We'll begin without restraints—harmless until proven otherwise."

"But Dr. Fontana said—"

"Mr. Thoreau is my patient, not Dr. Fontana's."

Dr. Fontana, head of psychology and psychiatry, was of the old school. He wasn't open to many new ideas, but Rachel respected and admired him. There was much to be said about time and experience lending a wisdom that could never be gained in a classroom. But that didn't keep Rachel and Dr. Fontana from clashing at times.

She approached the bed. The man's scalp was covered with a new crop of hair that was as inky black as his eyebrows. His face was hollow-cheeked and yellow-tinged—jaundiced, most likely, from overmedication. He needed a shave and a bath and clean hospital clothes.

"Mr. Thoreau," she said softly, "I am Dr. Collins."

In a head-injury case, the patient could appear to be totally incoherent when in actuality he wasn't. Rachel was always careful to guard her words, to not say anything that might cause undue distress.

"You're here at the University Hospital in La Grange, Iowa, because you were in an accident and hurt your head. I'm going to be helping to take care of you."

She watched his gaunt face for any sign of response and was rewarded with a slight movement beneath his closed lids.

"First of all, I'm going to make you more comfortable by untying your hands." She untied first one, then the other. His arms fell limply to his sides.

Now she could see that the backs of his hands and the insides of his arms were a mass of blue and yellow bruises—evidence of veins searched for but never found.

At most hospitals the attending nurse or doctor never tried to get an IV line started after the second try. It was policy to call in another attendant then. Apparently with Samuel Thoreau someone had tried again and again.

She felt the pulse on his wrist. It was slow due to the overload of drugs in his system. Then she examined the area at the base of his skull, finding a small red ridge of scar tissue. No sign of infection. A miracle. He'd healed despite everything.

Rachel was about to call the nurse aside with further instructions when the man's eyelids twitched, then opened.

She found herself being regarded by a pair of coal-black eyes set deeply in bruised sockets. The look in them made her think of a Holocaust victim. These eyes were empty. Expecting nothing. Wanting nothing.

Once again, anger burned in her. How could anyone treat a patient this way? They had violated one of the most important rules of medicine: First, do no harm. Apparently some institutions were still the stuff bad dreams were made of.

And then Samuel Thoreau did something that made her go weak with self-doubt, made her wonder if she'd just been fooling herself, made her fear that she might no longer have the emotional strength needed to survive this kind of journey, a journey that could take her deep into his psyche.

With defeated eyes, Samuel Thoreau looked up at her and whispered through dry lips, "I'll . . . be . . . good."

FOUR

IT WAS MID-APRIL. MOLLY ALWAYS UNCOVERED HER rosebushes in mid-April. But weather was unpredictable, and Molly could remember a year when the temperature had dipped below freezing the last of May. Roses could take the cold; they couldn't take a deep freeze.

But today, as Molly worked in her garden, pulling down the wire supports and raking the winter mulch from the bushes, she could feel the promise of warmer weather. There was a crispness in the morning air that would soon be chased away by the sun rays already penetrating the back of her sweatshirt. Earlier, she'd removed her jacket and now it lay on grass that seemed to have turned green overnight.

Off in the distance, from the vicinity of the towering blue spruce, came the call of a whippoorwill. And the previous night she'd heard the wistful hoot of an owl.

The rose garden was Molly's favorite place. She felt safe here. Whole. Austin's disapproval couldn't touch her here.

Her husband didn't like the outdoors. He hated wind and rain and sunshine. The only time the soles of his shoes touched grass was at the golf course. And he suffered that only because it was expected of him. It was part of his successful stockbroker image.

Molly dumped the last cartload of mulch into the compost pile, then picked up the shears and began pruning the dead wood from the bushes.

Roses were her passion. Or they used to be. Years before, while still in high school, she had grafted several of her own varieties. Some had won national honors and she'd been awarded a floricultural scholarship.

But there had been Sammy to take care of. And after that, she'd met Austin. Somehow she'd never gotten around to using the scholarship. But she still had her prize-winning roses.

"Here you are, Mother!"

Molly straightened to see her daughter, dressed in faded jeans and a baggy green sweater, striding across the yard, her straight, red-gold hair gleaming in the sunlight.

"I should have known I'd find you in the garden," Amy said with a teasing smile.

At the sight of her daughter, a familiar reverberation of fear knocked in Molly's chest. Why had Amy come on a weekday? Something must be wrong.

Why this fear? Why always this fear?

When Amy was a baby, Molly had been afraid to take her eyes off her. She felt that if she looked away, Amy might stop breathing. It was almost as if the strength of her love and her single-minded concentration was keeping her darling alive.

She had hoped that as Amy grew up, her own silly, irrational fears would subside. But they hadn't. They had only changed into different fears.

Maybe it was because Amy was so perfect. Molly had always felt that it had been an accident for her to have been bestowed with such a perfect child, a precious gift she didn't deserve. And she feared that one day the mistake would be discovered and Amy would be taken away from her.

"Is something wrong?" Molly asked, voicing her fear, willing her heart to stop its erratic beating.

Amy smiled, her sweet, wise, reassuring smile. "No, Mother."

Everything was okay. Molly had always felt that Amy was the adult in their relationship. She was the reasonable one, calming her mother's worries with quiet words.

Where had she come from, this person of light and laughter? Not from Molly. And not from Austin. Oh, she had Austin's flawless skin and her own brown eyes, but Amy's inner self was like no one else's . . . except maybe Sammy's. . . .

Kahlil Gibran had been right. Children came *through* their parents, not *from* them.

At age two, when most children were still unwilling to share their toys, Amy showed a sensitivity that had astounded Molly. The child's heart was broken over everything—a squashed bug, a sentimental commercial on televison.

"How's Uncle Sammy?" Amy asked.

So far Molly had been vague in her explanation of Sammy's problem. Amy knew he'd had an accident, but Molly hadn't told her of the VA hospital's diagnosis. And Molly didn't want Amy to see her uncle, not the way he was now. And if he didn't get better, she wanted Amy to remember the old Sammy. Not the Sammy with the empty eyes.

"He's been transferred to the University Hospital here in town," Molly told her. "But they don't think any of us should see him until they're done with his evaluation."

Molly had been skeptical when she'd found that Sammy's case had been assigned to a woman. But then she'd met Dr. Collins, and her fears were put to rest.

"Do they expect him to be there long?" Amy asked.

Unable to look her daughter in the eye, Molly said,

"He could be there weeks . . . maybe months. The lease on his apartment was almost up, so I drove to Prophetstown and boxed up all of his things."

"You should have told me. I would have helped."

She was glad Amy hadn't been there. Molly was trying hard to be strong. Before she'd gone to Sammy's apartment she'd actually been proud of the fact that she'd broken down only once, and that had been at home in the shower with the bathroom door locked.

But going through Sammy's things the day before had been too much for her. She'd ended up collapsing on the floor and crying until her eyes had practically swollen shut.

She'd been doing fine until she'd started boxing up his awards and magazine articles. Then she'd felt a sharpness in her throat, a sharpness she couldn't dislodge.

When she'd come across the framed black and white photos of herself and Amy, the tightness in her throat had intensified. It was the box of Amy's wrinkled drawings and faded construction-paper cards that had caused her to fall apart completely.

No, she was glad Amy hadn't been there to witness her weakness. And she didn't want her to know how bad things were with Sammy.

As always, Amy seemed to intuitively pick up on her mother's silent distress, and changed the subject. "Did you have any evening grosbeaks this winter?" she asked, glancing around the yard at her mother's bird feeders.

"They all came back," Molly said. "The whole family. One day I counted seven at one feeder. And I had dozens of goldfinches. They're such dainty eaters." Even though bird-feeding season was over, Molly left her feeders up all year around. Some birds chose to stay all summer, some didn't.

Molly peeled off her garden gloves. She had hothouse

roses to deliver to a local florist, but it could wait. Amy was there. "How about a cup of coffee?" she asked.

Amy flashed her sunlight smile and nodded. "Sounds wonderful." She bent and scooped up her mother's jacket, then linked her arm with Molly's. Together mother and daughter walked toward the two-story white colonial house.

They carried their coffee and a plate of cookies out on the deck overlooking the backyard. The house blocked the wind and the deck absorbed the sun's warmth, making a protected place to sit on a cool spring day.

Amy took a sip of coffee, then set her mug down, her elbows braced on the round patio table, chin resting on her hands. "I have something to tell you, Mother."

Again, Molly felt that flutter of fear.

Amy leaned closer, her eyes bright, a smile lifting the corners of her mouth.

"You're moving away," Molly said, voicing one of her many worries. First Sammy. Now Amy. Her brother and her daughter were both slipping from her.

Amy laughed. "No." Her smile left her mouth but not her eyes. "I'm going to have a baby."

Worse than moving! Something Molly hadn't even considered—a baby! Childbirth was too dangerous, too painful for her little girl.

Amy's bright smile became a little unsteady as she waited for her mother's reaction.

On one hand, Molly could see that Amy wanted her to be happy. But on the other, all Molly could think about was her own pregnancy. The morning sickness. At night, the leg cramps. The long, lonely hours of labor, the terrible fear, the terrible pain. She didn't want Amy to go through that.

"A-are you sure?" Molly asked, hating herself for disappointing Amy with her negative response. But maybe Amy was wrong. Maybe it was a mistake.

"Yes. I've been to a doctor. Chris is going crazy. He's more excited than I am. He's already read every baby book he can find, and he's making lists of names. Some of them are horrible!" She made a face. "He even called about Lamaze classes and was disappointed when he found out we couldn't take them until my third trimester."

The fear that had been gripping Molly relaxed. Chris wasn't Austin. And Amy wasn't Molly. "I'm so happy for you. You'll be a wonderful mother."

Amy smiled. Obviously relieved, she picked up an oatmeal cookie and took a bite.

Imagine, Molly thought. A baby. Her daughter was going to be a mother. And she would be a grandmother. . . .

Molly looked out past the deck rail to where two robins were hopping about the yard. Soon Amy would have a baby that she would love with a fierce, protective pain. She and Chris and their baby would be a family, the way it should be, the way it was supposed to be.

Children had never interested Austin. When Amy was in grade school, he'd managed to make a few token appearances at school programs. But his interest hadn't been sincere. They hadn't been a real family the way Molly had wanted them to be. They hadn't gone to the park together, or on picnics. Or on one of those horrendous vacations she'd always overheard other people moaning about, vacations she herself had longed for. But Amy and Chris would be different. They would be a family.

Amy's voice broke through Molly's reflections.

"Why have you stayed?" she asked quietly.

"What?"

"Why have you stayed with Daddy?"

How long had she known? Molly wondered. As intuitive as she was, maybe she'd always known.

"You know, I used to feel guilty," Amy said. "I thought you stayed with him because of me. I thought that maybe, when I got married—"

"Oh, Amy." Molly's hand flew to her heart. Had she pushed her only child into marriage? "Don't tell me that's why you married so young?" It was too terrible to think about, too terrible to consider.

"No, Mother. I love Chris." Amy's face was earnest, and Molly knew her daughter well enough to see that she was telling the truth. Amy was a terrible liar. Like Sammy.

"I thought . . ." Amy made an uncomfortable gesture with one hand. "I just wondered . . ."

Molly's gaze was drawn to her rose garden. The roses had been there as long as she had. They might not survive transplanting.

Molly had never bought a lottery ticket. She had never been one to take risks. She had always needed security.

"I guess I just didn't want to uproot everything," she said quietly.

A long time ago, before Sammy had been drafted, he'd gone to a concert and come back to his dorm to find that it had burned down. There was nothing left but a pile of smoldering ashes. Molly had tried to comfort him, but he had shrugged it off, spouting something about the heavy weight of earthly possessions. He'd even laughed, saying he felt a little lighter now.

At the time his answer had seemed callous. But now Molly thought she understood what he'd meant.

Yet he'd saved the pictures . . . and he'd saved little Amy's childish scribbles. Gifts of love.

Obviously, to Sammy, things not so earthly.

FIVE

SOME OF THE CONFUSION THAT HAD HELD SAMMY'S
brain in limbo for so long had lifted. Now he realized he
had to get busy. He had important stuff to do. Like
going fishing. Like feeling the sun on his face.

Like getting the hell out of here.

He'd been moved to another hospital. He remembered the ride over. At first he thought he'd died and
they were taking him to a cemetery. He'd thought, wow.
So this is what it's like to be dead. Your soul doesn't go
anyplace. It just stays in your dead body.

But then somebody—one of the attendants—had
slapped the side of Sammy's face.

"Wake up."

Slap, slap.

The attendant leaned over him, grinning. "You're
being transferred," he said. "Wanna know why? Because
you're crazy."

Sammy's arms were tied. He couldn't take a punch at
the grinning face, so he spit.

The grin turned to rage. "You son of a—" A pillow
was shoved against Sammy's face until everything went
black again. . . .

The next thing he was aware of was being wheeled
along on the gurney, blue sky and cotton clouds above.

But then the sky and clouds disappeared as the hospital's double doors opened wide and swallowed him.

So far the new place didn't seem as bad as the old one. It didn't stink.

Sammy had learned his lesson, though. He'd learned that he had to be good, learned that he had to be careful and not say the first thing that popped into his head. That was the difference between a crazy person and a sane person. A crazy person just didn't know when to keep his mouth shut.

He heard a movement in the hall.

Someone was coming.

Sammy was careful to keep his eyes closed.

The person came into the room, stopping next to the bed. It was *her* again. Not the nurse with the cigarette breath—she belonged to the other place. This person smelled good. Clean. And her voice, when she talked to him, was low and soothing.

Don't trust her, he warned himself. She was one of them.

"Samuel? How are you feeling?"

Samuel? He hadn't been called that in a long time. His mother used to call him Samuel. But only when he was in big trouble. Then his mother would shriek *Samuel Harden Thoreau.*

That had always been Samuel Harden Thoreau's cue to exit, stage right.

"Are you still tired?"

He felt her fingers touch his wrist, cool fingertips pressed gently to his pulse.

"You should be feeling quite a bit better."

He should probably respond in some way, so she wouldn't get suspicious, so she wouldn't suspect that he was faking it, that he was planning his big breakout.

It was a struggle to open his eyes. That surprised and worried him, but he finally managed to lift his lids.

Cream-colored walls. Bright lights. Swirling ceiling.

And a woman bending over him. A woman with short blond hair and a small, pointed chin. White jacket. Wire-rimmed glasses. A nurse. He didn't like nurses.

"I'm Dr. Rachel Collins," she said.

He didn't like doctors.

"We met this morning, but you may have forgotten. You were pretty tired. You're at the University Hospital in La Grange, Iowa."

He didn't like hospitals.

She wrapped something around his arm—a blood pressure cuff—then she linked the stethoscope to her ears. "I'm going to take your blood pressure, Samuel—"

"Sammy," he croaked.

God. Was that his voice? He sounded like a wimp. How the hell was a puny wimp going to pull off an escape? "Name's . . . *Sam-my*."

"Then Sammy's what I'll call you." She smiled at him. Real friendly. Not like the army nurse. He almost smiled back.

Whoosh, whoosh, whoosh.

The pressure cuff filled, reminding him that she was the enemy. No fraternizing with the enemy. Wouldn't do. Wouldn't do at all.

He felt the cold metal of the stethoscope touch his inner arm. He watched as she focused her attention on getting a reading.

She had a sad face, he decided. Even though she'd smiled at him, there was sadness in her. She didn't look like any doctor he'd ever seen. She wasn't big enough. Wasn't intimidating enough.

"We'll get you off this IV as soon as you're eating and drinking on your own. We can't have you dehydrating."

Sure. If he dehydrated, they could just sweep him into a little pile in the corner.

"Think you might feel like eating tomorrow?" she asked.

The enemy. She was the enemy. Keeping him here against his will. He didn't answer. She didn't seem to mind.

"Blood pressure looks good." She pulled the stethoscope from her ears and removed the cuff from his arm.

He let his eyes drift shut. Couldn't let her think he was getting stronger all the time. She might call in the goon squad to hold him down and tie him up and send him off to limbo again. No, he was gonna check out of this place first chance he got.

"Go ahead and rest. Later, maybe tomorrow morning, we can talk some more."

He didn't allow himself to respond. He wanted to trust her. He liked her cool hands and soothing voice. But she was the enemy.

At ten P.M. Rachel was still at her desk, catching up on paperwork, putting off leaving—as she often did. There had been a time when she couldn't wait to get home, when she rarely worked late, when she had left her desk littered with unfinished work. But that had been before . . .

Don't think about it, she told herself, pushing the painful thoughts away. It hurt too much.

She closed the file, turned off her desk lamp, and got to her feet. She would stop off on the patient floor before leaving, just to see how everything was going.

She didn't meet anyone on the way to third. The elevator moved silently, in seeming deference to the night. The doors opened and she walked down the hall to the nurse's station. Not a single light glowed in the switchboard.

"Quiet evening," the night nurse said. "Must be the waning moon."

A lot of night nurses insisted that the moon cycles affected the patients. And Rachel couldn't argue fact. There were more babies born during a full moon. And mental patients could be unusually troublesome during a full moon.

"How's Samuel Thoreau doing?" Rachel asked.

"Still sleeping."

"I thought I'd look in on him before I leave."

His room was at the end of the hall. The door was open, the unlit room cast in shadow by the lights filtering in from the hallway.

His bed was empty.

At first Rachel thought he must have been moved to another room, but then she saw the IV rack next to the bed, the needle dripping fluid onto the sheets.

On the other side of the room the bathroom door was partially ajar, showing darkness.

Had she heard a faint sound coming from inside?

She thought about calling an orderly, but then she remembered the way Sammy had looked up at her.

I'll be good.

She didn't want to do anything that might jeopardize their relationship. She needed to gain his trust. She wouldn't gain it by calling in an orderly.

"Sammy?" she whispered.

Silence.

She crossed the room. She was reaching for the light switch when the door crashed open.

He erupted from the darkness, flinging her aside.

Everything seemed to happen at once and in slow motion. Rachel lost her balance and fell backward, the soles of her shoes skidding on the polished floor. Her glasses were knocked from her face. She heard them skitter across the floor. She grabbed for something, anything to stop her fall, but her hand flailed at air. Her hip struck the floor. She cried out as her elbow connected with the concrete wall.

Sammy was getting away.

She knew he wouldn't get very far, dressed as he was in hospital greens. But when he was caught he would be thrown in solitary, something she had hoped to avoid.

"Sammy!"

He stopped, his silhouette framed in the doorway. His chest was heaving. Blood dripped from the back of his hand, where the IV needle had been ripped out, onto the floor. He looked conscience-stricken and confused. There was something tragically poetic about him with his short hair, dark eyes, and hollow cheeks.

She scrambled to her feet but didn't move closer. "Sammy. Don't go. Nobody's going to hurt you. You're safe here."

She took a step toward him.

He turned away.

From the hallway came the sound of running feet. Then two orderlies were there, grabbing him, one on each side.

The confusion in Sammy's eyes was replaced by rage and fear. He let out a cry of frustration, practically lifting both men off the ground. "I don't belong in this loony bin!"

"Don't hurt him!" Rachel cried.

"Easy, bud," one of the orderlies said. "It's gonna be okay."

But Sammy was beyond hearing them. He was like a child who had lost control of his own tantrum.

"Get your damn hands off me!"

The orderlies finally managed to force him to the floor, locking both his arms behind his back, one side of his face pressed to the linoleum.

He continued to thrash and hurl obscenities. An orderly pressed a knee to the back of Sammy's neck.

"I don't belong here, you bastards!"

His shouts echoed up and down the hall, which had been empty just minutes earlier. Now the doorways were filled with faces of patients, some curious, some frightened. Several nurses had materialized.

Rachel saw that in order to stop his ranting and before he could do any more damage to himself, she had to give him an injection of Thorazine.

His muscles were so tight she couldn't find a place on his thigh to stick the needle. She lay a hand against his shoulder. Beneath the cotton hospital gown he was like granite.

"Relax your muscles, Sammy." She almost told him that she didn't want to hurt him, but she knew he wouldn't believe her. Not now.

"Go . . . to . . . hell." The words were forced, one at a time, through gritted teeth.

He was staring at her with accusing eyes. Hostile eyes.

This was the last thing she'd wanted, the very situation she'd been trying to avoid. Now she might never gain his trust.

He didn't relax. He didn't bat an eye when she stuck in the needle. He just watched her, his face pressed to the floor.

Dr. Maxwell Fontana leaned back in his chair and slammed Samuel Thoreau's file down on his desk. Rachel, who was standing just inside his office door, couldn't help but flinch at the angry sound.

"This is a psychiatric hospital," he said, "not a bed and breakfast. The patient arrived here under restraint.

He should have remained under restraint until an evaluation was completed."

Rachel didn't try to defend herself because he was right. She'd screwed up.

Dr. Fontana ran blunt fingers across his bald head, the way he always did when he was deep in thought. "The man obviously had enough presence of mind to play possum on you. He is potentially dangerous. I want him kept in solitary until we can get a full evaluation. For God's sake, Rachel, if you're going to take a patient off sedation, put him in a room where he can't hurt himself or anyone else. That's what we have solitary confinement for. You're lucky to have gotten away with just a few bruises and a pair of broken glasses."

"It was my fault. I'll take full responsibility. And I'm sure it wasn't his intention to hurt me. It was an accident. I was just in the way."

"I'm not looking for someone to blame. I just don't want something like this to happen again." He picked up the file and flipped it open. "I took a look at his CAT scan this morning. Part of the memory lobe is damaged and very likely missing. He's going to be a difficult patient. Would you like the Thoreau case given to someone else?"

"No. I can handle it."

"I never meant to imply that you couldn't. I just didn't know if you felt emotionally ready." He let out a sigh. "Rachel, you know how I hate to come down on you like this. Forget what Freud said about work being the closest thing to sanity. I can't ignore the fact that you've been pushing yourself too hard. And I have to wonder if this episode was a manifestation of your own exhaustion."

"It was simply the way I thought the patient should be handled. I was wrong."

He pushed back his chair, came around the desk, and

sat on one corner. His faded blue eyes below bushy brows grew even more serious. "You can't keep running."

"I'm not running."

"Jennifer's been gone now . . . what? Three years?"

"Three and a half." She didn't want to discuss this.

"I've never been one to offer empty platitudes. A person never gets over something like the loss of a child . . . but there should be some healing. Some eventual acceptance. We doctors have a tendency to blame ourselves for everything that goes wrong. Especially when it comes to our own children. But the fact is, tragedies happen that make no sense, that have no explanation. No blame. But because we are doctors, because we are supposed to save lives, we feel doubly guilty."

She swallowed and looked down. She was rubbing her thumb across her palm. Over and over. Quickly she dropped her hands to her sides. "I'm better. I'm handling it."

But she knew he was aware of a time when she hadn't handled it so well, a time when she had fallen into a trap many doctors who were pushed to the limit of their emotional endurance fell into. In order to override her emotions, in order to keep functioning as a doctor, she had turned to the numbing effects of prescription drugs that were so readily available to physicians. It had taken an almost lethal dose of Valium combined with alcohol for her to see what she was doing to herself. And in the end she found that she'd only postponed the pain, postponed the reality.

"If you ever want to talk . . ." Dr. Fontana said.

She didn't want to talk. She nodded. "I know. Thanks."

He took the hint. "About Thoreau," he said, changing the subject. "Are you sure you want this case? This fellow is going to be a handful. I can give it to Sanderson."

She didn't know why the Thoreau case was suddenly so important to her, but it was. And she didn't like Sanderson. "No. I want the case."

"Okay." He closed the file. "But let me know if things get too rough and you change your mind. As far as immediate treatment, I suggest you let our boy cool his heels for a few days. Get him stabilized on a minimal dosage of Thorazine. Then when he's leveled out you can start over and get some kind of prognosis drawn up on him. I've spoken with his sister and it sounds as if our Mr. Thoreau is in trouble financially. No insurance, nothing to fall back on. She told me she'd planned on footing the bill herself, but when she asked me what the cost might be, the rough estimate I gave took her aback. So I suggested we put him on the student research program and she agreed. He'll make an interesting case study."

"Yes."

On the research program there would be no fee for his hospitalization and treatment. In return, Sammy would have to let students poke and prod him all they wanted. He would be a guinea pig. Rachel had the feeling Mr. Thoreau wouldn't like that one bit.

A handful, Dr. Fontana had called him. She suspected a handful was putting it mildly. Maybe that's why she felt so strongly about this case. Sammy Thoreau was amazingly indomitable. Most people, after going through what he had, would have died or given up. They would have been more than willing to let the drugs take over their mind and free them from the horrors of their condition. But Sammy had an inner resilience that was astounding. She couldn't turn her back on that kind of spirit.

SIX

RACHEL KNOCKED, THEN STEPPED INTO THE EVALUA-
tion room, shutting the door behind her. A week had
passed since Samuel Thoreau's attempted escape; this was
going to be their first session together.

Things didn't look promising.

Sammy was slumped in a straight-back chair, arms
crossed at his chest. He was wearing faded jeans, a baggy
gray sweatshirt, and white sneakers. His new growth of
hair was sticking straight up. A rebellious James Dean,
the embodiment of every mother's nightmare.

But Rachel suspected his insolent pose was just
that—a pose.

"You're not a doctor," Sammy said accusingly. "You're
a damn shrink."

Not the new beginning she'd wished for.

"Hope you're packing a hypo. I'm starting to lose the
buzz."

"I never deliberately misled you," she said. "A shrink
is a doctor."

Rachel sat down in the only other chair in the room.
She crossed her legs, smoothed her skirt, and settled her
clipboard on her knee. She usually used a tape recorder,
but she was afraid that Sammy might feel threatened by
it.

The room was empty except for the chairs and a camera attached to the ten-foot ceiling. All their sessions would be videotaped for later use by psychiatric and psychology students. It was reassuring to know that today's meeting was being monitored from an adjoining room by Jake, an orderly known for both his strength and gentleness.

"I want to know why I wasn't allowed to see my sister when she brought my clothes," Sammy said.

"You were asleep."

"Asleep? Is that what you call it? Try wasted. Or strung out on junk."

"I'm sure on her next visit you'll be able to see her."

He let out a rude snort. "Yeah. Sure I will."

"Do you mind if I ask you a few questions?"

He lifted his arm and frowned at an imaginary watch. "Go ahead and do your shrink stuff so I can get the hell out of here."

Her first question was standard. "Do you know where you are?" It was important to determine how disoriented the patient was. He was oriented times three if he knew who he was, where he was, and what day it was.

"I'm at a nut hospital in La Grange, Iowa, in the United States of America, on the continent of North America, on the planet earth, in the Milky Way galaxy."

His expression seemed to say, How'd you like that?

"Do you understand *why* you are here?"

He unfurled his arms and leaned close, elbows on his spread knees, eyes staring insolently into hers. "I hit my fucking head."

She nodded and made a couple of notes.

"Want to know how to spell that?" he asked. "F-u—"

"If you're trying to shock me, it won't work. I've seen my share of bathroom stalls."

She looked up in time to see a spark of interest flash

in his eyes. Humor. He had a sense of humor. She would remember that.

"Back to the question. You were in a car accident. Do you remember wrecking your car?"

"Sure. I remember driving down the road. And then this deer ran out in front of me. I swerved." He shrugged. "The rest is history."

"A deer? In the middle of the day?" The accident report said it happened at three in the afternoon.

Some of his insolence faded. "Maybe it was a cow. . . ."

Rachel suspected he was just saying what he thought she wanted to hear. Lots of patients played that game. But she wasn't here to back him into a corner. That wasn't her intention. Her intention was to gain his trust, become his friend so he would tell her what he remembered and what he didn't. She wanted him to admit that he needed her help. Only then could she give it.

"Let's back up a little. What is your full name?"

"Samuel Harden Thoreau."

"Where were you born?"

"River Bend, Iowa. My parents divorced before I was born. I never knew my dad. My mother died when I was fifteen."

All accurate according to his personal history file. "Who is the president of the United States?"

His eyes clouded over and he jumped to his feet. He paced, then stopped in front of her. "I'm not crazy."

"*Crazy* isn't a word we use here. No one is crazy. Some people just need help."

"Yeah, yeah." He waved a hand, leaning closer. "Well, I don't need your help. Because I'm not crazy. But I'll tell you what." He jabbed a finger her direction. "If I have to stay here much longer, I will be."

He began pacing again, stopping in front of the camera. "Big Brother is watching." He made a rude gesture with his hand. Then he turned and strode back to his chair, grabbed it and slammed it down directly in front of her. He plopped down on it so that their knees were just inches apart.

"I have a great idea," he said. "How about a little role reversal. How about I ask *you* some questions? I'll pretend I'm the shrink and you're the patient. What do you think about that?"

"It sounds fine. Ask me anything you like. That's what this is all about. Getting to know each other."

"You really should have a couch, but this will have to do. Okay, what's your full name?"

"Rachel Danielle Collins."

"Age?"

"Thirty-two."

"Married?"

"Divorced."

"Is Collins your married name or maiden name?"

"Maiden name."

"Any kids?"

She hesitated. "No."

"Ah." He nodded his head in true shrink fashion. "Kids get in the way, don't they? You're a busy woman. With an important career. Shrinking people. A kid would really cramp your lifestyle. And what about hubby? Was he a pain in the connubial butt?"

Their roles had switched with a vengeance. With the precision of a surgeon he had lasered in and exposed her deepest wound. But she had to hold her ground. She had told him he could ask her anything. She couldn't back out. Couldn't go back on her word.

"We just went our separate ways, that's all."

"Because you were too involved in your job? Did you neglect poor hubby?"

Maybe Dr. Fontana had been right. Maybe she should

have given this case to someone else. Someone stronger. Maybe he was too smart for her.

"Did you neglect him, Dr. Rachel Danielle Collins?"

He was zooming in, getting closer to her pain. She felt as if she were smothering.

"The truth," he said mockingly. "We have to tell the truth here."

"Yes. Yes, I suppose I did neglect him."

"Did your job come first, before your family? Was that it?"

"No . . . yes. Maybe. My job was very important. But so was my family."

"And now . . . now how is your life, Rachel? Neat and tidy? Do you live alone?"

"Yes."

"Are you satisfied with your life?"

She was lonely. She hurt. "Yes."

"What do you do at night when you go home to that empty house?"

She played the "if only" game. If only she hadn't taken Jennifer to the baby sitter that day. If only she hadn't gone back to work. If only the baby sitter hadn't gone to the grocery store. If only the light at the intersection had been red instead of green. If only . . .

"No, wait. Don't tell me. I'll tell you." He put his elbows on the arms of the chair and put the fingers of both hands together in front of his face, watching her over them. There was an intensity in his eyes that was almost mesmerizing. "Let's see. You go home and eat a TV dinner while you watch the news. Very important, news. Gotta know who the president is."

He closed his eyes, as if in deep concentration. "You brush your teeth, careful to do each tooth for ten seconds. Then after that you put some cream stuff on your face—you have nice skin. Then you go to bed. All by yourself. Nobody to bother you, nobody to call out to you in the middle of the night. Nobody to need you."

Oh, God.

Rachel had to stand up, had to get away, had to get some air, but she couldn't move. Her heart was hammering. Sweat had broken out on her forehead and her palms. There was a terrible pain in her chest from the breath she couldn't seem to draw.

Her clipboard and pen slipped from her numb fingers and clattered to the floor. Papers scattered. She dropped to her knees and began frantically gathering the papers, her hands shaking, the papers rattling like dry leaves. Her pen. She couldn't find her pen. Her—

"Rachel . . ."

She looked up. *He* was holding it out to her.

She had to get away. Had to get out of here.

She grabbed the pen and scrambled to her feet, the clipboard clutched protectively to her chest.

"Tell me something, Rachel," Sammy said as she hurried away from him and his questions.

She paused at the door.

"Who shrinks the shrink?"

That night Sammy was lying on his back in bed, hands behind his head, staring up at the ceiling. He'd been given a shot to make him sleep, and it was beginning to take effect. The night before they'd given him a pill. He'd held it under his tongue until the nurse left, then stuffed it under the mattress. But they were on to that trick, because fifteen minutes later the nurse came back and found his hiding place.

He had to give them credit. They were on the ball.

He shouldn't have come down on the doc so hard, he decided.

Jeez. What was he saying? She was the shrink. He shouldn't feel guilty for fighting back. But he did.

He was scared. Something was going on, and he couldn't understand it. There had been that deal with the president. Who the hell *was* president? He didn't know. He should know who the damn president of the United States was. And there were the questions about the car wreck. He couldn't remember a damn thing about any car wreck. He couldn't even remember what kind of car he'd been driving.

And cars were his thing.

When Dr. Collins had asked him about the accident, her expression had been a little odd, as if she knew something she wasn't telling him. And that scared him.

And he couldn't quit thinking about that first nurse, the one who smelled so bad. Who told him he was thirty-eight.

A lie. They were all a bunch of damn liars, twisting things around, confusing him.

His eyelids started to droop. Sleep beckoned. Next time . . . maybe next time he wouldn't be so hard on Dr. Rachel Collins—if he ever saw her again.

Sammy set up his chair the way he had the day before. "Let's get down to the important stuff."

He'd been surprised to see Dr. Collins again. He figured she'd give his case to somebody else. He was even more surprised when she agreed to try the role reversal again.

"Go ahead," Rachel said.

He could tell she was bracing herself for an attack. He would surprise her. He settled in across from her. "Have you ever been to Disneyland?" he asked.

His efforts were rewarded with a slow smile and a relaxing of her shoulders. "Twice."

"Mr. Toad's Wild Ride?"

"Yes. More times than I can count. I love the butler."

"The Matterhorn?"

"No."

"No? You went to Disneyland and you didn't go on The Matterhorn?" he asked in disbelief.

"I was afraid I'd throw up," she said a little sheepishly. "And I make it a point to never ride anything with a warning sign beside the entrance."

"The Matterhorn's the biggest rush I've ever had. Well, almost," he added as an afterthought. "I went there and spent one whole day just riding that one ride. As soon as it was over I'd get off and walk right back to the end of the line."

He suddenly realized that she was watching and listening very intently.

Uh-oh. Shrink trap. Make it look like you're asking the questions, then suddenly you're answering your own damn questions. She was sharp. Really sharp.

"How old were you when you rode on The Matterhorn?" she asked.

Shrink trap.

He frowned. He'd just graduated from high school. He'd driven there with a couple of buddies, Harper and Luke.

Spent the summer in California. How long ago *had* that been? Not long. Not long at all. But there were other memories. Vague ones. Of some guys in fatigues and camouflage

helmets. Sammy could remember holding a camera, taking pictures . . . of what?

Dead guys.

Taking pictures of a pile of dead guys.

A uniformed officer jerked the camera from his hands and smashed it on the ground. He could see the film lying there in a tangled heap, exposed to light.

But he'd never been in the army. Had he? Sammy squeezed his eyes shut, trying to block out the image.

"Sammy?"

Rachel Collins was leaning close. Behind her glasses her eyes looked concerned.

Green eyes. Compassionate eyes.

He straightened his back and shoulders. "How old was I when I rode The Matterhorn?" He pretended to give it some thought. "Eighteen. I was eighteen." Just a while back.

"Some time ago, then?"

A trap. He couldn't let her see that he was mixed up or he'd never get out of there. He had to make it look as if everything was cool, as if everything made perfect sense. "Yeah," he said. "A long time ago."

SEVEN

RACHEL FELT AS IF SHE AND SAMMY HAD MADE SOME headway yesterday. He had actually conversed with her in a friendly manner. So today she'd brought along the Wechsler Memory Scale, hoping that he'd be ready to begin standardized testing.

As soon as she opened the door to the windowless evaluation room, she could see that things weren't going to go as she'd anticipated.

Sammy was seated in his typical sprawled pose. He appeared relaxed, but Rachel knew all about false body language, and she sensed that Sammy's pose was a carefully cultivated act. For one thing, his arms were crossed at his chest, his hands jammed under his armpits. Hands were a giveaway. Even when a person seemed totally composed, their nervous hands told a different story.

He was thin enough to cause concern, and his eyes were shadowed. His chart showed that he wasn't eating.

She stepped into the room and closed the door. "Are you still hiding your pills under the mattress?"

He looked up at her and smiled without parting his lips—a secretive smile. "I don't like Thorazine," he said. "Gives me indigestion."

Rachel made a mental note to check with the nurse to see if he'd been taking his medication.

She sat down and Sammy immediately came out of his slouch and pulled his chair close so that he was facing her, his knees just inches from hers, his expression smug.

Her initial reaction was to shift away, but she knew he was trying to intimidate her by invading her space.

"Would you like to choose a subject to talk about today?" she volunteered.

He leaned back in his chair and crossed his arms again. "Ladies first."

She wished he would stop thinking of her as the enemy. They would get nowhere like this. His distrustful attitude reminded her of the school delinquent in trouble with an overly strict principal.

She rolled her shoulders, making herself relax. She smiled and met his cocky gaze. "What kind of music do you like?"

Music was usually a good topic of conversation. Everyone liked music in some form or other, and from experience she'd found that most people could get quite involved in a discussion about music.

"Rock." He paused. "And roll. How about you? Do you like rock and roll?"

"Yes. I like all kinds of music." It was true. And she hoped to show him that she had an open mind.

He unfurled his arms and leaned close, his elbows braced on the knees of his faded jeans. A flash of cunning lit his black eyes, causing alarm to stir deep inside her.

"Do you know what rock and roll means?" he asked. "Do you know where the phrase comes from?"

"I never really thought about it. I always supposed it had to do with movement . . . maybe dancing."

"You got the movement part right."

This was another one of his little games. He had that look on his face, the one that said he had baited a trap and was now waiting for her to step inside.

He was charmingly transparent.

"I don't know," she said, deciding to leave the conversation open and let him play his hand.

"Rock and roll is slang for sex. Back in the fifties a New York disc jockey came up with the name. It was a secret joke that got out of hand because none of the straight people knew what it meant."

He smiled, and the smile was ornery and sexy at the same time.

She adjusted her glasses. "How very interesting."

"So be careful. If some guy comes up and asks you if you want to rock and roll, he might be asking you if you want to get laid."

"I'll remember that."

She wished he'd quit staring at her that way. What message was he sending? Just seconds before she'd been thinking how transparent he was. Now she didn't know if he was teasing her because he thought she was unattractive, or if he just liked to talk about sex.

Somehow she refrained from checking to see if her clothes were all in place. Instead, she flipped opened her folder and pulled out the Wechsler Memory Scale test. It was usually the first oral test given in a memory-loss case.

"I'm going to ask you some questions," she said, settling the folder on her crossed knee.

"I thought we were supposed to get acquainted."

"I think you're ready for some simple tests." She uncapped her pen, twisting the plastic cap on the end. "I'd like you to count backward from twenty."

He rolled his eyes, settled back in his seat, and counted down from twenty.

When he was finished, she checked the box labeled Accomplished. "Now recite the alphabet."

With obvious disgust he complied.

"Now count forward in threes."

When he reached 360 she stopped him.

"Being a shrink sure is a gravy job," he said.

"I told you the test was easy."

"You know what your problem is? You don't have any attitude. Doctors have to have an attitude. You have to act like you know all the answers even when you don't."

"An attitude?"

"Yeah, doctors are all bluff." He shifted his hips. "Is it true what they say about shrinks?"

"What's that?"

"I always heard people become shrinks because they want to figure out their own problems. Is that true? Have you got a lot of problems, Rachel?"

She had to be careful. He was trying to steer the conversation toward her personal life. He was seeing if he could upset her again. "Everyone has problems. Problems are a part of living. I'm here to help people learn to deal with those problems. Not run from them."

He pursed his lips and nodded his head in mock wisdom. "Oh . . . I see."

"Shall we get back to the test?"

"You're the doctor."

She gave him a short story to read, then asked him to tell her what he'd read. After that she read sequences of numbers, then had him repeat them to her. Then she had him reverse the order of the numbers.

She showed him a picture—a street scene—then put it away and had him draw what he could remember.

He let out another heavy sigh and took the pencil and tablet from her outstretched hands.

He drew with long strokes, his head bent over the page. When he handed it back he hadn't missed anything. Birds, clouds, flowerpot in the window, the manhole cover in the street—they were all there. He didn't possess much artistic talent, but everything was recognizable. There was even something endearing about his unself-conscious drawing.

Now he was ready for the last part of the test, which was called paired-association learning. She gave him twenty pairs of words. The first ten were easy associations. The last ten were difficult. When she finished with the list, she went back and gave him the first word. He was supposed to remember the second of the pair.

He got a perfect score. She'd never had a patient get a perfect score.

"So, doc. What's all this mean?"

"It means you have excellent short-term memory."

"I told you there was nothing wrong with me."

But she knew a person could have a high score and still be found highly amnesiac when tested with other procedures.

She knew Sammy didn't know who the president was. And she suspected that he wasn't sure about his trip to Disneyland. Yesterday Rachel had consulted with Sammy's sister. Molly had told her that Sammy had gone to Disneyland right after graduating from high school. But as far as she knew, he hadn't been there in several years.

"So, when do I get to check out of this joint?"

"You can't leave here until a release form is signed."

"Well, sign it."

"It can't be signed until you complete the tests to our satisfaction. Tomorrow I'll give you the one that deals with long-term memory. It focuses on things we call publicly rehearsed, which is no more than common knowledge. The second part is devoted to things that happened during certain time periods. It's rather like playing Trivial Pursuit."

"Trivial what?"

"Pursuit. It's a game." She jotted something down on her tablet.

"What are you doing?" he asked suspiciously.

"Just making some notes."

"Let me see that." He jerked the clipboard from her

hands and turned it around. "Trivial Pursuit." He tore off the page, crumpled it, and tossed it to the floor. Then he shoved the tablet back at her. "You wrote that down because I hadn't heard of it. I don't *play* games. That's why I've never heard of it."

"That's not why I wrote it down. I wrote it down because I thought you might like to play it someday."

"You're lying." He jumped to his feet. His chair tipped and crashed to the floor behind him. "I'm not going to be around here long enough to play any damn games. I want out of here. *Now.*"

Rachel knew that most patients shouldn't be pushed too hard at first, but she was beginning to think that a hard push might be what Sammy needed. "If you left, where would you go?" she asked.

He didn't answer.

"Would you go home? Would you go back to finish high school?"

"No. I've already graduated from high school."

Yet he hadn't been surprised by her question. "Then college. Would you go to college?"

His eyes were unfocused, his mind somewhere else, trying to make sense of his thoughts. "I went to college for a while . . ." All his former cockiness was gone; his voice was low with uncertainty.

"Then what? What did you do after college?"

She could see him struggling to retrieve, but he was unable to do so.

"I'm not crazy."

"Nobody said you were. You've had an accident and you've had some memory loss."

"I don't have any damn memory loss. Didn't that test just prove it?"

"Who is the president of the United States?"

He turned his back to her. His shoulder muscles beneath his T-shirt were drawn tight; the hands at his sides were clenched. "Nixon," he said without conviction.

"Have you ever heard of Watergate?"

"Watergate? Isn't that the Democratic headquarters in D.C.?"

His controlled nervousness had turned to panic. She could sense it all around her, seeming to fill the small room.

He'd had enough reality for now. She didn't want to have to sedate him again.

He had recalled high school and a little college, so, trying to pick a subject he might be familiar with, she asked, "Have you ever heard of Kennedy?"

"*President* Kennedy? Or Bobby?"

"President."

"He was assassinated by Lee Harvey Oswald. By a bullet fired from the book depository."

"That's right."

"In Dallas," he continued. "It happened in Dallas. 1963."

"Yes."

She wanted to ask him how long ago that had been, but he was too upset. She'd pushed him far enough.

"I've never been to Dallas," he said.

He was talking more to himself than to her, reminding her of a child trying to convince himself that there weren't any monsters under the bed.

"I've never been to Dallas either," she said. But Rachel knew Sammy had. In his file she'd come across an article he'd written on the conspiracy controversy.

"Or Houston." His face was chalk-white. "I've never been to Houston."

He set his chair upright, then sank down on it. He lifted one hand in front of his face and examined it very closely, as if expecting to find skin that was old and wrinkled. In truth, Sammy looked younger than thirty-eight. He could probably pass for thirty.

"I think we've talked enough for today," she said.

"No shit." He blew out a long breath, then buried his face in his hands.

Rachel stood and motioned to the camera, signaling Jake to shut off the videotape so he could come and escort Sammy back to his room.

She turned away from Sammy. The sight of him subdued bothered her more than she'd expected. She didn't like to see him humbled.

She heard the door open, but she couldn't watch as Jake led Sammy away.

After they were gone, Rachel lowered herself into the chair Sammy had just vacated. She sat there a few moments, staring down at her hands, which were lying in her lap. They were shaking. She clenched them into tight fists, trying to make them stop. But the shaking was coming from deep inside her.

She needed a drink.

It had been months since she'd felt such an overwhelming urge for something to settle her nerves. But she felt it now.

Dr. Fontana had been right. She'd taken on too much too soon. Maybe if Sammy liked her, if he at least trusted her, then things would be different. But to him she was the enemy. He wouldn't want help from the enemy.

But to step aside, to turn his case over to Sanderson . . . Sanderson was an ass. He was abrasive and totally unsympathetic. Somewhere along the line he'd lost his compassion, if he'd ever had any to begin with.

But maybe that's what it took to survive.

She couldn't figure out why Sammy was getting to her like this. Was it because she knew of the mental suffering that lay ahead for him? Suffering was something she understood all too well.

Memory loss was a tragedy, because memory was more than just the power of remembering. Memory was a treasury of personal intimacies, sweet souvenirs of the times of a person's life. Only thorough testing would tell for certain, but Rachel was afraid that Sammy had lost many of those precious souvenirs. And she was afraid he was going to have a hard time coming to grips with that loss. For him, the nightmare was only just beginning.

She took a deep, stabilizing breath, then checked her watch—10:30. She'd been with him a little over an hour and already she was exhausted.

They weren't right for each other, it was that simple. They clashed. It happened sometimes. He was too intense and cunning for her; she was too cautious and unsure for him. She had failed before she'd even begun.

First, do no harm.

A doctor had to know when to say she'd been beaten and step aside, admit defeat.

Maybe she could talk Dr. Fontana into letting Mark Elliot take Sammy's case. That way, she could oversee everything from a distance.

That decision made, Rachel closed her eyes and tipped her head back, feeling hollow.

Chicken.

Sammy knew he was chicken. He could feel his heart thumping in his chest. His skin was damp with sweat. But his mind was clicking along, sorting, cataloging, putting everything in order, heeding the voice of logic. But Sammy didn't want to hear the voice of logic. He wished he could just shut it off.

Because he was chicken.

For a few moments back there with Dr. Collins, he'd half expected to look down at his hands and find them wrinkled and yellow-nailed. Find out somebody had pulled a Rip Van Winkle on him.

Son of a bitch.

Big Jake, the hospital bouncer, was striding along beside him, escorting Sammy back to his room.

But Sammy didn't want to go back to his room. It was too empty. Too quiet. Too conducive to thought. And he didn't want to have to listen to the thoughts that were running rampant through his head, careening off his skull.

He glanced over at Jake. Man, the guy was big. "How about we go and get a cup of coffee?" Sammy asked in the most pleasant voice he could dredge up.

Jake smiled. "That would be nice, but I can't leave the floor."

"Then how about a game of cards? You like to play cards?"

"Sorry. I've got to escort another patient in just a few minutes."

Escort. Hospital talk for guard.

Sammy quit walking. He stood there, hands at his waist. Jake took a few steps, then realized Sammy wasn't coming. He stopped and turned, his bushy eyebrows raised in polite question.

"How old would you say I am?" Sammy asked. His heart was thundering again. He could feel it in his temple, feel it in his fingertips.

"How old? I don't know. I'm not very good at ages."

"Come on. Just give it a shot."

Jake's dark eyes did a quick inventory of Sammy, from his short hair to his sneakers, then back to his face. "I don't know." He shrugged. "Thirty-one . . . thirty-two?"

Sammy could feel panic crawling through him. His lungs seemed to constrict. The edges of his vision became blurry. Check-out time.

You're thirty-eight, Sammy, came the taunting voice of that other nurse, Brunhilde.

The hag had been telling the truth.

The clues had been there all along; he just hadn't wanted to see them. Obvious things like clothes and hairstyles.

His own clothes were the same ones he'd always worn. The jeans with the button flies and the faded T-shirt with the Iowa State emblem. He remembered buying the T-shirt at the university store. His buddy Jay had been with him. As they were leaving, Sammy had flirted with the good-looking girl at the cash register only to find out she was married and had a baby at home.

Now Sammy thought about some of the clothes he'd seen in the hospital halls. They'd been a little . . . *different*. And the hairstyles—Dr. Collins's was pretty tame, but some of the nurses had hair that was obviously dyed and lacquered and stuck up about a foot in the air.

What had happened to the natural look? What had happened to bell bottoms? Why wouldn't they let him watch television, or read any magazines or newspapers?

Sammy glanced over his shoulder. They were standing in front of the men's rest room.

He'd been chicken long enough.

He lunged, shoving open the door with such force that it crashed against the wall.

To the right was a row of stalls, to the left, four sinks. Above the sinks was a mirror that ran the length of the wall.

Before he could change his mind, Sammy ran to the mirror. With the palms of both hands braced against the cold porcelain sink, he forced himself to face his reflection.

A gaunt, hollow-eyed stranger stared back.

Oh, God.

The man in the mirror wasn't him. It couldn't be him.

Not this guy with the sunken cheeks and haunted eyes.

From the edges of his awareness came the sound of hushed voices. People were standing in the doorway, talking about him. He heard the word *sedate*. But he didn't care. He didn't glance away, didn't take his eyes off the reflection before him.

He raised a hand and touched the side of his face. The man in the mirror did the same.

You're thirty-eight, Sammy.

They both cringed.

No! It wasn't true. Only weeks before, he'd gotten that brown envelope in the mail. His draft notice. *Report for duty.*

He'd gone to tell his buddy Jay, only to find that Jay had gotten one too. It seemed that after kicking them both out of college for starting a riot, the good old dean hadn't wasted any time turning both their names into the draft board.

"*No!*"

Sammy made a fist and smashed the mirror, shattering the image in front of him. Again and again he hit it while glass flew around him.

Suddenly hands were grabbing him from behind, pulling him away.

"Calm down, buddy."

Jake's voice. Jake's hands on his arms. But Jake didn't understand what was happening, didn't understand Sammy's terror.

Sammy fought, but fighting with Jake was like fighting a bear.

Sammy's arms were pulled back even tighter, making his shoulder joints twist in their sockets. He bent his knees, thinking about hurling Jake over his head.

No dice.

Suddenly Sammy was shoved forward, his body slammed against the floor, his face pressed to the cold tile, one massive knee crammed into his back, his hands pinned behind him.

"You're going to cost me my damn job," Jake panted from above. "I got a wife at home with a baby on the way."

Sammy tried to speak, but he couldn't draw a breath, couldn't make a sound.

The door crashed open.

"What's going on in here?" came Rachel's stunned, outraged voice.

Good old Rachel. Rachel would save him.

"I don't know," Jake said. "One minute he was asking me if I wanted to play cards, the next thing I know, he was in here, flipping out."

"Let go of him."

You tell him, Rachel.

"Give him the hypo, then I'll let him go."

"Let go. *Now!*"

Then Rachel was shoving Jake away—or Jake was letting himself be shoved. "Can't you see he's not breathing?"

With the three hundred pounds off him, Sammy sucked in huge lungfuls of air, then immediately went into a paroxysm of coughing.

Free to move, he rolled away from them both, facing the wall, his knees drawn up to his chest, waiting for his lungs to relax, waiting for the black dots in front of his eyes to go away.

Little by little the pain and coughing and blackness subsided. He began to breathe normally.

From behind him he heard Rachel say, "Wait in the hallway, Jake."

Jake mumbled something that Sammy didn't catch.

"No," Rachel said. "No more hypos. Just wait outside."

Jake shuffled away. "I'll be right outside the door," he said, loud enough for Sammy to hear. "Right outside."

Sammy listened while Rachel moved closer, stopping when she reached him. "Sammy . . ." From the direction of her voice, he could tell that she'd crouched down beside him. Then he felt her hand on his shoulder, urging him to turn around. "Sammy . . ."

He stayed curled away from her. He even started to tell her to leave him alone, but then he realized that he didn't want her to leave him alone.

"Sammy, you're bleeding. Let me look at your hand."

He untucked his hand from where he'd been hugging it to his stomach. He was surprised to see she was right.

The knuckles of his right hand were split open. There was blood on the floor, blood on his T-shirt, blood on his jeans.

He rolled over, then scooted to a sitting position. Without looking up, he extended the injured hand to her and waited for her to take it.

Her touch was cool and comforting. But for a doctor, not all that steady.

She examined his hand. "You somehow managed to miss the tendons, but you're going to need stitches."

"You're shaking," he observed.

He was close enough to hear her draw a deep, trembling breath. "I'm sorry," she whispered. "I haven't handled your case very well. I was trying to protect you, trying to make things easier for you."

He'd come this far. He couldn't chicken out now. "Rachel . . . how old am I?"

He looked up. She wasn't wearing her glasses, and he was surprised to see a glimmer of tears in her green eyes.

She swallowed. Then, not taking her eyes from his, she said, "Thirty-eight."

He squeezed his eyes shut and took a deep breath. Time ticked away. . . .

When he opened his eyes again, she was still holding on to his hand. And with a strange detachment he noted that she'd wrapped his bleeding knuckles with white paper towels. He hadn't even felt her do it.

His throat was tight. He swallowed, but it didn't help. His vision blurred.

A frightening sound—a hoarse sob—rose from deep inside him. His lack of control terrified him.

Then, to add to his horror, he began to cry. And once he started, he couldn't stop.

He was so alone. He needed to touch and be touched.

Blindly, he reached for Rachel, grabbing fistfuls of her lab coat. He pulled her close and buried his face against her chest.

EIGHT

RACHEL STEPPED INTO HER APARTMENT, NUDGED THE door shut, and tossed her coat and patient files on the couch.

The apartment was small—one bedroom with the kitchen separated from the living room by a high Formica counter. But its size suited Rachel.

Several months after Jennifer's death, Rachel put their home up for sale and moved into the tiny apartment. It was near the hospital, and she didn't have to worry about taking care of the yard. There was a handyman who did that. And he fixed things when they broke. And more important, the apartment held no memories.

She'd considered leaving work early that day. In her thoughts she'd pictured herself arriving home to go directly to the highest cupboard in the kitchen. She'd imagined reaching all the way to the back, past the faded plastic bowls and empty glass vases to pull out a fifth of scotch.

She hadn't had a drink in months. Some time ago she'd faced the ugly realization that alcohol and drug dependency was a self-centered way to live. And she didn't want to be self-centered. But she kept the bottle as security, just in case a day like today came along. A day when everything fell apart.

But then the incident with Sammy had occurred, changing her whole perspective, not only on the day, but on Sammy's case and the role she was playing in his recovery. Just when she'd thought she didn't matter, just when she'd decided she was actually a hindrance and that he'd be better off with someone else—even Sanderson the jerk—Sammy had reached out for her.

And now she couldn't let him down. She also knew that in order to help him, she had to start believing in herself.

She'd always thought she was good at reading people, but she'd been wrong about Sammy. Just because he could dish it out, she'd thought he was tough. His act had fooled her. He wasn't tough at all. He was scared and trying his best to hide it.

Rachel went to the kitchen and opened the freezer. Her hand automatically reached for the TV dinner on top of a stack of four—one for each remaining day of the week—then stopped. Tonight she would have something different. A sandwich? Yes, a sandwich.

She shut the freezer and opened the refrigerator. It was almost empty, the light bulb glaring nakedly from the back.

Her mother had always said that an unobstructed light bulb was a sign of a bad wife and mother. She'd also said that good mothers didn't work outside the home. Good mothers didn't seek personal satisfaction.

And in the end her mother had been right. People with empty refrigerators *did* make bad mothers.

Jennifer's funeral. That was the last time Rachel's mother had spoken to her.

"Why couldn't you have been home with your child?" she had demanded while a cold rain struck the canvas cemetery tent above their heads and turned the sky an ugly gray.

Rachel had looked away, searching for something to

distract her mind. Her gaze had been unwillingly drawn to three grave diggers waiting under a tree, shovels in hand. They had been smoking and talking in loud, thoughtless voices. She hadn't wanted such people to be the last to tend to her daughter. She imagined them laughing and telling crude jokes as they shoveled dirt.

Cold seeped through her, and Rachel suddenly realized she was standing with the refrigerator door held wide.

She forced the bleak images from her mind and grabbed the rumpled lettuce, knotted bag of wheat bread, and the six-ounce jar of mayonnaise, almost emptying the refrigerator in the process.

She fixed the sandwich and poured herself a glass of milk, then sat down to eat in the solitude of her cramped kitchen. Her thoughts began to ramble again, going down paths she always tried to avoid.

Years earlier, when she'd dreamed of becoming a doctor, she'd never imagined herself at the age of thirty-two, spending her evenings alone.

Take responsibility for your own actions.

Like so many people who marry young, she'd married the wrong man. Psychiatrists were notorious for being unable to foresee and therefore prevent their own problems, and she was certainly no exception. She'd ended up sharing her life with a man who couldn't share. A man who had wanted a maid, not a wife. A man who took but never gave.

But Rachel hadn't allowed herself to bend to his will, and within a year David had moved back to the only place he'd ever referred to as home. Back to his mother. The year before, Rachel heard he'd remarried. Well, she hoped he'd found the right woman this time. Someone who liked being a doormat.

She finished her sandwich, rinsed her plate and glass, then went to the bathroom and took a shower.

Afterward, she spent the evening going over Sammy's file. It was stuffed full of the articles and information Molly Bennet had brought to the hospital.

She discovered that Sammy hadn't become a writer until he'd gone to Vietnam. Before that he had written scathing essays for his high school and college newspapers, but Rachel guessed the articles had been done more in fun than anything else.

Still, they had been enough to get him duty as army reporter. And with the sale of a stark, painful, uncomfortable and equally unforgettable article to *Rolling Stone,* Sammy Thoreau became an overnight folk hero.

There were stacks of reviews. One in particular caught her eye.

With a sense of self-recognition, Sammy Thoreau's writing touches something deep within us all. He has a way of clarifying emotions we ourselves have always felt but have lacked adequate words to describe.

And another one:

In *Through the Looking Glass, A Soldier's View*, Samuel Thoreau has given a first-hand account of the horrors of war in all its stark, shameful glory. We want to look away, but the magnetic power of his prose is too strong to ignore.

Possibly the reason Rachel had never heard of Sammy was that after Vietnam he went the way of most folk heroes: He slipped into oblivion. He continued to write, but not with any regularity, and certainly not with the same passion. His later stories seemed to lack spark, almost as if he'd given up, or was simply putting in time. Some were funny, some were sad, but they were all a little removed, as if he'd distanced himself somehow, as if he were holding back.

Rachel sat across from Sammy. They had been in the evaluation room five minutes, and so far there had been no mention of how he'd cut his knuckles. She'd already decided she wouldn't discuss the incident unless he brought it up. It was probably something he'd rather push aside, at least for now. There would be time to deal with it later.

Today Sammy was quiet, too quiet. There was no cocky body language. He hadn't pulled his chair close to hers. He was docile, answering questions when asked, not speaking unless spoken to.

Dressed in jeans and a black T-shirt, he sat, elbows on his knees, soles of his sneakers flat on the floor, his body bent forward, his hands clenched between his spread knees.

She had started the day's session with the standard who are you and where are you questions, all of which he'd answered quietly and without hostility.

Now she held a stack of nine by twelve pictures facedown in her lap. "I'm going to show you a series of portraits," she told him. "Let me know if you recognize any of these people."

He lifted his head to meet her gaze. With dismay, she saw that the light was gone from his dark, soulful eyes.

Above all, she must make sure he got that light back.

She held up the first picture.

"Charlie Chaplin."

"Right." She went on to the next.

"Albert Einstein."

"Right again." She lifted the next card.

"Dustin Hoffman."

"Yes."

"Beatles." Another card.

"Timothy Leary." And another.

"Charles Lindbergh." Another.

He hesitated this time. Then he shook his head. "I don't know."

"Gerald Ford. Does that name sound at all familiar to you?"

He thought a moment. "Wasn't he a member of the Warren Commission? I know—he wrote *Portrait of the Assassin*."

Portrait of the Assassin? She'd never heard of it. She checked the notes on the back of the card. Gerald Ford, along with John R. Stiles, had indeed written *Portrait of the Assassin* in 1965. Ford later became president in 1974, of which Sammy obviously had no memory.

They were getting closer to pinpointing the area where his memory stopped, which she knew could very likely be a ragged edge.

"Now I'm going to ask some questions," she said, putting the stack of cards aside.

"Go ahead."

"Who is Neil Armstrong?"

"First man on the moon."

She checked her test sheet. The first man walked on the moon in 1969.

"Neil Young?"

"Musician. Wrote *Heart of Gold*."

She would have to check the date on that.

"What is the minimum voting age?"

"Eighteen."

Before 1971, the voting age had been twenty-one. "Have *you* ever voted?" she asked.

He frowned, thinking. Then he shook his head. "No."

From earlier questions, she knew he still thought

Nixon was president. Nixon's first administration was 1969 to 1973.

"How much does a gallon of gas cost?"

"Around thirty-five cents."

"The cost of a movie?"

"Two bucks."

"What was the last movie you remember seeing?"

He thought a few seconds. *"M*A*S*H."*

"How much would you pay for a newspaper?"

"Fifteen or twenty cents."

"Cigarettes?"

"Forty."

"A record album."

"Three or four bucks."

"Candy bar?"

"Ten or fifteen cents."

And so the questions went.

Hour after hour, day after day.

By the middle of the following week, Rachel had all her re-

search compiled and was ready to meet with Molly Bennet—a meeting she wasn't looking forward to. It was going to be hard telling Molly that her brother had permanent, irreparable memory damage.

But at least she wasn't a harbinger of death.

Once when she was a first-year resident like Mark Elliot, she'd been in the room when a neurosurgeon had told a mother and father that their child was going to die. She had been amazed at how well the doctor had handled the situation. He'd used just the right words, just the right amount of compassion. She'd even caught herself wondering if it was all an act, if he really felt anything at all.

An hour later, she'd found that same composed, dignified surgeon hiding in a closet, crying.

Molly didn't like this. She didn't like the serious expression on Dr. Collins's face. She had smiled at her when she'd come into the office, but Molly had also detected sympathy combined with trepidation in that smile.

"Have a seat," Dr. Collins said, indicating the chair in front of her desk, a desk stacked high with files and folders.

Molly didn't want to sit down. She was too nervous to sit down. But she sat anyway. Perched on the edge of the cushioned chair, her purse gripped tightly with both hands, she waited.

"As you know, we've been conducting tests on your brother all week. We've run CAT scans and numerous neurological studies, plus a battery of memory tests." Dr. Collins clasped her hands together over a file. "The conclusion we've drawn is that Sammy has some memory impairment."

Memory impairment? That didn't sound terribly threatening. At least she hadn't said that Sammy was crazy. Molly began to feel a little less scared.

"I'm sorry to tell you that quite a large part of Sammy's memory is gone."

Gone? "Do you mean he has amnesia?"

"I don't like the word amnesia. It can be misleading."

"But he will get his memory back, won't he? Eventually?"

Dr. Collins took a deep breath. "People tend to think of memory loss the way it's portrayed in movies," she explained patiently. "A knock on the head and everything is fine. That won't happen to Sammy. I'm sorry, but there's no chance of his memory returning."

No! It wasn't true! Molly had heard about people who'd gotten their memory back. Had she simply traded one inadequate doctor for another?

Dr. Collins must have seen the disbelief in her face, because she went on to say, "In instances of emotional trauma, memory *is* sometimes regained. But that isn't your brother's case." She stood and reached across the desk. "Let me show you something."

She opened a big manila envelope and withdrew an X ray. "The brain is the most complicated and mysterious part of the human body. There are a lot of things we have yet to learn." Dr. Collins attached the X ray to a viewer screen on the wall and flipped on the light.

"This is a CAT scan of Sammy's brain. One of the things we *do* know is that this section"—with a pen, she indicated an area on the lower part of the brain—"is what is called the memory lobe. It's the place where memory is stored and retrieved. Some people who have been through severe emotional trauma still have memories stored in this lobe; they've just lost the ability to retrieve them. Sammy's case is different. Part of his memory lobe is missing. That means there is nothing there to retrieve."

She flicked off the light and sat back down. "I know you won't appreciate this now, but Sammy is very fortunate. He can still learn and build new memories. Many amnesiacs can't. In fact, Sammy is quite remarkable in his ability to retain. His test scores are some of the highest I've ever seen."

Molly felt numb with shock. Deep down, she'd known something was seriously wrong with Sammy, but she hadn't been willing to face it. She hadn't wanted to lose hope, because losing hope would have meant she'd failed him.

The doctor's voice went on, penetrating the fogginess in Molly's mind.

"As far as we can tell, Sammy's memories didn't end with a specific date. Imagine a piece of paper torn in half, its edges ragged. His last memories are like that. He remembers Vietnam, but he doesn't have a clear memory of himself in Vietnam. Sammy doesn't know you're married and he doesn't know you have a daughter."

"What happens now?" Molly managed to ask. "Will I be able to see him?"

"Yes, but Sammy's state of mind is very fragile. He's not ready to be overwhelmed with new and frightening information. The hardest thing will be getting Sammy to accept what has happened so he can begin a new life. What he needs is reassurance. He needs to know that you are here for him."

Dr. Collins began straightening Sammy's file, slipping the reports back inside. She looked up, and Molly thought she detected a glimmer of a tear behind the doctor's wire-rimmed glasses. But no. It must have been a reflection on the lens.

NINE

MOLLY WAS COMING TODAY AND SAMMY COULD HARDLY
sit still. He'd been eager to see her from the beginning.

He and Dr. Collins were in a place he'd immediately
labeled the fake living room, because you couldn't have
a real living room in a hospital. It had table lamps and
wallpaper and overstuffed chairs. But it didn't have a
lived-in feel. There was no personality here. It could
have belonged to anyone.

Sammy was sitting in one of the overstuffed chairs.
The thing had swallowed him. His ass was almost on the
ground. His knees were practically level with his chest,
and the armrests were so high he felt like the statue of
old Abe at the Lincoln Memorial.

Dr. Collins had apparently been swallowed by one of
the chairs before, because she'd opted for the firmness of
solid wood. She was sitting at the round table, head
bent, scribbling in that notebook of hers.

At first all of her note taking had bugged him. But
now he kind of liked it. It gave him the opportunity to
really check her out.

He was still checking her out when she closed the
notebook and looked up.

Caught in the act.

Sammy quickly redirected his gaze, shoved himself
out of the ridiculous chair, and paced to the window.

Today he'd had his first real glimpse of the world since his accident. When he'd first stepped into the room, he'd been afraid to approach the window. He didn't want to see something totally unfamiliar, something right out of *The Jetsons*. But except for the cars, everything had looked pretty normal.

Now he kept going back to make sure it was all still there.

After he'd finally comprehended what had happened to him, when he'd realized he'd lost a substantial part of his life, it had seemed like a nightmare within a nightmare. He couldn't handle it. Dr. Collins had told him he probably wouldn't get any of his lost memory back, and in desperation he'd latched on to the word *probably*.

Hadn't she told him that the brain was pretty much unexplored territory? And that most doctors didn't like to admit how little they really knew about it?

Sammy also knew lots of things happened that couldn't be explained. Like people waking up after being in a coma for twenty years. Or coming back to life after being pronounced dead.

He'd already decided he was going to be one of those unexplainable cases. He'd already decided he was going to get his memory back. It might take time, but it would happen. He just had to wait.

They were several floors up, but he could see the cars in the parking lot well enough to know they were pretty strange. Different from the cars he was used to. Practically clones of each other, most being small and bizarrely aerodynamic.

"What make is that?" he asked, pointing to a red sports car leaving the lot. It had a spoiler on the hood and mag wheels.

Dr. Collins came over and looked, frowned, then

shook her head. "I'm not sure. I don't know much about cars. I'll pick up some car magazines for you."

He nodded, only half listening.

He stood watching her as she stared out the window, the harsh, unforgiving sunlight pouring across her face.

She passed the direct-sunlight test. No zits. No huge pores.

He usually went for girls with a tan. Dr. Collins didn't have a tan at all. In fact, her skin was almost colorless except for a slight tint to her cheeks that almost matched the pink in her soft-looking lips.

She had great legs—from the knees down, anyway. More than once he'd caught himself wondering what she was hiding under that baggy lab coat.

Rachel.

He liked that name. He couldn't remember ever knowing anybody else with that name. In his mind, he usually thought of her as Dr. Collins. He'd started calling her Rachel to taunt her, to let her know he wasn't intimidated by her doctor status. But she hadn't seemed to mind. In fact, she hadn't even seemed to notice. But he knew she *had* noticed, because she noticed everything. After all, that was her job. She was a shrink.

He usually went for girls with long hair. He liked the way long hair felt sliding across his bare skin. But looking at Dr. Collins, he decided he liked her short hair. It didn't make sense, but the length actually made her look feminine, made her look sexy.

She glanced up and caught him staring again. This time he didn't look away.

He smiled.

She adjusted her wire-rimmed glasses—something she did quite a bit, usually when she was a little nervous. At times he liked to make her nervous. It gave him a small sense of power, made him feel a little in control of a situation where he had no control.

In his mind he went over what he knew about her. Divorced. No kids. Single. Lonely? He wondered if she was ever lonely.

"How old did you say you were?" he asked.

Her light eyebrows rose in surprise. Her pink lips parted to form words. "Thirty-two."

He hadn't paid any attention to that when she'd first told him, and until he'd accepted his true age, he'd thought of her as older than he was. Come to find out, he had six years on her. Weird.

"What are you smiling about?" she asked, smiling a little herself. She had small, perfect white teeth.

"I'm older than you."

"Thirty-eight isn't very old."

"It's double my life." He mentally shifted gears. "Double the life I remember, that is."

Actually, now that he'd gotten over the initial shock, the whole thing didn't seem quite real. Sometimes he could even laugh about it. Either that or cry. And he sure wasn't going to do anymore crying.

He tried to stop himself from looking down, but he couldn't. His gaze fell to his knuckles. Fifteen stitches. Stupid, Thoreau. Really stupid.

He wondered what she'd thought about him, hanging on her and crying like that. Probably thought he was a real wienie. He didn't want her to think he was a wienie.

He'd never lost it like that before, and it scared him. From now on he had to be careful. No more flipping out.

A light touch on his arm made him turn around.

Dr. Collins was looking up at him. "Your sister should be here anytime. I'm going to leave you two alone. But in case you need me, I won't be far, just down the hall."

He didn't get it. She was acting like this was going to be hard on him. From the concern he read in her expression, he could tell she was wondering if he could handle it. Of course, after he smashed that mirror, her doubt was understandable. . . .

But he *wanted* to see Molly. He'd wanted to see her all along. Maybe Dr. Collins thought they were the kind of brother and sister who fought all the time. There was nothing further from the truth. There was only one time he could even remember Molly raising her voice, and he'd deserved it. He'd deserved it a lot more than once.

"Don't worry," he told Dr. Collins. "I promise I won't go nuts."

"I never thought you would." She smiled, and he thought he detected a touch of sadness in that smile.

For him?

For her?

Maybe she missed her husband. Maybe that's why she was sad. She'd probably loved him. Well, sure she'd loved him. She'd married him, hadn't she? Then he had a thought that jarred him a little. Maybe she still loved him.

She gave his arm a reassuring pat. "I'll be down the hall."

The pat made him feel comforted and irritated at the same time. Comforted, because he liked it when she touched him. Irritated, because the casualness—hell, the *motherliness*—of her touch made him feel like a little boy.

As soon as she left, Sammy went back to staring out the window. But the streamlined cars zipping through the parking lot failed to hold his interest. His thoughts returned to Molly.

Quiet, dependable Molly. He'd grown up secure in the knowledge that she would always be there for him whenever he needed her.

Maybe they had always gotten along so well because they were complete opposites. She was cautious where he was reckless. She was stability and home while he dreamed of adventure and travel to faraway places.

He smiled to himself. Whenever he thought of Molly, he thought of flowers. Not soft, shy violets, or pale petunias, but brightly colored, dramatic roses.

In high school he'd written a story about Molly and her roses. About how they were an extension of herself. She was so quiet, her roses so vivid.

From behind him came the rattle of a doorknob.

He turned.

Standing in the doorway, holding a single red rose, was Molly. An older Molly. A Molly with streaks of gray in her brown hair.

Appearing a little unsure, she stepped inside the room and shut the door behind her. But that was Molly. New situations, new places, were always hard for her, always made her nervous. The secret of getting Molly to relax was to drown her in conversation until she gradually adjusted to her new surroundings.

An overpowering feeling of family, of belonging, filled him. God, it was good to see her.

Not hesitating, Sammy crossed the room and wrapped his arms around his sister, pulling her close.

She seemed smaller than he remembered, frailer than he remembered.

She sniffled. A small, trying-to-get-control-of-herself sniffle.

Only minutes ago he'd sworn that he was done with being a crybaby, but the sound of his sister's distress caused a suspicious tightness in his own throat. He blinked, swallowed, and set her away a little, so he could look at her. "Don't cry, Molly-o."

"It's just so good to see you." Her eyes trailed from him to the rose she held in her hand.

"You still have your roses, I see."

He felt her stillness, sensed her sadness.

"Yes."

How could one word convey so much pain? What had happened? He wanted to ask, but he knew he was on unstable ground. With his memory loss, he had no way of knowing which words would bring comfort, which would bring pain.

Careful, so the thorns wouldn't prick her fingers, he took the rose.

She still chewed her nails. He found an odd reassurance in that. He recalled all the times she'd tried to quit, all the remedies she'd used from Tabasco sauce to gloves.

But she still chewed her nails. And the world outside wasn't filled with Hovercrafts and plastic trees and smog. Maybe things hadn't changed so much.

Sammy made a quick search of the cupboards until he found a green soda bottle. He filled it with tap water, stuck in the rose, then set the bottle in the middle of the table.

"Remember the time that storm came up?" he asked, pulling out the chair Rachel had vacated earlier and sitting down. "A tornado had been spotted five miles out of town, heading in our direction. Branches were blowing off trees. And where were you?" He shook his head, giving her a what-am-I-going-to-do-about-you look. "You were out in the backyard, rescuing your roses."

The shared memory was having the effect he'd hoped for. Molly was beginning to relax. Her eyes softened as she focused on the past.

Palms flat on the table, she slid into the seat across from him. "Remember how you tried to get me to come in? But I wouldn't." She smiled. "So you got a pair of scissors and helped me cut all the blooms."

"I couldn't leave you out there by yourself."

Just as they had snipped the last blossom, the rain had come and the wind had tried to rip the roses from their bleeding fingers. They had raced to the house, their arms loaded with yellow and red and pink flowers, their hair plastered to their heads.

And they had stood there, just inside the door, while the civil defense siren blared and the wind rattled the windows.

"You're crazy, you know that?" Sammy had gasped between lungfuls of air. "Risking your life for a bunch of flowers."

"Not flowers. *Roses.* There's a difference. And just you wait and see," Molly had said with earnest intensity. "Someday my roses will be in every florist shop in the country!"

Now, without having to ask, he knew her roses hadn't made it to all those florist shops. Something had happened to her dream. Something had happened to Molly.

Sammy had been prepared for an older Molly, a fatter or thinner Molly. But not a changed Molly. Not a Molly who had given up, who had quit.

Was that what happened when people got older? Did their dreams die?

He felt angry at himself, at the years and the part of him he could no longer remember, at the person who had stood idly by while his sister's dream faded.

She had always been there for him. Who had been there for her?

Molly was watching him closely. He could read the distress in her eyes.

"What about the time you got up on the table in that pizza parlor?" she said, as if deliberately steering the conversation away from roses. "You stood there and said you'd fight anybody in the place!"

Sammy laughed, remembering.

"And the entire building was full of little kids and grandparents! I can still see their faces." She laughed. "What an awful thing for you to do to all those people."

"Me? It was Jay's idea. He bet me ten bucks that I wouldn't do it."

"When you two were together, there was no telling what would happen."

When the laughter finally died down, Sammy asked, "How's ol' Jay doing?"

Molly's smile faded. "I—I don't know," she said, suddenly training her eyes on the tabletop.

Sammy tried to think, tried to remember. "The last time I saw him . . . was . . . was . . ."

Sammy had gotten his draft notice in the mail. He'd jumped on his motorcycle and ridden over to Jay's house, wanting sympathy. When he got there, Jay's face had been pale, all his freckles standing out in contrast to his colorless skin. In his hand had been a draft notice.

"Look's like we're going together, bud," Jay had said.

"Guess so."

Jay had tried to smile, tried to make a joke of it. "Get kicked out of college together, fight together, die together."

Right now there was a hollow feeling in Sammy's stomach. Jagged memories filtered back. Though four years older, Jay had been his best friend. Until Molly came along, they had been inseparable. There had even been a time when Sammy had been jealous of his sister and Jay's closeness, jealous of Molly for coming between them.

Sammy looked at Molly's left hand. A wedding band. "You're married," he said, the hollow feeling moving to his throat.

She pulled her hand back, hiding it under the table. "Yes."

"But not to Jay."

"No."

"What happened?"

Molly wouldn't look at him. All he could see was the top of her head.

"Molly?"

"Oh, Sammy . . . I was afraid this would happen. I shouldn't have mentioned the pizza parlor. Maybe I shouldn't have come today."

"Come on, Molly. I've always been able to depend on you. Tell me the truth."

"It's not fair. You took it so hard the first time. You shouldn't have to go through it again." She looked up, her eyes swimming with tears. The choked words, when they finally came, didn't surprise him. "Sammy . . . Jay is dead."

"Vietnam?"

She pressed her lips together, then nodded.

He felt as if all the air in the room had been sucked out. His lungs hurt. His throat hurt.

He wanted to yell. He wanted to jump up and bang his head against the wall.

Instead, for Molly's sake, he curled his hands into tight fists and told himself to hang on. He crossed his arms on the table and hid his face.

I won't be a crybaby, he told himself as he felt a flood of tears welling up inside him.

His best friend Jay had been dead for years, and he hadn't even known.

When would the nightmare end? When would he wake up and find out this was all a warped dream?

He felt a hand on his shoulder. Molly's hand. "Do you want me to get Dr. Collins?"

He couldn't speak, so he only nodded.

TEN

IT WAS SUNDAY MORNING. RACHEL DIDN'T USUALLY stop at the hospital on Sundays, but she wanted to check on Sammy.

She pulled into the hospital parking lot, turned off the car engine, and set the emergency brake. From across the nearby hills came the plaintive echo of church bells, a normally comforting sound, but not today. Because today was no ordinary Sunday. Today was Mother's Day.

A joyous occasion. A day of flowers and candy and pastel dresses tied with pink sashes. Flat-brimmed straw hats perched on baby-fine hair. A day for mothers. And daughters.

Rachel squeezed her eyes shut and gripped the steering wheel tighter.

No matter how well Rachel thought she was doing, grief never failed to take her by surprise. She would go along, thinking she was getting better, when from out of nowhere would come grief, its impact hitting her as hard as that very first blow.

Everyone knew holidays were tough to get through for victims of severe loss. It was only to be expected. Making it through a holiday was like surviving a critical illness. But accepting that didn't make things any easier.

Rachel drew in a long, shaky breath, exhaled, then got out of the car and headed for the hospital.

Sammy Thoreau had been moved to a long-term facility, which meant he was in a larger room that was more like living quarters.

It was there that Rachel found him pacing back and forth.

As soon as her footfall sounded in the doorway, he swung around. The second he realized who it was, his frown turned to a smile. "Dr. Collins!" He bounded across the room, his energy buffeting her like a gust of ocean wind.

"I have a great idea. Let's go somewhere. Blow this hole for a while. What do you say?"

Restless, pent-up energy met bewildered sorrow. It took Rachel a moment to gather her thoughts.

"I could leave here for a while, couldn't I? Just an hour or two?"

The irrational side of her wanted to say yes. But the practical doctor knew he was too unpredictable, his psyche still too raw.

"Sammy . . . you're not quite ready. Maybe next week . . ."

"Next week!" He raked his fingers across his scalp, making his bristly hair stand on end. "I'm nothing but a guinea pig," he said in frustration. "A laboratory specimen. A damn freak show." He began pacing again.

She could certainly sympathize with him. He'd spent the past few days being evaluated by a team of psych students, which she had argued against, but Dr. Fontana had insisted Sammy start earning his keep.

"I've got to get out of here," Sammy said, his voice edged with panic. "Just for a while. For an hour. A few minutes. I need to breathe."

His gaze shifted around the room, seeking a solution, seeking an escape, finally coming to light on her once more. "I'll be good, I swear." He drew a finger across his chest. "Cross my heart."

The desperation in his eyes was almost her undoing. What he was suggesting wasn't all that irregular. It was only a matter of signing a pass. But he wasn't ready. *She* wasn't ready.

He was watching her closely, the way he always did. "You're not going to let me go, are you?" he asked.

"Sammy—"

"Don't say it. You don't have to say it. I can tell by your face." In a matter of seconds he'd gone from excited to disappointed to angry.

"I can read you like a book. A *boring* book. You have to get home to your boring little life. Your boring little apartment. Your boring TV dinners."

He was venting his frustration on her. Normally she wouldn't mind; normally she would have encouraged it. But not today of all days.

He was moving toward her, closing the space between them. She took one step back, then another, until she was pressed to the wall with nowhere to run. And he was still coming, his expression not so much angry now as analytical and a little cruel. Or was it hurt? Defensive?

"You're afraid," he stated. "What are you afraid of, Rachel?"

"Nothing."

"Tell me the truth. You're afraid of me, aren't you?"

"No."

"Yes. I've seen it in your face before, I can see it in your face now. Sometimes you look up from that clipboard of yours and catch me staring. And I can tell it bothers you. Why does it bother you, Rachel?" When she didn't answer, he asked, "Do you ever wonder what I'm thinking when I'm watching you?"

She swallowed.

"Want to know?"

She shook her head.

"No? But you're a shrink. You're supposed to want to

hear my deepest, darkest secrets. Isn't that right? My deepest, darkest desires."

His voice was rough, threatening . . . and, heaven help her, sensual.

She brought up her hand. Fingers splayed, she pressed against his chest, trying to hold him back . . . but he didn't move. She knew she could scream for help and someone would come. But she also knew Sammy would never hurt her. At least not physically. But his words . . . they were a different thing altogether.

"Sometimes when I look at you," Sammy whispered, his face only inches from hers, "I get horny. Did you know that, *Doctor* Collins?"

"Sammy." Once again she shoved the solidness of his chest, but it was like shoving against something set in concrete.

"You know what else?" he asked slowly, thoughtfully. "A lot of times I wonder what it would be like to . . . *kiss* you."

From his emphasis on the word *kiss,* she knew he was insinuating much more than a kiss.

She felt her own panic wind higher. This had to stop. Immediately. "I'm your doctor. You're my patient. There can be nothing sexual between us."

"So *you* say."

"So the physician's rules of ethics say."

"Screw the rules. Screw ethics." His voice dropped, became more intimate. "Tell me, Rachel. How long's it been since you were . . . *kissed*?"

That inflection again. And now he pressed his body firmly against hers so they were touching from chest to knee.

His head came down; his mouth drew nearer. Heavy lids half hid dark pupils.

In the fraction of a second before his lips met hers,

conscience won. She turned her face away. His mouth brushed her burning cheek.

He straightened slightly. Enough to look at her.

"Let me go," she said with a surprisingly level voice.

Confusion and anger and wounded pride were reflected in his eyes. By drawing away from his kiss, she'd struck a blow to his ego. But she couldn't have let him kiss her. She was his doctor. He was her patient. It was unthinkable.

All sensuality was gone from his expression. Anger had taken over. And anger was his defense.

Dismayed, she knew she was in for it. He was going to come at her with all he had.

"Let's see if I remember this right," he said sarcastically. "You used to be married, but your husband left you because you were a lousy wife, because your job came first before your family. Isn't that the way it was?"

Something cold curled deep inside her.

Despair.

She leaned her head against the wall. She squeezed her eyes shut. "Yes," she whispered hoarsely. "That's the way it was."

She no longer had to worry about sticky hands, or toys scattered on the bathroom floor. She didn't have to worry about spilled Kool-Aid or scraggly dandelions left on her pillow.

She swallowed. "When I look inside my refrigerator . . .
I can see the light bulb."

She had to get out, to get away from Sammy. She needed to go home. To get a drink. To fade away . . .

Who had she been kidding? She was no doctor, not anymore. She didn't belong there. She was more messed up than her patients.

She forced her eyes open.

Sammy's face was still looming over hers; the long,

hard length of him was still pressed to her. But his eyes were different. The anger was gone. There were parallel frown lines between his dark brows. He was watching her as he so often watched her.

"Rachel?"

He was clearly confused. He moved back slightly, still maintaining a light grip on her arms. "I'm sorry. I . . . get so damn frustrated. I—are you okay?"

She tried to think of the right words, professional words. Doctor words. Words that would make everything normal again. But she couldn't.

No, I'm not okay, because it's Mother's Day. And I won't be getting any warm, wet kisses or a plaster handprint with a pink bow on the top. . . .

She tried to look calm. "I have to go."

"I don't think—" Sammy cast a glance over one shoulder, toward the door she'd left ajar. She recognized alarm in his face. Worry. He guided her toward a chair. "You better sit down. You look a little . . . funny."

She didn't sit down. Instead, she managed to shrug away from his hands. "I don't have time. And I'm sorry I can't take you anywhere, but I'm busy. I have a lot of things to do."

If she could just get away, just get home, then she would be okay. Then she would never make herself come back here again. Ever.

She wasn't aware of walking, but suddenly she was out of the room, moving toward the elevators.

She should tell Sammy good-bye, but she had to get home right away. She didn't want anybody to find her crying in a closet.

ELEVEN

THE NEXT DAY SAMMY SAT ON THE EDGE OF HIS BED, waiting for Dr. Collins to stop by and get him for their session.

He'd done it again. He'd lost his head. So what was new? He could make excuses. He had a million. He was upset about Jay's death. He felt guilty as hell about letting Molly down, about not being there when she'd needed him. He hated the fact that he'd been turned into a damn sideshow. Poked and prodded and given the third degree by a bunch of psych students with superior attitudes. He hated being reduced to the status of a nobody.

But right now he felt like a nobody.

Rachel had come to his room at the wrong time, just when he'd reached the end of his self-control—what little self-control he had.

But there was no excuse for hurting her, for striking out at the very person who was doing all she could to help him. Why had he said such cruel things? It wasn't like him to be mean. Obnoxious, yes. Mean, no.

He got up from the bed and began pacing. He couldn't wait for her to get there. When she came, he'd say something funny to make her smile. Maybe even make her laugh. Then everything would be okay.

He suddenly remembered that he'd been pacing yesterday when she'd shown up, so he stopped. Calm. He had to stay calm.

He sat back down on the bed to wait.

When the knock came and the door to his room opened, it wasn't Dr. Collins standing in the doorway. It was somebody Sammy had never seen before.

"Hi. I'm Dr. Elliot. But you can call me Mark."

He didn't look like any doctor Sammy had ever seen. He supposed his black curly hair was short enough to look professional, but the clothes . . . Sammy had never seen a doctor dressed in faded jeans, a loud Hawaiian shirt, and basketball sneakers. His one concession to doctorhood was the red stethoscope draped around his neck and his gold name tag. Guess that made him official. From the tag, Sammy noted that he was a resident. Guess that made him *somewhat* official.

Sammy wanted to see Rachel, not someone who looked like a tourist at Knott's Berry Farm.

"Dr. C. won't be coming today," Mark said, entering the room with a springy stride. He was one of those guys who walked on the balls of his feet. "I'll be working with you instead. Don't worry. We'll have a good time."

"Why isn't she coming?"

Mark shrugged. "I don't know. Maybe she has a headache or something. Or maybe she just needed a day off. I'm familiar with all her cases. I always take over when she's gone." He looked at his watch. "I haven't had breakfast. What do you say we hit the cafeteria, then catch *Jeopardy!* in the lounge?"

"*Jeopardy!?*"

"On television."

"I know what it *is*." He was just having a little difficulty adjusting to the idea of such freedom. Rachel had been so controlled, so cautious. Now this guy was saying anything goes.

"I don't know. . . . Maybe I should wait until Dr. Collins gets back."

"You've got it all wrong. We're supposed to take advantage of her absence. Have some fun. Play a little hooky. It's no big deal. We won't leave the hospital. All we have to do is take the elevator to the basement, turn right, go down a few corridors, and we're there. Easy."

Yesterday Sammy would have given anything to get away. But he had imagined Rachel being with him, going with him. He felt safe when she was around. Without his saying anything, she seemed to know where his head was. She understood his fears.

"In Dr. Collins's notes, she said you need help adjusting to everyday things." Mark stood in the doorway, waiting. "What could be more everyday then eating?"

True. But since his accident, food had held no appeal for Sammy. He ate only enough to keep the IV out of his veins. But he could surely handle a trip to the cafeteria.

He ended up following Mark, wondering what Rachel was going to think when she got back.

She'd be pissed.

In the end, it wasn't too bad. Sammy didn't have any trouble handling the excursion. Maybe it was because Mark was a nonstop talker. Sammy had never been around anybody who talked so much. Sammy even caught himself wondering if Mark wasn't raiding the old pharmaceutical cabinet.

"I'm having real girl problems," Mark said around a mouthful of blueberry muffin.

Sammy sat with his shoulders hunched, his hands locked around a ceramic coffee cup, trying to ignore the interested glances of a couple of young nurses at a nearby table.

"I can't ever get a date," Mark said. "Try one of these." He slid half a muffin across the table. "They're made with real blueberries."

Sammy didn't want to be rude, so he picked up the muffin and took a bite. Mark was right. It wasn't half bad. Better than that, it was good.

"And the few times I do get a date," Mark went on, "I think, Oh, boy, now we're cooking. I've finally found a girl who's looking for more than a pretty face and hard body. Then you know what always happens?"

Sammy shook his head.

"They want me to psychoanalyze them. Solve all their personal problems. Like I'm some kind of Mr. Know-It-All. What really gets me is when they start talking about their *boyfriends*, for God's sake. What would you do in a situation like that?"

Sammy shrugged. "Charge by the hour?"

Mark laughed, blowing out a few crumbs. "Believe me, I've thought about it. But working around here is like living in a small, gossipy town. Everybody knows everybody else. It's easy to get the reputation of a jerk. A guy can do fifty great things, but let him do one lousy thing . . ." He shook his head. "It erases everything else and goes on your permanent record."

When they finished in the cafeteria, they went upstairs to the lounge to watch television and play cards.

Later that night, Sammy realized it had been nice shooting the bull with Mark, being with somebody who wasn't watching his every move, somebody who wasn't waiting for him to do or say something crazy. Yeah. It had been okay.

But that didn't mean he wasn't looking forward to seeing Rachel tomorrow.

But in the morning Mark was back.

"I'm not sure when we'll be seeing Dr. Collins again," he said when Sammy asked about her.

Sammy tossed out a few more offhand questions about Rachel, but Mark's answers were all vague and evasive, which was unusual for Mark. Sammy didn't like it. Something wasn't right.

Once again they ate in the cafeteria, then went upstairs to play cards.

"I can't believe you actually get paid for doing this," Sammy said as he shuffled the cards.

Mark was sprawled out in a chair, half of his attention on the television blaring in the corner, the other half on Sammy and the card game. "Look at this lady cry." Mark pointed to the TV. "She's the best crier I've ever seen."

Sammy dealt the cards. "Aren't you supposed to be doing doctor stuff?"

Mark raked in his cards and gave Sammy a bland look. "Like what?"

"Well, like changing bedpans, or taking somebody's temperature. Like giving me some tests."

"You're all done taking tests. In fact, I think you're ready to leave the grounds for a little while. You need to get out. Have some fun."

Sammy knew he should be glad, but instead he was skeptical. He couldn't help but wonder what Mark thought was fun. "What do you have in mind?" he asked suspiciously.

"Anything. You name it."

Sammy had an idea. "What do you say we go by Dr. Collins's house?"

Mark's bland expression became serious. "I don't think we better. How about going fishing? I hear the catfish are biting."

Sammy knew he was trying to steer him in another direction, but he didn't turn. "Dr. Collins might like to fish," he suggested. Sammy knew it was nuts, but he just had a bad feeling about all this and he knew he wasn't going to quit worrying until he saw her and made sure she was all right. Until he could tell her he was sorry.

Mark put his cards facedown on the table. "I wasn't supposed to tell you this, but you're going to find out sooner or later. And anyway, I make it a point to never lie, especially to my patients." He paused and gave Sammy his complete attention. "Dr. Collins isn't coming back."

Sammy didn't think he heard right. "What?"

"She's not coming back," Mark repeated. "She quit."

Sammy stared at him in disbelief. "This isn't some fast food joint where employees just come and go. Doctors don't just . . . *quit*."

Mark shrugged. "Rachel did. For personal reasons."

Sammy knew differently. It was because of him. Because of the way he'd treated her. "It's my fault," he said with conviction.

"You didn't have anything to do with it," Mark told him.

But Mark didn't know what had happened Sunday. He hadn't seen Rachel's face when Sammy had taunted her. Hadn't seen the way she'd drawn away.

"You don't understand. I kept pushing her. Goading her."

"It wasn't you. Listen." Mark glanced behind him, checking to make sure no one was listening. The other patients were obediently watching television. The lady on the screen was crying again. Her cheeks were wet. Her nose was even running.

Mark rounded his shoulders and leaned closer. "Dr.

Collins has some personal problems you don't know anything about."

"Her husband," Sammy said, piecing it all together.

"Not her husband. From what I've heard from a few people who knew him, he was a real jerk. She's lucky to be rid of him. No, this has to do with her kid."

"Kid? She told me she didn't have any kids."

"She doesn't. Not anymore. Over three years ago, her little girl died."

Sammy felt as if somebody had punched him in the stomach. All of his cruel words came rushing back at him.

"Sunday was Mother's Day," Mark said. "Holidays are tough for survivors. They can set everything off. " He shrugged. "I guess that's what happened to Rachel."

Your job came first before your family. Isn't that the way it was?

Self-loathing crawled through him. Sammy didn't deserve to get better. He didn't deserve anyone's help, especially Rachel's.

In the next second he knew he had to see her. He had to tell her he hadn't meant any of the things he'd said. He'd been feeling sorry for himself and he'd wanted to hurt somebody.

And he had.

He jumped to his feet. "I have to see her."

From Mark's expression, he could see there was no way in hell he was going to take him to her house. Mark's eyes narrowed. "Calm down, buddy."

"I *am* calm!"

Sammy knew it was happening again. He knew he was losing control, but he was beyond caring. With one hand he swept the cards from the table, but it didn't make him feel any better.

He had to see Rachel.

He didn't care about the patients who were getting to their feet and shuffling away uneasily.

Screw them. Screw them all.

Mark was coming around the table. Sammy pressed an open hand to his flowered shirt and shoved. Mark staggered back and Sammy dove for the door. Then he was off and running down the hall for the elevator. He slammed his palm against the button, then looked up at the lights above the door. The elevator was on the first floor.

Sammy's eyes darted back the way he'd come. Mark was running toward him, all of his cool gone.

To Sammy's left was an exit sign. A stairwell. He jerked open the door and took the steps three at a time, airborne most of the way. He crashed to the first floor landing and pulled open the door. As he ran down a brightly lit hall, he was peripherally aware of the startled faces on his left and right.

Screw them.

And then he was at the glass front doors. Beyond them, through the mesh wire, he could see a wide sidewalk leading away to a winding street.

With both hands he grabbed one rail of the double doors and threw all of his weight against it.

Nothing happened.

He grabbed the other and shoved.

Locked. They were both locked!

He rattled the metal rails, moving from one door to the other. Back and forth. Behind him, he could hear several pairs of pounding feet.

He was a goner.

He let out a sob of frustration. He'd screwed up again. There was no way out.

Defeated, he leaned his forehead against the cool metal of the door, hardly feeling the pain when he banged his stitched fist against the glass, not caring that he was bleeding again.

TWELVE

THE TELEPHONE WAS RINGING.

Rachel tugged the pillow around her ears and rolled over, trying to drown out the sound.

But she couldn't drown the nagging guilt. A doctor never ignored her ringing phone.

Then she remembered that she didn't have any patients anymore. There was no reason to answer the phone.

The ringing finally stopped. The rigidness was just beginning to leave her muscles when the phone rang again.

She couldn't talk to anyone now, couldn't pull herself together enough to make coherent conversation, even to a siding salesman or magazine solicitor. She just wanted to be left alone. . . .

As soon as silence descended she reached out, groping blindly for the phone, finally managing to knock the receiver to the floor.

There.

Relieved, Rachel fell back against the mattress.

Telephone receiver in hand, Mark Elliot sat with his sneakered feet propped on a corner of Dr. Collins's desk, listening to the busy signal. He hung up and tried again.

Still busy.

He suspected she was home and had taken the receiver off the hook.

He hung up. What do we do now? he wondered.

It had been almost twenty-four hours since the Sammy Thoreau catastrophe. It had taken Dr. Fontana only two seconds to remove Sammy from Mark's care and turn him over to Sanderson.

And everybody knew Sanderson was an ass.

His actions yesterday had certainly proved it. He'd taken one look at Sammy, ordered a full dose of Haldol *plus* morphine, then shipped him off to solitary.

Of course, Sammy had pulled that punch, and a good one it had been. Mark had almost applauded, but caught himself just in time.

Now Sammy was back to square one. Back to the very state he'd been in when he'd arrived, the only difference being that this time he wouldn't have Dr. Collins on his side. He wouldn't have anybody on his side.

Sanderson . . . Mark wouldn't send a cat with a fur ball to Sanderson. He wouldn't send his worst enemy to Sanderson.

He tried Dr. Collins's number one more time.

Busy.

Coming to a decision, he hung up, let his feet drop to the floor, and headed outside to the bike rack where he'd left his ten-speed.

Dr. Collins lived only a couple of miles from the hospital. On his bike, Mark was able to weave through traffic and cut down alleys, getting to her place in under fifteen minutes.

Even though he knew she wouldn't answer, he knocked on her front door.

No answer. Big surprise.

Strictly out of habit, he knocked again. He always

knocked twice. In case somebody was flushing the toilet or something.

He thought about yelling, but her place was one of about twenty-four apartments. He didn't want somebody to call the police. It looked bad when a doctor was arrested for disturbing the peace. And he'd had a few warnings already.

He tried the knob. It turned, but he didn't push the door. Did he dare? Dr. Collins wasn't his superior anymore. She couldn't get him fired or anything.

What the hell? He pushed it open, slipped inside, and shut the door after him.

Quiet. Stuffy. Empty.

Dark. The curtains were closed. As his eyes adjusted to the dimness, he could see that there was no bric-a-brac anywhere, nothing to make the place cozy. It didn't look like anybody lived there.

From where he stood near the front door, he could see into the living room. Beyond that, the kitchen. Ahead of him were stairs, presumably leading to the bedroom.

"Dr. Collins," he whispered.

Why was he whispering? She wouldn't be able to hear him if he whispered. "Dr. Collins!" he shouted.

No answer.

He moved through the living room, looking for signs of recent activity. A pair of shoes had been left near the couch. He moved to the kitchen. There on the counter he found a couple of empty fifths of scotch. On the floor, a broken glass.

Directly above his head the ceiling creaked. He froze, feeling the flutter of a nervous heart palpitation in his chest. Suddenly he felt like a criminal caught in the act.

DOCTOR CAUGHT BREAKING AND ENTERING.

Of course, the door had been unlocked. Didn't count if the door was unlocked.

He heard another series of creaks. Then the sounds of

movement continued across the ceiling to the vicinity of the stairs.

He had the sudden ridiculous urge to drop to the floor and make himself very small. He quickly dismissed the idea. If she found him like that, he'd look pretty damn stupid. Instead, he kept his eyes trained to the foot of the stairs, where he could see the carpeted edge of one step sticking out.

And then there she was. The person he thought of as Dr. Collins. She was standing at the foot of the stairs, not looking like Dr. Collins at all.

He'd always been secretly attracted to her, but he'd known she was too old for him. Or, rather, she would think *he* was too young for *her*. But she didn't look very old at all. She looked like a kid. A lost kid.

She was wearing a huge black T-shirt that almost touched her knees. The dark color did nothing for her, making her pale skin seem even paler than usual. Her usually neat blond hair was a mess. It was sticking up in places, and the roots were a little dark, as if she hadn't washed it in a while. Her eyes had huge purple shadows under them.

She looked like hell.

She was staring at him, frowning. "Mark?"

Her shoulders were hunched. Her arms were crossed at her waist, as if her stomach hurt. "What . . . are . . .you . . . doing . . . here?" she whispered hoarsely.

"You really should lock your door," he said. "Anybody can get in."

She blinked and gave him what he figured was supposed to be a smile. "So I see."

He'd come to tell her about Sammy, come to talk her into coming back. But she didn't look in any shape to hear anything.

Since he was always thinking about food, he said, "How long's it been since you ate?"

She frowned, thinking, then shook her head. "I don't know. What day is it?"

Oh, boy.

He could see that she was trying to pull herself together, trying to make sense out of finding him in her kitchen.

"What are you doing here?" she asked again, her eyes squinted against the dim light. "I left everything at the hospital, all the instructions." Then her eyes widened a little, enough for him to see just how bloodshot they were. Her arms dropped to her sides and she took a couple of steps toward him. "Sammy. Something's happened to Sammy."

He couldn't lie. His face had always been an open book. But he didn't want to hit her with everything right now. He needed to get some food in her first.

"It's Sammy, isn't it?" she asked.

"Yeah, but it's nothing that can't be straightened out. Listen. Why don't I make you something to eat? While you're eating, I'll tell you all about it."

Slowly, as if it hurt for her to move, she sank down on the edge of the couch, pressing a hand to her forehead. "That would be nice," she whispered. "But I don't think there's any food in the house."

"Okay. Tell you what. I'll go get some. What would you like? Chinese?"

If possible, her face paled even more. "I don't think so."

Chinese. Brilliant, Elliot. "McDonald's. How about McDonald's?"

She nodded.

He sat down on the arm of the couch and lifted her wrist, pressing his fingers to her pulse. "For a doctor, you sure take crummy care of yourself," he told her.

Her pulse was a bit slow, but nothing unusual, especially if she hadn't eaten in days. He touched her forehead, then her neck. No fever. But there were fine lines around her eyes and mouth that he'd never seen before. Dehydration. Alcohol did that to a person.

She looked up at him with her bruised eyes. "What do you think, Doc?"

He felt sorry as hell for her. Just sorry as hell. "I think Sammy was right."

She frowned, clearly puzzled. "Sammy?"

"He said somebody should check up on you."

Without seeming to be surprised, she said, "Sammy knows everything. He has X-ray eyes. He sees things I don't want him to see."

Mark could see that Sammy had also been right about his being the cause of Dr. Collins's distress.

Before leaving for McDonald's, Mark went to the kitchen and swept up the broken glass so she wouldn't cut her bare feet. Then he brought her some water. "Just sit here and drink that. I'll be back in a few minutes."

A couple of hours later, after Rachel had eaten and showered, she felt a little more human. Not a lot, only a little. Her hands still trembled and her head still hurt. But those were minor problems.

Mark had told her about Sammy. Now she had to decide what to do.

She was afraid. So afraid. But she knew she had no choice.

Rachel had no problem getting in to see him. Most of the staff weren't aware that she was no longer an employee of the hospital.

She went into his room by herself.

Sammy was lying on his back in bed, his face turned away, toward the blank wall.

Thinking he was asleep, Rachel moved quietly. But when she reached his bedside she saw that his eyes were open, staring at nothing.

Fear and grief gripped her, worse than the first time she had seen him. The first time he had been a patient, facts on a chart. Now he was Sammy.

She touched his arm. "Sammy."

With a drug-induced weakness, his head came around until she could see his face, see into his soulful eyes. Beneath their glazed opaqueness she was relieved to note a flicker of recognition.

She didn't know how long she stood there, held by a strange sense of communion. But suddenly she felt his fingertips brush hers. Then he caught her hand in his.

She had expected him to beg for his freedom. Instead, with a voice that was hoarse and shaky and incredibly weak, he said, "I—I'm so-rry."

That was when she knew she would do anything for him.

She fought to keep her own voice steady. "There's nothing to be sorry for."

Pain flashed in his eyes, and he rolled his head in denial.

He squeezed his eyes shut, then opened them. "I . . . hurt . . . you."

"You didn't mean to."

"I—I'm sorry."

She somehow managed a tremulous smile. "There's nothing to forgive. I know you didn't mean it."

He immediately relaxed. He let out a relieved, shuddering breath, then his eyes fell shut. His grip relaxed.

He had dark smudges under his eyes. He hadn't been

shaved. His jaw was blue-tinged, the growth of beard filling in the hollows.

She was amazed by how fast his hair had grown. It was over an inch long, coming in shiny and as black as his eyebrows.

She leaned closer. Slowly, she lifted her hand, bringing it to the side of his face, stroking his hair back in a soft, soothing motion. "Sammy?" she whispered.

His eyelids twitched, then came partially open and he stared up at her.

"I'm going to get you out of here," she swore. "I promise."

"I want the Thoreau case back," Rachel said, the palms of both hands pressed against the files that cluttered Dr. Fontana's desk.

With blunt fingers he rubbed the top of his bald head. "I told you you'd always have a job here, Rachel. But I can't jerk a patient around on your whim. It's not fair to Sammy Thoreau, and it's not fair to Dr. Sanderson."

"But all the work I've done with him has been wasted!" She swept her hand toward the door. "He's in solitary again!"

"You can't be sure he wouldn't be there anyway, even if you'd stayed. I'm sorry, Rachel. I want you back. You're one of the best we have, but forget about Thoreau. We'll start you off fresh, on an easier case. Your day patients are a different matter. Most of them don't even know you've been gone, and the others saw Mark Elliot, which they were accustomed to doing occasionally anyway."

Rachel felt like shouting, but that wouldn't get her anywhere. She forced herself to remain calm and to keep her voice level. "I think Sammy Thoreau would be better off in my care."

"I'm not so sure. I think you've become too emotionally involved with this case. I think it would be in your best interest to move on to somebody else."

She couldn't believe he was siding with Sanderson. The thought made her furious. But then, she'd witnessed Sanderson's act around Dr. Fontana. He was a real suck-up. She had always thought Dr. Fontana was smart enough to see through him.

"What if I talk to Sanderson myself?" she asked.

Dr. Fontana let out a tired sigh, and she knew she was making headway. "Go ahead and talk to him," he said in weary defeat. "But I don't think you'll have any luck."

She could have kissed the top of his head. "Thank you!" Then she was off.

She found Dr. Sanderson in the cafeteria. She didn't want him to know she'd come just to find him. Sanderson didn't like her. He'd never forgiven her for not going out with him. If he realized how much she wanted Sammy's case back, he might use it to get even.

Rachel paid for a cup of coffee, them moved slowly in the direction of Sanderson's table. When she reached it, she said, "May I talk to you a moment?"

He smiled up at her, white teeth flashing against his tanning-booth tan. His eyes rested on her breasts. "Sure. Have a seat." He motioned to the empty chair beside him. She remained standing.

"You have a case of mine—Samuel Thoreau. I appreciate your taking over for me while I was gone. I just wanted to let you know I'm back, so you don't need to look in on him tonight. I'll send Mark Elliot to pick up his patient file."

Feeling she'd bulldozed him fairly well, she started to walk away.

"Wait a minute."

She paused.

"Thoreau's my case now. And anyway"—his eyes

trailed from her breasts, to her crotch, to her breasts—
"he's too much for a little thing like you to handle."

How did a person get to be like Sanderson? Was he
born that way, or did he have to learn to be a creep? Did
he have a father and uncles out there who were just as
disgusting as he? What a frightening thought.

"Thoreau is a very physical patient," Sanderson
drawled. "I wouldn't want you to get hurt."

"He's not violent."

"Not violent? His outbursts are the talk of the entire
ward. The nurses are afraid of him. And what about
this?" He pointed to a bruised area on his cheek.
"Thoreau hit me . . . after he tried to kick me."

Rachel would have loved to have seen that. No
wonder Sanderson put him under sedation. Sammy had
made him look like a fool.

She attempted to smile, but felt she was failing
miserably. "I think Sammy responds better to women.
Men make him angry. Why not let me take him off your
hands." She looked at his red cheek. "Especially since
you two obviously don't get along."

Sanderson noisily swallowed a mouthful of coffee.
"You want this guy pretty bad. What's the deal, Rachel?
Got the hots for a patient?"

Rachel fought the urge to slam a fist into Sanderson's
other cheek. "You should know all about that, shouldn't
you?" she asked instead.

His eyes narrowed and he actually seemed to lose
interest in the contemplation of her bra size. "What are
you talking about?"

"I could tell Dr. Fontana some things that could get
you put on suspension. Maybe even make you lose your
license."

"You don't have anything on me."

"How about that patient Mary Osborn?"

"What about her?"

"You told her that having sex with you would cure her of agoraphobia, isn't that right?"

He paled. "Why, you little bitch."

She had been bluffing. Now she felt ill knowing that something she had only suspected was true. "It makes me sick the way you pass yourself off as a doctor," she said.

"You're just bent out of shape because you never get any. Maybe if you pried those skinny legs of yours apart sometimes—"

"I'll send Mark Elliot to pick up the Thoreau file. And from now on, don't go near any of my patients. Especially Sammy. And remember—I'll be watching you. If you ever pull anything like you pulled on the Osborn case again, I'll turn you in to the board."

Hate flashed from his eyes and radiated from his entire body. "Go ahead and take Thoreau. You two deserve each other. If we're lucky, he'll end up breaking your damn neck."

"Maybe. Or he might even get well."

THIRTEEN

SAMMY STOOD IN FRONT OF THE MIRROR, RUNNING A small black comb through what there was of his hair. His big problem was that he had a couple of cowlicks, one on each side of his head, and his hair was still too short to do anything but stick straight up, especially in those two spots.

He usually tried to avoid mirrors. His reflection didn't fit the mental image he had of himself: Sammy Thoreau at nineteen. But maybe that really wasn't so weird. Even people who hadn't gotten their brains rearranged in a car wreck didn't always have accurate self-images. Old Al at the pool hall once told him that he always got a jolt whenever he looked in the mirror because he thought of himself as eighteen.

Sammy gave up on his hair and tossed the comb on the edge of the sink. He wasn't going to be so shallow as to let a little thing like hair get him down.

Yesterday Molly had come to visit. And Rachel—he always thought of her as Rachel now—was coming today. She was going to take him somewhere. He didn't know where, and it didn't matter. Just as long as it was out of there. Just as long as she came along.

He switched off the light, walked the few steps to his bed, and sprawled on his back, locking his hands behind his head.

The ceiling didn't tilt for a nice change. His fingers didn't tingle.

He'd been straight for three days. Three days since he'd opened his eyes to find Rachel, with her cap of smooth blond hair, leaning over him like a sweet angel of mercy. He couldn't remember what he'd said, or what she'd said. He remembered only the incredible relief he'd felt at seeing her and knowing she'd make everything okay.

Now that he was clear-headed, he was once again waiting to get his memory back, but he wasn't too worried. It was only a matter of time. Only a matter of finding the right trigger.

He just had to remember to be good until his memory returned, just as good as hell.

He had to admit that there had been a few times when it had been hard. More than once he'd caught a wisecrack forming in his head, getting ready to slip out his mouth. But he'd always managed to stop himself.

A master of self-control.

Rachel had told him that Sanderson hadn't been very gung-ho on giving up his case. But lucky for Sammy, he had stepped aside. He didn't know how Rachel had done it, but everything was back to the way it had been before. And now both he and Rachel had to be especially careful, because everybody would be watching them, waiting for them to screw up.

A knock sounded on the door. Then Rachel was there, standing in the doorway. But this was a Rachel he'd never seen before. She was wearing a pair of jeans, a pale yellow T-shirt, and white sneakers. For a few seconds he forgot all about being good. For a few seconds he just lay there, staring.

She looked great.

He sat up, swinging his feet to the floor, his hands on the bed.

Her jeans were old. They'd spent a lot of time touching the curves of her body. The T-shirt was big, but the cotton fabric clung to the tops of her breasts and fell in soft folds to her hips.

He'd been wondering what she looked like under that white lab coat. Now he knew.

Wow.

Seeing her brought the previous night's dreams rushing back in one horny wave. He dreamed about her almost every night. And in his dreams he kissed her. On the mouth. And that wasn't all he did to her. He ran his hands up her rib cage, his fingers daring to skim the swollen undersides of her breasts—

"Ready?" Rachel asked, startling him out of his hot daydream.

He remembered he was supposed to be on his best behavior. A model patient. He pushed himself to his feet, then motioned toward the door. "After you."

He followed the sweet rhythm of her hips as she led the way.

Her car surprised him. He didn't know what he'd been expecting. Maybe a station wagon with wood panels on the sides. But what he found was a little black sports job with bucket seats and a five-speed stick.

"What'll this do?" he asked, cupping his hands to peer through the window at the tachometer. "Ever open this baby up all the way?"

"No, but I doubt it would do over eighty. It's only a four cylinder."

"A four cylinder?" He couldn't keep the disappointment from his voice.

"But it's fuel injected."

"Fuel injected. Wow."

A memory hit him. He could see himself tooling down a backroad, a motorcycle under him, the wind snapping his long hair around his face.

"I used to have this Harley," he said, his eyes checking out every detail of the car's instrument panel. "There was nothing I liked better than taking it out on a hot summer night. You know, the kind of night where it's too hot to sleep. I'd find a deserted country road and open her up. Nothing feels better than flying through those pockets of icy night air. When I stopped, my skin would be cold. After that, I could always sleep." He'd like to do that again. Have that sense of total freedom.

"I wonder whatever happened to that bike?" he said, as much to himself as to Rachel. "I wonder if I still have it?"

"Molly would probably know."

"Yeah. I'll have to ask her. I could take you for a ride on it."

"I'd like that."

He was looking through the window again when she asked, "Would you like to drive?"

His head came up. She was dangling a set of keys in front of him. "Are you serious?"

"Why not?"

"Are you forgetting what put me here in the first place?"

She smiled. "I trust you."

Before she could change her mind, he snatched the keys from her hand. He was no fool. He unlocked the door and folded his body into the sun-baked car, stretching his legs out in front of him.

It wasn't until then that he realized she was still standing by the passenger door, waiting. Shit. Should have opened the door for her. He'd have to remember that next time. He reached across the seat and unlocked her door.

When she was settled beside him, he stuck the key in the ignition. The gearshift was a standard H pattern, with the exception of an additional fifth gear. He put in the clutch and shifted to neutral, starting the engine at the same time.

Rachel reached across his chest, showing him how to open the power windows, letting in fresh air.

The stereo was in the center of the dash. It had the same green digital displays he was becoming accustomed to seeing on everything. He reached for the radio dial, ready to switch it on, when her hand touched his, stopping him. He looked up, puzzled.

You couldn't cruise without tunes.

"Maybe we shouldn't listen to music," she said. "You don't want to overstimulate yourself."

Overstimulate. He laughed, loving her shrink vocabulary. "Don't worry. I like to be *overstimulated*."

"Sammy, I'm not kidding."

"Neither am I."

He knew what was bothering her. Nothing stirred memories like music. But he wanted his memories stirred, his thoughts stimulated. It might help. It just might be the trigger he was waiting for.

On the other hand, he could see from her uneasy expression that Rachel needed reassurance. She needed to know he wouldn't hear a song from yesteryear and flip out. "You worry too much," he told her. "I'll be okay. I swear."

He turned the dial through several stations until he heard a familiar Beatles number. He left it there and settled back.

"You have to fasten your seat belt," Rachel said.

"What?"

"Your seat belt. It's a law."

"No shi—" He caught himself. But he was sure she'd caught him too. "No kidding?"

"No kidding."

He had a little trouble figuring out how it worked, and to his delight Rachel ended up helping him. She showed him how to snugly anchor the belt over his shoulder and hips. When she was leaning across him, the fresh scent of her hair filling his head, a soft breast grazing his chest, he decided there were some definite benefits to this memory-loss stuff.

He was still thinking about the way she'd felt as he guided the car through the lot, down the parking ramp, and into the street.

Air rushed in the open windows, bringing smells of exhaust fumes and freshly mown grass. As they moved under towering oaks and maples, the sun cast dappled patterns on the hood of the car. Above, white clouds moved across an incredibly blue sky.

He took a deep breath. It was a good day to be alive.

He'd never been very familiar with La Grange, but he knew that down the hill from the hospital and to the left was a highway that led out of town. After spending weeks cooped up in a tiny room, he wanted to move, to go fast. To see the world fly by.

At the bottom of the hill, he hung a left, loving the way the little car cornered, loving the tight shifting pattern and the feel of the engaging gears, the increasing whine as the engine wound higher.

Within five minutes they were cruising down a four-lane highway, the stereo blaring and the wind rushing in.

He glanced at the speedometer. Sixty-five. It seemed like he was doing a hundred. Maybe that's the way old people felt when they got in a car. Maybe that's why they drove so slowly. To them, maybe it felt like they were breaking the sound barrier.

He had a vague memory of a park somewhere in the area. He kept his eyes peeled, and pretty soon he spotted a green information sign. With his craving for speed satisfied, he slowed, then pulled off the highway onto a narrow blacktop road with no center line.

They were enveloped by trees and the musty smell of woodland. The air around them instantly turned cooler. Contrasting light and shadow flickered over them like a strobe.

They passed a play area where kids were swinging and shrieking and having a great time. Sammy thought about stopping. Maybe Rachel would like to swing.

When he glanced in her direction, the bottom fell out of his stomach. Her face was white and pinched.

The kids.

She was thinking about her daughter.

Seeing her pain, understanding the cause of it, gave him the same hollow punch he'd felt when he'd found out she had a kid who had died.

He was still carrying around a huge amount of guilt over what he'd done to her, what he'd said. Only yesterday he'd attempted to bring up the subject so he could apologize, but she had steered the conversation in another direction. Not wanting to hurt her again, he hadn't pushed. But he had wondered, as he had all those days ago, who *she* talked to, who *she* went to for help. He didn't know much about inner healing, but he did know that three and a half years was way too long to grieve.

He drove on, past the playground, until the sounds of children's laughter faded and was replaced by the call of birds.

He turned left down a narrow dirt lane, and discovered that it led to a small clearing surrounded by trees. There was no one else around. A perfect place to stop.

Pulling to the edge of the road, he cut the engine and looked over at Rachel. Color was coming back to her face. "Come on," he said, pulling the handle and shoving his shoulder against the door. "I've been wanting to do this for a long time."

What he really wanted to do was erase the look of

bleakness from her face. He didn't want her to be sad on such a great day.

He got out and shut the door, inhaling the fresh air while sunshine warmed his head and shoulders.

Four days ago, when he was doped and in solitary, he wouldn't have believed he'd ever be standing in the sunlight. Four days ago, he had begun to think that he'd never feel the sun again.

A door slammed.

Good. She was coming.

He smiled and moved to the middle of the clearing. Without hesitation, he lay down on his back in the grass.

He cast a quick glance over his shoulder. Rachel was standing not far from the car, a tiny, questioning smile playing about the corners of her mouth.

He patted the ground beside him as if it were a couch—or a bed. "Come on. There's plenty of room."

She hesitated.

"Come on, try it. Lying on the grass is great therapy."

She moved closer. When she reached his side, she gingerly sat down. If he stretched out his arm, he would have been able to touch her.

"You're not doing it right," he told her. "To fully appreciate this moment, you have to lie on your back like this so you can look up at the sky."

He watched her until she was flat on her back, head on the ground.

"That's the way. Doesn't it feel good?"

"A little scratchy."

Her face was turned toward him. He could see grass blades poking her cheek. "That's because you're looking at me. You're supposed to look up at the sky."

"Oh." She looked up.

"Now. You should be familiar with this kind of thing. It's what I call nature's Rorschach test. See that cloud?" He pointed. "A perfect elephant."

"I don't see any elephant."

"Aw, come on, Rachel. You're not trying." He shifted his body so he was closer to her. So their hips and shoulders were almost touching. He pointed again, moving his finger as he talked. "See, there's the trunk"—he drew a curve—"and that big round cloud"—he made a circle—"is the ear."

"I see it now! Oh, and look, there's a baby elephant holding on to its mother's tail!"

He shot her a quick glance, wondering if she was pulling his leg. But she was totally serious, totally caught up in the game. He looked up again, but couldn't see any baby elephant and finally had to give up on that particular shape. They continued to take turns, pointing out various clouds. When they got tired of that, they both closed their eyes.

Sammy could hear his own heartbeat, hear his own breathing. The sun was warm, soaking through his T-shirt and jeans. Birds called from distant trees. An occasional breeze moved across his skin, stirring the hairs on his arms.

And Rachel was beside him, just like one of his dreams. . . .

He may have fallen asleep. He wasn't sure. But sometime later the orange glow behind his eyelids dimmed. He opened his eyes. A cloud was moving across the sun. He turned his head. Rachel was still lying on her back, her eyes closed, her chest gently rising and falling. Was she asleep?

He rolled to his side so he was facing her, his elbow on the ground, head braced on his palm. "Rachel?" he whispered, not wanting to wake her if she was really asleep.

"Mmm?" she asked drowsily, without opening her eyes.

"Just checking. I thought you were asleep."

"I am," she mumbled, barely moving her lips.

He smiled.

Between them, the grass was thick and green and dotted with yellow dandelions. He liked dandelions. They were pretty and resilient. A good combination.

"Want to play another game?" he asked.

She yawned and covered her mouth. "What kind of game?"

"The sensation game."

"I've never heard of it."

"It's easy. Just keep your eyes closed. That's it. Now tell me what you hear."

She was quiet, and for a moment he almost wondered if she'd fallen asleep again.

"Birds," she said. "Lots of birds."

"Okay. What do you smell?"

"Grass . . . and damp ground."

"What do you *feel*?"

She hesitated. "A breeze. A soft breeze. Sometimes it's warm. Sometimes I feel a stir of cooler air."

"You're really good at this."

He picked a blade of grass, leaned closer, and stroked it across her cheek. "Now what do you feel?"

Her brows drew together in a frown. "A feather?"

"No." Once again he stroked her face, this time trailing the green strand from her cheek to the fullness of her bottom lip.

Her brow relaxed. "Blade of grass."

"Yep. Now, how about this—keep your eyes closed." He picked a dandelion, then touched the flower lightly to her neck.

She giggled and pulled away.

Rachel giggling? He let the soft petals touch her cheek.

Her brow furrowed again as she tried to put a name to

the sensation. When she couldn't, he trailed the bloom down her cheek to her lips.

"A flower," she said right away. "A dandelion."

"You have a very sensitive mouth, Rachel," he said, his voice sounding a little tight, a little odd, even to himself. "Now, how about—"

"I think we should stop," she broke in. She didn't sound sleepy anymore.

They couldn't stop now. "The game's almost over. Come on. Just one more guess."

"Okay." Her answer came a bit reluctantly.

"Keep your eyes closed," he warned.

"I'm not a cheater," she said, indignant.

"I didn't think you were." She wouldn't be indignant for long. She would be mad. Just mad as hell. But he could be good for only so long. And Rachel was too much of a temptation.

He leaned forward. Without making contact with any other part of her body, he touched his lips to hers. A feather-light brush.

As soon as his lips skimmed hers, Sammy heard her quick, indrawn breath. At the same time, he felt an incredible surge of desire rush through him.

He pulled away slightly, his lips inches from hers. "Did you guess, Rachel?" His voice was tight.

"Your mouth," she whispered, her eyes still closed, as if she didn't dare open them.

Before she could move away, he touched his lips to hers once again. Softly. As softly as he'd touched them with the flower.

She gave another little jolt of surprise, and drew in a breath that parted her lips.

Desire made him weak and hot. He could feel the fullness of her bottom lip between both of his. It was all he could do to keep from moaning out loud. He slanted

his head . . . and immediately felt the intimate wet-
ness of her mouth.

He wanted to be inside her, if only with his tongue in
her mouth.

He was dimly aware of her fingers clutching his upper
arms. And of his own breathing, harsh and irregular.

He had memories of other kisses stolen in the backseat
of his '64 Chevy. But they were hazy.

Crystal-clear were his dreams of Rachel. And now his
dreams meshed with reality.

Without conscious thought, without relinquishing
contact with her mouth, he positioned himself over her,
urging her knees apart with his hips until he was where
he wanted to be—between her thighs, his hardness
pressing against her warmth.

His kiss deepened. His tongue slid past her lips, into
the moist recesses of her mouth.

As he made love to her mouth, he could almost feel
another part of him buried in her.

He began to move his hips.

Stroking . . .

One hand lifting her closer . . .

Desire winding tighter . . .

Suddenly an uncontrollable shudder went through
him, then another and another. He plunged one last
time before collapsing on top of her.

Then, little by little, the world filtered in. Gradually
he became aware of his surroundings. The sun beating
down on his back. The sound of his ragged breathing,
the thudding of his heart. Rachel below him.

He'd made love to her with his clothes on.

He couldn't look at her. No way could he look at her.
So he hid his face against her neck, breathing in her
sweet scent. He could feel her pulse beating against his
cheek.

Hands began to stroke his back. Reassuring. Comforting.

"Sammy, it's okay."

No, it wasn't. Maybe in her book—her shrink book—but not in his. He squeezed his eyes shut, sucked in a deep breath, then rolled away. With his back to her, he curled to a sitting position.

He was so damn embarrassed. He couldn't remember ever being so embarrassed. He locked his arms and his knees and stared into the distance. Somehow the trees didn't look as green as they had earlier.

What an idiot.

He felt her hand on his shoulder. "Sammy, there's nothing to be embarrassed about. Sexuality is a perfectly normal thing. Physically, you're thirty-eight, but your sex drive is probably more like that of a nineteen-year-old."

Sex drive! Here he was, totally mortified, and she was doing her shrink thing. An analytic appraisal of his sexuality was the last thing he needed.

He made a frustrated sound deep in his throat and shrugged his shoulder away from her hand. "I can't believe you're analyzing this. Do you have to analyze everything?"

He knew what she was doing. Putting him in his place. Treating him like a child. Like a nut patient. But that's not what he wanted. He wanted her to *want* him. He wanted her to think of him as a man, not as a boy.

He continued to focus on the grove of trees, unable to look her in the eyes. "You think I'm just some horny kid, don't you?" The truth hurt.

"I think you're confused," she said in a soft, controlled shrink voice. A voice he hadn't heard in a while. He'd been foolish enough to think their relationship had moved past that. Guess again, Sherlock.

"You're very vulnerable right now," she was saying.

"Very susceptible. It's only natural for you to have certain . . . feelings for me."

Don't do your shrink thing. Please don't do your shrink thing.

"A doctor and patient share intensely emotional secrets that they would never share with anyone else. Not their wives or their husbands, not their friends or their lovers."

It began to occur to him that she sounded as if she were speaking from rote, reciting words from some crusty old manual. He could almost see it.

Patient-doctor relationships: How to handle your aggressively affectionate patient.

He was beginning to feel like a kid who'd been caught with a *Playboy* under the mattress.

He couldn't stand it anymore. He forced himself to look over his shoulder at her, and what he saw practically knocked him breathless.

She looked as if somebody had been making love to her.

Her lips, the lips that were usually pink, were red and swollen from his kisses. There was a blush in her cheeks.

Could he have been off so much? When he'd first started kissing her, he could have sworn she'd responded, could have sworn she had kissed him back, had touched him in a way that wasn't shrinkish at all.

He could have sworn she'd wanted him.

And even now, as he stared at her without speaking, the color in her cheeks darkened. Then her eyes shifted away and he knew. He *knew*.

His confidence returned. If he'd been standing, he probably would have swaggered. He had it all figured out. *She couldn't admit to wanting him.* Like she'd told him before, any relationship between them was unethical.

Denial. Wasn't that the psychological term for what she was doing?

Okay, Rachel. For right now I'll play along.

He shoved himself to his feet, then extended a hand to help her up. For a second she hesitated, then put her hand in his. And, by God, her hand was trembling.

Oh, Rachel, he thought as he looked into her light green eyes, you have so many secrets. Someday you're going to tell me a few. But not now. Now we are both too fragile.

His eyes never leaving her face, he brought her hand to his mouth and pressed a kiss on her knuckles. "He was crazy, you know," he said.

Her bemused expression faded to puzzlement. "Who?"

"Your husband. He was crazy to leave you."

He had never thought of himself as a particularly insightful person. So it surprised him when he suddenly understood the difference between himself and Rachel. He met problems head-on. He yelled, he raged, he banged his head against the wall and put his fist through mirrors. Rachel, on the other hand, ignored her problems, hoping they would go away.

Well, she had one problem she might eventually have to face. Because he wasn't going anywhere. At least not for a while.

FOURTEEN

A WEEK LATER RACHEL WAS FINISHING WITH THE LAST of her outpatients. "I'll see you again next week," she told Mrs. MacLacklin as she walked the elderly woman to the office door. "Is someone here to drive you?"

"My son is waiting outside." The woman glanced slyly up at Rachel. "You're not married, are you?"

"No."

"Neither is my son."

Rachel simply smiled and continued to usher the woman out the door. "Good-bye, Mrs. MacLacklin."

"Bye dear."

With Mrs. MacLacklin gone, Rachel checked her watch. Four o'clock. Sammy and Mark would be here anytime. For the past two days, Sammy had been bugging her about going downtown to a used record store. He seemed obsessed with the idea, so today they were going to a place called Strange Days.

She hurried to the bathroom, splashed some water on her face, and ran her fingers through her hair.

Sammy. . . .

She had to be very careful. The other day at the park she had come face-to-face with herself, face-to-face with the truth. And the truth was that she was attracted to Sammy Thoreau. Up until that point she had been fooling herself; she had been telling herself that she was interested in him solely as a patient.

Now she knew better.

It was a joke among impaired doctors that M.D. stood for massive denial.

It was no joke.

As she took off her lab coat and hung it on the rack near the door, she thought about what had happened between them. It was certainly a memory that was never far from her mind. Sammy hadn't been the only one to lose control that day. If he hadn't been so embarrassed over what had happened, he may have seen the effect he'd had on her, seen that she, too, had been to blame. But thankfully he hadn't noticed. And thankfully she had managed to dredge up some of that old professional attitude, enough to bluff her way through.

So far Sammy hadn't mentioned what had happened. And she didn't think it was due to embarrassment. There had been nothing in his actions that told her he even remembered. He was like a child in the way he had totally dismissed it from his mind. If only she could do the same.

Yes, she must be very careful. She had to make sure they didn't end up in the same situation again. The last thing Sammy needed was more problems in his life. And the last thing she needed was to fall for a patient.

That's why she'd asked Mark to come along. As a third person, he would make a perfect buffer. And she knew Sammy liked him.

The two men arrived in a bustle of noise and talk and laughter. Mark was dressed in his usual loud shirt. Sammy was wearing a black T-shirt, jeans, and white sneakers. Every time she saw him, he looked healthier. His color was good. His eyes were bright, the shadows almost gone. He was gaining weight.

His looks went beyond anything traditional or classical. His face was too open, too vulnerable-looking. Yet he was the kind of person whose presence you could actually *feel*. His sister had best described it when she'd said he was more alive than most people. His soul burned brighter.

"Ready?" Sammy asked. Even though he was standing still, she could sense his excitement, his eagerness for them to be on their way.

"Ready."

They ended up crowding into the elevator with four young nurses. Two of them were whispering behind their hands while casting glances in Sammy's direction. The object of their interest shifted uncomfortably and kept his eyes focused on the numbers at the top of the elevator.

They stopped on the second floor, and Sammy had to step aside in order to let them off.

As soon as the door slid silently closed and they were moving again, Mark said dryly, and not without a twinge of envy, "I think we just saw four women who would love to change your bedpan."

Outside, the day was warm, the temperature nearly eighty degrees. Since the store was only ten blocks away, they decided to walk. Rachel approved of the idea, hoping both Sammy and Mark would burn off a little excess energy before they reached their destination.

This was the first time she'd seen Sammy and Mark together, and she was beginning to wonder at the wisdom of the outing.

There was no order to their walk. Sometimes they moved forward three abreast, but more often than not, Sammy and Mark were staggered, either trailing behind or ahead. Sometimes they walked backward, sometimes pivoting on their heels, turning like a flower to the sun whenever an attractive woman happened by. Then the two men—had she thought men?—would nudge each other with their elbows and put their heads together in discussions that usually ended in a burst of laughter.

Rachel was thankful when they made it to the store without getting arrested.

The record store was dark and clammy and musty, the cement floor damp and uneven, smelling and feeling like a place that never dried out completely, not even in winter. Near the front door was a rack of magazines, and Rachel noticed that some of them were magazines Sammy had once written for.

He walked past them without so much as a glance. He also went past the current record releases. He was heading for the back of the store, toward the used albums.

Rachel had hoped Sammy and Mark would both behave once they were inside, but she should have known better.

"Check out these hooters." Mark was holding up an album with a picture of two futuristic-looking women on the cover. Their breasts were covered with metal bras that could have been made from a car's bumper.

Sammy shook his head. "You know what really ticks me off?"

Mark slid the album back in its slot. "What?"

"Bras. I thought they'd all been burned. I thought they were obsolete."

"Jogging," Mark said. "Jogging brought back the bra."

"Bummer."

Mark nodded his agreement.

"I thought you came to look at albums," Rachel said, feeling a little left out. But there was no way she was going to get into a conversation about hooters and bras.

"We did, we did," they both said, putting their heads back down and tending to business.

"Led Zeppelin IV," Sammy commented to no one in

particular, holding up an album. "'Stairway to Heaven.'"

"Good song. I know the chords," Mark said.

"No kidding? I know the notes."

"Yeah?"

"Yeah."

"Grass Roots." That was Sammy.

"The Band." Mark.

They continued to throw names back and forth. And Rachel decided that this was exactly what Sammy needed—to see things that were familiar, to know that the world wasn't completely brave and new.

"Vanilla Fudge."

"Sam the Sham."

"Dylan. 'All Along the Watchtower.'"

"Great song. Ever heard the Hendrix version?"

"Faster, but just as good."

"Yeah. Hey look, The Troggs."

"'Wild Thing,'" Sammy said.

They began to sing. And their voices were amazingly awful.

Rachel pressed a hand to her mouth, trying to smother the laughter that was building inside her, but to her horror her laugh escaped in a loud, uncontrollable burst.

The singing stopped. Two pairs of insulted eyes glared at her from across a sea of tattered album covers.

She was still trying to catch her breath when a person she assumed was the owner appeared at her shoulder.

"Can I help you find something?" he asked in an unthreatening manner. He was bald on top, his hair long on the sides.

Thank God they weren't going to get tossed out on the sidewalk.

"We're just checking out your records." Sammy's long fingers continued to flip the albums.

"Is there anything in particular you're looking for? A certain song? A certain year?"

Sammy shrugged. "Late sixties and early seventies." He glanced over at Mark. "How about you?"

"I'm just along for the ride."

"Take your time," the man said. "Look around all you want."

Now that she'd wiped the tears from her eyes, Rachel couldn't help but notice that the man was staring at Sammy in an intense way. Her heart gave a small jump of dread.

"Hey, you're Sammy Thoreau, aren't you?" he finally asked.

Sammy's head came up. "Yeah." His surprised and cautious expression seemed to say, How did you know?

The man's previously sober face broke into an excited grin. "I've read all your stuff. I really liked that article you did on the whales. It was funny, but at the same time you really made a point, really hit the reader with a gut punch."

Sammy's hands had dropped to his sides, the records unimportant now. He took a step back. "Thanks."

"I haven't seen anything by you in a while. Do you have something in the works?"

"Ah . . . yeah. Sure," Sammy said automatically.

"Great."

Sammy's dazed, panic-filled eyes moved from the man to Mark, finally settling on Rachel. And there they stayed. "Time to go?" he asked, his voice emotionless. But Rachel wasn't fooled.

She looked at her watch. "Yes. We have to be going."

"Before you leave—" The man hurried over to the wooden counter and came back carrying a spiral tablet. He stuck it and a pen in Sammy's hands. "Could I have your autograph?"

Sammy held the pen limply in his hand, looking as if

he'd never used one before and wasn't quite sure what to do with it.

With a cracked yellow fingernail, the man tapped the blue-lined paper. "My name's Max. And my wife's name is Judy. Could you write both our names?"

"Sure," Sammy said, sounding just the opposite. He put pen to paper, then, in perfectly formed letters, he slowly wrote out both names, then finished with his own. He handed the tablet back to Max.

"Thanks, man. Judy will really get off on this."

Rachel watched as Sammy hauled in deep breaths. She stepped close and slipped a hand through his arm. "Come on." She steered him toward the door. He stumbled on the uneven floor, then caught himself.

Once outside, they walked in silence for perhaps a block before Sammy stopped and grabbed Rachel by the arm, swinging her around to face him. "What the hell was that all about?"

Mark stepped in closer, but not so close as to be threatening.

"I don't like surprises," Sammy said. "And I don't want any more of them. I want to know who the hell I am, and why Max wanted my autograph."

It was too soon. Too fast. "I'm not sure if you're ready," Rachel said truthfully.

Sammy made an exasperated sound and let go of her arm. With both hands he reached up and raked his fingers through his scruffy hair. "This *not knowing* is driving me crazy. I'm afraid! Afraid of what's going to happen next! What'll it be? Am I going to walk into a store and have a woman I've never seen before come up and say she's my wife? Or have some strange kid call me Daddy? Will I go to visit a friend only to find out he doesn't live there anymore because he's dead? And worse than that, find out he's been dead for ten years?"

People were walking past, casting uncomfortable glances their way.

Sammy took a deep, shuddering breath, and when he spoke again, his voice was lower, more controlled. But Rachel could detect a tremor in it as he enunciated his next words, one at a time. "I just want to know what the hell's going on."

"I'm sorry about your friend Jay," Rachel said, trying to remain calm for all their sakes.

He'd been doing so well. She hated to see him fall apart like this. She wanted to shelter him.

But that was wrong, she told herself. These knocks were to be expected. To make progress, he had to fall down.

"You don't have a wife," she told him. She caught Mark's eye. "What do you think?" she asked him. For all his boyishness, she trusted Mark's judgment. He seemed to have a sixth sense when it came to human nature.

"I think Sammy's right. He needs answers, and if he's asking the questions, then he's ready. He should have access to his file."

She nodded.

Sammy didn't move. He stood in front of her, his hand clasped in white-knuckled fists. "I take it I'm . . . some kind of writer."

This was exactly what she had feared, exactly what she had hoped to avoid for a time, until he was more stable. "You *used* to be a writer," she told him. "But you can't think about who you were, you have to think about who you want to be."

"Are you saying I can't be who I was before?" He walked a tight circle, coming back to face her. "I thought you said my storage and retrieval skills were fine."

"They are. And there's no reason why you can't be a writer again, but an important element in any life goal is the desire to pursue that goal. You may no longer *want* to be a writer."

In memory-loss cases such as Sammy's, it was best not to put too much emphasis on who they used to be. It wasn't uncommon for the patients' likes and dislikes and oftentimes their skills to change. She knew of a football player who never picked up another football; a successful stockbroker who never stepped inside another office, but took up commercial fishing instead.

It wasn't so much that they couldn't do the same things they once did. They simply no longer had the desire because their interests had changed.

She knew it was going to be hard enough for Sammy to deal with all those lost years, all those lost memories. She didn't want him to feel pressured into being somebody he could no longer be. Instead of his chasing the old Sammy's dreams, she wanted him to chase his own.

FIFTEEN

SAMMY WAS AS NERVOUS AS HELL. IF HE SMOKED, HE'D be lighting one cigarette after another.

Right now he was pacing the carpeted floor of the phony hospital living room, waiting for Molly to arrive along with her husband and daughter.

He should be tired. He hadn't slept at all last night, not after reading his file. But he wasn't tired at all. He was too keyed up to be tired.

He'd known Molly was married, but it hadn't seemed quite real. And he sure hadn't thought about her having a kid. That blew him away. And something else that blew him away was finding out that he was a smart-ass writer. He knew he was a smart ass because he'd read the articles that had been attached to his profile.

Looking over them, he'd felt as if he were reading somebody else's writing. And that piece he'd done on Vietnam was some of the best stuff he'd ever read. It made him feel in awe of himself, of the person he used to be. He could never write like that.

Vietnam . . . that was the hardest thing for him to grasp. He had a few disjointed memories of the place, but they were hardly more than faded snapshot images. They didn't seem a part of him at all.

After going through his file, he'd insisted on meeting

Molly's husband and daughter. And so here he was, waiting for them to arrive.

And he was just nervous as hell.

With one finger he dug at the knot in his tie. It was strangling him, shutting off his air. He'd found the tie in the bunch of clothes Molly had dropped off. He hated dressing up, he especially hated ties, but he wanted to make a good impression. Of course he hadn't gone so far as to give up his jeans for a pair of dress pants.

He gave the knot another tug, wishing Rachel hadn't left. He felt better when she was around. She'd made a special trip to the hospital to see him earlier, and she had straightened his tie, smiled up at him, and said he would do just fine.

And he would. Right? What was there to screw up about meeting his sister's family?

They would come, and everybody would have a great time. They would sit around and swap stories, maybe laugh a little over old times. One big happy family. That was what he wanted. What he needed.

Nothing he couldn't handle.

He paced the room about twenty more times, then there was a shuffling outside the door. His visitors had arrived.

Sammy received his first jolt on seeing Molly's daughter, Amy. Stupid of him—he'd known she was old enough to be married, yet in his mind he'd been picturing a kid. But Amy was all grown up. That really threw him.

He was still trying to grasp the idea of an adult Amy, when Molly and her husband stepped inside the door.

Austin. The guy's name was Austin. Sammy's eyes went from Molly—she looked as nervous as he felt—to Amy, then back to Austin.

He had a flash from childhood. Sitting in a dentist's waiting room, thumbing through one of those kids' magazines, the one with the round-headed Timbertoe family. Somewhere inside they always had a scrambled picture. Maybe a chef flipping pancakes with a shovel. Or a person dressed for snow skiing, ready to dive into a pool. Incongruous things. Sammy got that same unpleasant feeling now, looking at Austin Bennet.

This three-piece-suit guy couldn't be Molly's husband.

But obviously he was.

Confused and not quite ready to confront the Austin dilemma, Sammy looked at Amy again. She was pretty in an old-fashioned way. There was something tranquil about her. She made him think of those dreamy photographs of turn-of-the-century women. She was made up of the same sepia tones with her sunset hair and creamy complexion.

There was no mistaking whose daughter she was. She had Molly's gentle eyes and Molly's gentle smile.

"Hi, Uncle Sammy."

Uncle Sammy.

Another surprise. He hadn't been expecting to be called uncle. Another memory flashed across his mind: He and Jay were sitting on the bumper of Jay's car, drinking beer and watching a red sun sink below a corn-field-and-oak-tree horizon.

"Think you'll ever have kids?" Sammy had asked, the sunset and beer making him mellow and reflective.

"Yeah. Someday," Jay had answered in the same lazy tone. "Molly will make a great mom. Look how she's been with you."

Sammy had agreed. Molly had taken good care of him. The best.

And now Sammy stood in front of Molly's child, a child who wasn't a child. A child he had watched grow up, maybe carried on his shoulder. A child he couldn't remember. A child who should have been Jay's.

And he didn't know what to do.

Should he hug her? He didn't feel like he knew her well enough for that. He'd never approved of people who gave out token hugs and kissed the air. Better off not to do it at all than to fake it.

Amy relieved the awkwardness by striding across the room—man, was she tall—and giving him a quick hug. When she pulled away, he caught a glimmer of tears in her light-lashed eyes.

"It's good to see you," she whispered, giving both his arms a squeeze that put an added emphasis to her words, that said she meant them.

Nice kid, his niece.

Molly and Austin were still hovering just inside the doorway, Austin with his hands thrust inside the pockets of his dark dress slacks, a surly expression on his generic face.

There was something going on that Sammy couldn't quite grasp. It was easy to see Austin would rather be checking out market trends, or reading the paper . . . or getting a root canal than standing there.

They stood in an irregular circle, the kind a gym teacher would feel compelled to straighten out. No one knew what to do or what to say as they waited for Austin to act out at least a perfunctory greeting.

Sammy decided he sure as hell wasn't going to say hello first. Let the smirking stuffed shirt do it.

But then he caught the look Molly shot her husband, an obvious plea for civility, and Sammy immediately felt guilty with himself and mad at Austin. Especially when Austin gave no indication that Molly even existed.

In the second it took for that silent and telling exchange—or *un*exchange—everything fell into place.

Austin was the one who didn't belong in the picture. He was as incongruous as a snow skier surfing on Big Sur. He was totally wrong for Molly.

Even as a child Sammy had understood that Molly wasn't a strong person, that she needed someone to look out for her. Because Molly was a nurturer. She poured her strength into the people she loved, saving none for herself.

Something she'd never been good at was handling disapproval. If someone as much as frowned at her, she would cry. And from the looks of things, Austin did a lot of frowning. And disapproving. Hell, the air was thick with his disapproval.

Molly needed somebody to cherish her, somebody who could appreciate her capacity for love, not take advantage of it. Not drain the life from her and steal her dreams.

Molly waved a nervous hand toward the couch. "Why don't we all sit down?"

A perfectly normal suggestion.

But again Austin insulted Molly by ignoring her. He kept his eyes pinned on Sammy. "So here you are," he said, rocking on the heels of his alligator shoes.

His voice was deep and cultured, taking Sammy by surprise. He'd been expecting something a little more nasal.

"In the nut house," Austin finished.

"Austin—" Molly tried to break in, but her husband waved her away as one might a pesky gnat.

"I've got to hand it to you," he continued. "You really pulled it off this time."

Molly took a step closer, looking as if she planned to jump between them if need be. "Austin, you promised."

His eyes didn't even flicker in her direction. "Of course, I can't say that I blame you for wanting to forget some of your past. Like the ass you made of yourself at my promotion party. Dressed in camouflage, roaring into the country club on that motorcycle of yours. You never could make a quiet statement." He shuddered.

Sammy had never seen a man shudder. It was very
strange. But he wished he could remember the motorcycle scene. He wouldn't mind seeing footage of that.

"Or that time you lost some stupid bet and ended up
shaving your head on local TV." From Austin's expression, a person might think he'd just stepped in something unpleasant.

Sammy's feelings toward his brother-in-law had
started out as just plain dislike, because of what he'd
done to Molly. But now Austin was really pushing
it. . . .

"Actually"—Austin cast a glance around the tidy
room—"this is just the place for you. You can't get into
any trouble here. And where else can you sit around and
watch TV all day without having to worry about footing
the bill?"

Sammy was only vaguely aware of his clenched hands,
his clamped jaw. He hadn't wanted to cream anybody
this badly for a long time, not since the time he'd come
home from school to find Molly crying. It had taken him
a while to get her to tell him what was wrong, but when
she did, Sammy went a little crazy.

Virgil Chapin, a gang leader who was dangerous
because of his gorilla size and low IQ, had dragged Molly
into the boys' rest room, ripped off her blouse, and
shoved her back out into the crowded school hallway.

Sammy had been so enraged that he hadn't thought
about being eight years younger than Virgil. He hadn't
thought about being a good hundred pounds lighter,
either.

He'd ended up getting the biggest pounding of his
life. But one thing good had come of it. He'd met Jay.
Jay had happened along and jumped into the fight. It
had helped to even out the odds, but they'd both ended
up getting their butts kicked.

"Come on," Austin taunted. "Why don't you admit

you're playing this memory-loss joke for all it's worth? Why don't you admit you're faking?"

Sammy took a couple of deep breaths. *Don't lose it now.* "You know what's wrong with you?" he asked, giving himself points for the steadiness of his voice. It practically bordered on boredom. He could be a phony too.

"What?"

"Your face. It's too symmetrical. And when a face is symmetrical, it has no character." Sammy brought his right arm back. He was sick of this guy.

"Sammy! No!"

Molly. Damn.

Sammy halted in mid-swing. It gave Molly enough time to throw herself at him. She latched onto his arm with both hands, hanging on to him with all her weight.

"Don't! You'll be put in solitary again!" she cried.

Funny, she wasn't worried about her husband. That made Sammy feel good.

Maybe he'd learned something over the past couple of weeks, because he suddenly realized that the satisfaction of smashing Austin's face wouldn't be worth it. It wouldn't be worth solitary, and it wouldn't be worth disappointing Molly. And to hurt Austin would be to indirectly hurt Molly.

And if that wasn't enough, he kept seeing Rachel smiling up at him. *You'll do fine.* Sure he would. Such faith. Such blind faith.

But it worked. He couldn't let either of them down. Not Molly. Not Rachel.

Slowly, he lowered his arm. "On second thought," he said with a lot more maturity than he felt, "I don't want to do you any favors."

He felt everyone relax. Molly let go of his arm.

Austin rolled his shoulders and straightened his spine. "You always were all bluff," he said, not sounding as sure of himself as he probably intended.

Sammy laughed a mocking laugh. "We'll have to do this again sometime, brother-in-law."

"Why can't you ever act like a normal person?"

"Maybe because your idea of normal and my idea of normal are two totally different things."

"Ever since I've known you, you've always been mixed up in some uproar, some scene. Why don't you just grow up?" Finished, Austin headed for the door. "Come on, Molly." The words were flung back over his shoulder. "Amy."

"Good-bye, Uncle Sammy." Amy grasped his arm and gave him a kiss on the cheek before following her father out of the room.

"I'm sorry," Molly said.

"Bad idea, huh? A reunion."

"You and Austin never did get along. Putting you two in the same room has always been like throwing two cats together in a burlap bag." She kissed him good-bye and was turning to leave when Sammy put out a hand to stop her.

"Molly . . ." He glanced at the door, then looked back at her. "Why?"

That single word held so many questions. Why had she married him? What had she ever seen in him? Why did she stay with him?

She'd had a tough life. He knew it couldn't have been easy for her, barely a kid herself, having to take care of a younger brother. She'd given up so much for him. She deserved better than Austin Bennet.

Molly stood in front of him, staring down at her clasped hands with their chewed nails. "Jay died, you know, shortly after arriving in Vietnam." She paused, then hit him with something that almost knocked him out. "And I was pregnant."

Pregnant? Molly?

Why not? he reasoned. She was in love. She and Jay had planned to marry. "Amy?" he asked.

She shook her head. "No. Amy is Austin's child. We were married a week when I miscarried." She looked ready to cry, and he wished he'd kept his mouth shut. His memory loss was hard on him, but it was also hard on Molly. She shouldn't have to relive the agonies of her life. "You don't have to say anymore. I'm sorry."

She shook her head, seeming intent on getting it all out now that she'd started. "At the time, I thought it was important to have a father for my baby. And Austin was there. He was solid. Stable. He seemed to be everything that was lacking in my own life. I was just too naive to realize that the reason it was lacking was that I never wanted it in the first place. And of course, with Jay gone"—she shrugged—"nothing really seemed to matter."

"I would have taken care of you," Sammy whispered.

"I know. But you had enough problems. And you were still in Vietnam."

"Vietnam . . ." He shook his head. "I'm sorry. I don't remember."

"That's okay. There are some things that are better off forgotten."

Her eyes held a faraway look as she focused on the past. "It's hard to believe, but Austin and I have been together almost twenty years. And in all that time, I truly think he's been faithful to me." She shook her head, as if the idea amazed her. "He's given me no reason to leave."

"No reason? Come on, Molly. It doesn't look as if he's given you any reason to stay. Don't answer if you don't want to, but think about this—are you happy?"

"Happy?" She took a deep breath. "Is anybody really happy?"

"I'd like to think so."

"It seems so terribly selfish."

"It's not selfish to think about yourself sometimes."

"Maybe you're right." She straightened a little, as if shaking herself free of all dark thoughts. Then she tilted her head and gave him a smile, an old-Molly smile. "Austin will be out of town this week and I'd like you to come for dinner. I hope you don't mind, but I already asked Dr. Collins, and she agreed to bring you. I'll fix all your favorite things. How does that sound?"

"Great. It sounds great."

Her smile and her sudden enthusiasm made her look younger.

Fleetingly, he wondered if Dr. Collins could be classified as one of his favorite things.

SIXTEEN

MOLLY LEANED FORWARD AND OPENED THE OVEN DOOR. Dry heat blasted her eyes, carrying the smell of apple pie.

The crust, with its design of leaves and apple blossoms, was just beginning to turn a golden brown. Five more minutes and it would be done. She closed the door, its hinges creaking.

She was nervous and excited about tonight. She knew it was silly, since Sammy had been eating her cooking most of his life, but she couldn't help it. After all, this was his first trip to her house since the accident.

She glanced around the kitchen. Her pastel ceramic plates were out. So were the tall glasses for tea, the hamburger buns, ketchup and mustard, and the sweet pickles Sammy liked. The potato salad was done and in the refrigerator. Earlier that morning she'd finished the baked beans and now they were just waiting to be reheated. Everything was ready.

Five minutes later she removed the pie from the oven and set it on a rack to cool.

She checked her watch. Four-thirty. They would be here in a half hour. Just enough time for her to change before starting the charcoal.

Upstairs in the bedroom she shared with Austin, she threw on clean clothes: a pair of jeans and white blouse.

As she dressed, she thought about the horrendous meeting at the hospital. It was her fault. She shouldn't have begged Austin to come. She should have known better, especially after seeing how angry he'd been when he'd found out she'd had Sammy transferred. Of course the anger had died as soon as she told him that the cost of Sammy's treatment wasn't coming out of Austin's pocket.

Still, when Austin had agreed to visit Sammy, she should have known that he wasn't doing it out of the goodness of his heart. Austin didn't function that way.

She tucked in her shirttail and zipped her jeans. Then she picked up a brush and ran it through her straight, shoulder-length hair. The reflection in the mirror above the dresser was that of a middle-aged housewife. More than middle-aged. There were fine lines at the corners of her eyes and mouth. Her mousy hair was becoming streaked with gray.

Sammy hadn't been quite able to hide his shock when he'd first seen her. *You've changed,* his dark, expressive eyes had told her.

I'm still the same Molly inside, she'd wanted to tell him. But was she? Really?

She tried to remember what she had been like twenty-some years earlier. She and Sammy had lived in a cramped apartment. Sammy had his paper route, Molly her florist job. It had been hard. But now, looking back on those days, she felt a wistful longing.

It had hurt to see the puzzlement in Sammy's eyes.

She knew it would be hard for him to understand. It had taken her years to figure it all out. She used to wonder why Austin had married her. But then one day she realized it was because he thought he could control her, thought he could mold her into the perfect, dutiful, unassuming wife. A prop. She was no more than a prop in his orderly life.

She leaned a little closer to the mirror. Maybe some lipstick? Or a little mascara? She shook her head. She'd never worn any. Why start now?

Several years earlier Austin had tried to talk her into wearing makeup, but she'd resisted. Makeup made her look garish and feel foolish. She just didn't have the face for it. She knew she'd never been pretty, never been the kind of girl who turned boys' heads. More often than not, if they did look her way, it was to sling out some cruel comment, the way boys who hung in brave groups often did. There were many times she'd gone home in tears.

But then she'd met Jay. Jay, with his blue eyes and freckles. His teasing smile. Little by little he had coaxed her out of her shell. Little by little she had learned what it was like to be adored by a man. And loved.

For years he'd lived down the street from them. Several times she'd seen him from a distance. And then Sammy had gotten into that awful fight, and suddenly he and Jay were inseparable. Jay was Sammy's big brother, surrogate father, and best friend all in one.

And Molly had loved him with every bit of passion in her young girl's heart.

Over the past several years she'd managed to quit thinking about him as much. But Sammy's accident had brought it all back. The forgotten feelings. The forgotten dreams.

She *had* changed. Inside and out.

But Sammy was adjusting. With each visit she noticed small differences, could see signs of maturing. Sammy was adaptable. He always had been. Unlike her, he was at home wherever he went. He could make small talk with anybody, kids and adults alike.

Yes, he was adjusting. Getting better. And Molly was beginning to realize that some things were better off forgotten.

After returning from Vietnam, Sammy had changed. He wasn't the same old Sammy. When he laughed, his laughter hadn't rung out as richly, wasn't as infectious, as heartfelt. And sometimes, when he thought no one was looking, she would glimpse a haunted bleakness in his face that mirrored the horrors he must have witnessed.

But now she could see some of the old Sammy again, the Sammy she'd known and loved before Vietnam. And she wanted him to be that Sammy again. A Sammy with no darkness in him.

She recalled a time when she hadn't seen or heard from him in several weeks, so she'd stopped by his apartment to make sure he was all right. He'd been home from Vietnam about two years, but sometimes she felt as if he were still there. As if, in a way, he'd died along with his best friend.

She knocked and knocked, and waited, then knocked some more. Finally she heard faint sounds, as if someone were stumbling around inside. Then the door was flung open and Sammy stood swaying before her. As soon as he saw her, he straightened his shoulders a little, trying to make it appear as if everything were normal. But she knew better. She watched as his bloodshot eyes squinted against the hazy midmorning light.

"Hi, Molly-o."

His voice was gravel-rough from too much drinking and smoking and too many restless, sleepless nights. He was dressed in cutoffs and a wrinkled, unbuttoned shirt, most likely thrown on when he'd heard her knock. He hadn't shaved in several days.

Behind him the apartment looked like a scene from a detective movie—where the bad guys ransack the place in search of evidence. His writing desk was littered with empty food cartons, the typewriter keys dusty even though she knew he had an article long overdue.

He dragged fingers through his shaggy hair, then cast

a sheepish glance over his shoulder at the chaos. "Maid's day off," he muttered.

Nine o'clock in the morning and he smelled like stale whiskey, beer, and cigarettes.

Sammy, what are you doing to yourself? she wanted to ask. Instead, she said, "Did you go to your grief meeting last night?"

He waved her words away. "I don't need anybody to tell me I'm feeling guilty because my buddy's dead and I'm alive." He kicked at the cans on the floor, sloshing more beer onto the carpet.

Molly needed air. She crossed the room and tried to open the window, but the wood was swollen from high humidity.

Sammy nudged her out of the way. "Don't you know air's bad for you?" he asked, shoving open the window with a squeak of wood against metal. Cool air rushed in, diluting the stuffiness. "Full of exhaust fumes and factory fumes and things we don't even know about."

She rarely got after him for anything, but she couldn't help it this time. "You don't seem too concerned with your health."

Sammy plopped into the nearest chair. With elbows on the armrests, he rubbed a hand across his face, then looked up at her, an all too familiar bleakness in his dark eyes. "Funny, isn't it? The way we thought we were so indestructible. That nothing could touch us." He shook his head, seeming stunned by it all. "We thought we'd stay young forever . . . thought we'd live forever."

But life had turned out to be so much harder than any of them had ever dreamed. . . .

From downstairs came the sound of a ringing doorbell, pulling Molly back to the present, to her life with Austin and the dinner guests she was expecting.

At first Sammy's condition had given her a shock. But now Molly hoped Sammy's memory never returned. He was better off like this. Better off not knowing that Jay had been killed saving Sammy's life.

The evening went perfectly. Sammy grilled the hamburgers while Rachel and Molly brought the rest of the food out to the deck. The weather couldn't have been more cooperative. The temperature was just right. Not too hot, not too cool. There was barely a hint of a breeze, just enough to waft the scent of roses their way, but not enough to cause the napkins to blow around the yard.

Rachel and Sammy praised the food. "Your brother once accused me of eating nothing but TV dinners," Rachel said. "And it was true. A home-cooked meal is a treat."

Rachel was such a strong person, so poised, so self-assured that Molly couldn't help but feel a little intimidated by her, no matter how nice she was. It was nothing Rachel had said or done, but rather the things Molly had *never* done. Next to Rachel's, Molly's life seemed bland and terribly unimportant.

When they had finished eating, Rachel and Molly began to clear the table, with Molly protesting when Sammy insisted on helping.

"I want to help," he said. "I like it. It makes things feel normal."

When the dishes were done and Sammy had gone back outside, Molly paused by the buffet, thinking about showing Rachel some of the framed pictures that were set on a delicate crocheted runner. There were indentations on the cloth, evidence of the frames she'd removed earlier, pictures that could upset Sammy.

There was only one of Molly and Sammy together. It had been taken on the front porch of their home the first day of school. Their neighbor had taken it with her new camera—a Swinger. Molly couldn't remember the woman's name, but she remembered her singing, *Take the shot. Count it down. Zip it off.*

"I was such a homely child," Molly said, passing the picture to Rachel. "Boys used to tease me all the time." She smiled. "When Sammy was about eight or nine, he saw *The Scarlet Pimpernel.* After that, he started leaving little anonymous poems around to boost my ego. They were all signed Your secret admirer. I went along with it, but I always knew it was Sammy. Even though he tried to disguise it, I recognized his handwriting."

Rachel was smiling. Her eyes had a faraway look, as if she were imagining an eight-year-old Sammy hiding notes in shoes, in books, in laundry baskets.

Molly showed Rachel photos of Amy as an infant, Amy as a toddler, Amy as a grade-schooler.

Since she didn't know very much about Rachel's personal life other than the fact that she was divorced, she asked, "Do you have any children?"

Slowly Rachel put the pictures back on the crowded buffet. "I had a child," she said quietly. "A little girl. She died three and a half years ago."

The stark, pain-filled bleakness of her words cut straight through Molly's heart. "I'm so sorry. . . ."

Suddenly Rachel was no longer strong and self-assured. She was a mother who had lost a child.

I'm so sorry. What empty-sounding words. The thing Molly most feared had happened to Rachel. The loss of a child.

How had she stood it? How had she survived?

Watching her closely, seeing the way Rachel's fingers turned white around the glass she held, the way her eyes turned from the pictures and searched the room for something soothing to seize on, Molly realized, with mingled pain and fear, that Rachel hadn't survived.

Would anybody ever get over something like that? She knew she never would.

Behind them, the sliding door opened. "Better hurry up. Sun's going down."

His gaze fell on Rachel, his expression immediately showing concern.

Rachel's face was passive, only her eyes registered discomfort. Maybe worry. Anyone else would think she merely had a headache coming on, if they noticed anything at all.

He knows her so well, Molly thought with a small shock.

Sammy came across the room to her. "Rachel?"

She gave him an unsteady smile and waved a hand at the array of pictures. "I was just looking at baby pictures."

Instant understanding smoothed the lines from his brow. Without Rachel seeming to notice, he worked the glass from her clenched fingers.

"Are you okay?"

She blinked and nodded.

He took her hand and ushered her toward the sliding door. "You've got to see the sunset. The colors are unbelievable."

Sammy had always been sensitive, but this was more. He seemed to be in tune to Rachel in a way he'd never been to anyone before—except possibly Mary Dawn, a girl he'd dated in high school. And this bond between Sammy and Rachel worried Molly. There was more to it than a simple doctor-patient relationship.

An all too familiar feeling of dread filled her. A need to shelter Sammy from harm, to protect the person she loved.

Sammy and Rachel were out the door when Sammy stuck his head back in. "Coming?" he asked.

It was strange, this feeling of contentment. Sammy hadn't felt it in a long, long time, certainly not at all since his accident. And he could only surmise that all those endless days of staring at hospital walls had given him a new appreciation of things.

He knew it wasn't cool to get a charge out of potato salad and iced tea and just sitting around shooting the bull. But he did.

He was sitting, elbows resting on the wooden arms of the deck chair. For once he didn't have the urge to jump to his feet. For once the tightly coiled restlessness inside him was gone. For the moment he was content.

The food had made him nostalgic, each bite bringing all the good things of summer. Kid things, innocent things. No school, big grassy parks, and baseball diamonds. Fireworks and the sulfurous smell of sparklers.

Good things.

Rachel's and Molly's voices, hushed by the vastness of the night sky, drifted around him. Light from the kitchen window cast shadows across the deck. Moths beat their wings against the screen, and every once in a while a June bug would smack against the glass.

In the distance, cicadas sung madly in a chorus that rose to a frantic crescendo before dipping to silence, then starting again. Nearby, at ground level, crickets chirped.

"I love the sound of crickets," Rachel said drowsily, her voice coming out of the darkness beside him.

"They say you can tell the temperature by counting how many times a cricket chirps in a minute, then adding forty," Sammy said.

"I read that in *The Farmer's Almanac*," Molly said.

Sammy yawned. "There you go. Has to be true. And I used to think it just meant they were trying to attract a mate." Sammy shifted in his chair, sitting up a little straighter. "What do you say we check it out? See if it works."

Molly quickly got into the spirit. She jumped up and

went to the window so she could see the hands on her watch. "You two count. I'll keep time."

They had barely started when Rachel laughed, saying, "Stop! Stop! I lost count. Let's start over!"

Sammy hadn't even honed in on a cricket yet. He tilted his head. He could hear a loner near one corner of the deck. Sammy leaned over and touched Rachel's arm. "Hear that guy?" He pointed. "Off by himself? Let's both count him and see what we come up with."

Rachel agreed, and the chirp count began.

"Forty-one," Sammy said a minute later.

"Twenty-seven," Rachel said.

"Twenty-seven? How'd you get twenty-seven out of that?"

"Well, I counted some of the long chirps as one."

"You were supposed to count them as two."

"How do you know? Are there rules for this?"

He could hear the laughter in her voice, and it made him feel good to know that he wasn't the only one enjoying the evening.

This was all so normal. So right. He wanted to jump up and shout to the world, See, I'm a regular guy. I'm just sitting outside, listening to crickets. Nothing odd here.

Over the past few weeks he'd spent a lot of time trying to convince himself that he wasn't crazy. And sometimes he almost believed it. But other times, like the day of the Austin Bennet disaster, he'd get bummed.

He would start thinking about his situation, and the horror of it would grab him by the throat. To top it off, he had those damn students to cope with. They would file in and out of his room, going over his tests, asking him annoying questions. All of them had the same expression: curious, a little amazed, and excited. Making him feel like some sort of freak.

And the horror would grow. He would begin to fear

that he was never going to get well, that he was never going to get out, never get his memory back.

That night, before Rachel had stopped by to get him, he'd been bummed. The aftermath of twenty-some psych students.

But now he felt good.

"Just in case anybody's interested," Molly said from her position near the window, squinting at a round thermometer mounted on the sill, "the temperature is seventy-nine."

"Hah!" Sammy slapped a palm against a thigh. "What'd I tell you? A long chirp counts as two."

They tried it again, two more times, both counts ending in good-natured arguing.

They were all still laughing when a door slammed somewhere in the house. The laughter died. Sammy looked up in time to see Molly stiffen.

"Molly!"

The shout came from inside.

"Austin," Molly whispered in disbelief.

Indignant footfalls could be heard coming closer. Then the deck was suddenly flooded with harsh yellow light, almost blinding them after the near darkness. They were criminals trapped by a spotlight. Sammy resented that he'd been made to feel the wrongdoer, instantly realizing how Molly must feel most of the time.

"Austin . . ."

All the lightness, all the joy, was gone from his sister's voice. There would be no more cricket counting tonight.

"What are you doing home?" she asked.

Austin scowled at Sammy, but as soon as he noticed Rachel his face became passive.

Gotta put up a good front.

"I finished early, so I decided to drive back from Chicago tonight," he said in a tightly controlled voice.

But it didn't fool Sammy. Sammy knew he really

wanted to shout and demand to know what Sammy was doing at his house.

"We just had dinner," Molly explained. "There are some leftovers, if you're hungry."

Austin ignored her question, which was no big surprise.

"Did you get the oil changed in the Mercedes?" he asked instead.

"Oil?"

"Can't you remember anything? I told you to take the car in and have it gone over!" He sounded like a spoiled child.

"I'm sorry. I forgot. I'll reschedule it for tomorrow."

"Tomorrow! I wanted it done today. The appointment was for today!"

It was easy for Sammy to see what was going on. Austin was deliberately trying to humiliate Molly in front of them. And it was working. She suddenly appeared smaller. The joy that had briefly illuminated her face was gone.

Sammy shoved himself to his feet. While June bugs dive-bombed around them, he faced Austin, forcing a smile to his lips. "Just what did you need done to your car, Austin? A little going-over, you say?" He rubbed his hands together. "I can take care of that for you. No problem."

Earlier Molly had shown them around. Sammy knew right where to find Austin's silver Mercedes.

Without looking left or right, Sammy struck out, striding purposefully to the door, almost jerking it off the hinges as he opened it. Behind him came the sound of shuffling chairs and scuffling feet.

Austin's panic-filled voice filtered to him. "Forget the car!"

But Sammy was a man with a mission. "Don't sweat it." The words were flung back over his shoulder, complete with an airy movement of one hand. "This won't take but a couple of minutes. Then we can all sit down and have some apple pie."

He shoved open the garage door so hard it banged against the wall. He flicked on the light, revealing Austin's prized possession.

To his right was a set of golf clubs. Pricy clubs. Sammy had played golf before. Just enough to know he hated the sport and the white shoes that went with it, which was a stupid reason to dislike something.

Now he had a reason.

He jerked out a nine iron. Then, grasping it like a baseball bat—he'd always liked baseball—he swung it in an arch and smashed the hood of the car.

Behind him came Austin's agonized shout of disbelief, his voice quaking with emotion, making Sammy even more furious. Sammy swung again. The impact sent jarring pain up his arms to his shoulders. But he welcomed the pain. He loved the pain.

Anger fed anger. It felt good to let go. Total, unrestrained release. He didn't want to lose his anger. Had to hold on to his anger.

Again and again he lifted the nine iron, shouting as he went. "Materialistic bastard!"

Wang, wang.

"Cares more about his damn car than he does my sister!"

Wang, wang.

Behind him, along with Austin's shouts, he could hear Rachel's and Molly's raised voices. He pretended they were both cheering him on. Again and again he raised the club. Austin was every guy he ever hated. He was the bully who'd dragged Molly into the boys' bathroom, the bully who'd teased her and called her names.

"Sammy! Look out!"

Rachel's voice.

He swung around in time to see a club arcing toward him. He ducked and sidestepped.

Austin missed him and stumbled forward, catching himself. Sammy and Austin faced off, clubs in their clenched hands. Sammy could feel the sweat pouring down the sides of his face. His breathing was coming in loud rasps.

"Come on, you son of a bitch! Hit me!" Sammy moved the club back and forth in a taunting motion. *Swing at me, you bastard. Give me a reason.* "Come on. What are you waiting for? Come on."

Austin slowly lowered his club, but didn't let go. "Get out of here before I call the police."

Sammy saw Rachel edging past Austin, coming in his direction. Rational Rachel. He didn't want to face her logic. He didn't want to let go of the rage that was pumping through his veins. He knew if he looked at her, he would be a goner.

"Sammy."

He forced himself to concentrate on Austin.

"Sammy."

He couldn't help it. His eyes were pulled to Rachel's. Tonight she wasn't wearing glasses. Her eyes were the palest green he'd ever seen. The irises were outlined by black.

He felt her fingers skim his knuckles. "Let go," she said quietly, her eyes locked with his. "Put it down."

Suddenly he felt like a child who'd been caught breaking a window. A child who'd been insisting he was old enough to play with the big boys, only to find out he wasn't. "He's a son of a bitch," he whispered brokenly. "You know he's a son of a bitch."

She nodded.

His anger was gone, replaced by the same dark depression that had hung over him earlier. He hadn't helped Molly at all. What was he trying to prove? Would he ever get his act together?

Sammy loosened his grip. The club clattered to the cement floor. He was hypnotized by Rachel's soothing eyes. He couldn't pull away. Didn't want to pull away.

"Sometimes . . . I'm such a dumb ass. . . ." he choked out.

Rachel did something that surprised him, that completely knocked him out. She smiled. And it was a great smile. A smile that was totally unrestrained, a smile that lit a spark in her pale green eyes.

She placed a hand on each side of his face, her gaze holding his. "Sometimes," she whispered in a voice that was meant just for him, "you're wonderful."

SEVENTEEN

SHORTLY AFTER THE CAR-BASHING INCIDENT, RACHEL noticed a change in Sammy.

He wasn't as rash or outspoken. She could tell that he was making a strong, conscious effort to behave. He was also accepting responsibility for his actions—a sure sign of growing independence. He even told her that he planned to pay for the damage done to Austin's car as soon as he began earning an income.

Suddenly Sammy was progressing at a remarkable pace. He and Rachel still had their daily sessions, but he was doing so much on his own that there was hardly any need for them anymore.

He was catching up on everything that had happened over the past twenty years. Filling in the blanks, if not with his own memories, then with someone else's. He hounded Molly. He read autobiographies and biographies, fiction and nonfiction. He read scientific textbooks and entertainment magazines. When he wasn't reading, he was watching documentaries or movies or music videos.

About a month after the disaster at Molly's house, Rachel stepped out of the hospital elevator to hear laughter coming from down the hall, from the vicinity of the patients' lounge. Odd, she rarely heard laughter on this floor. She followed the sound, stopping when she got to the open doorway of the lounge.

Sammy was standing in front of a captivated audience, and it looked like he was performing magic tricks.

He was dressed in his customary T-shirt and faded jeans, over which was a green hospital gown worn backward so that the opening was in the front. The ribbons were untied, and the hem hit him at mid-thigh.

The room had been rearranged. Chairs had been shoved around so that they all faced the same direction, toward Sammy. Instead of staring blankly at a television screen, the patients were watching him, their expressions full of anticipation, as if they knew something good was about to happen.

Well, Rachel mentally corrected herself, if not something good, then at least something exciting. Something different. Because that's the way it was when Sammy was around.

It wasn't until then that she noticed her presence in the doorway was causing a mild wave of distraction. She was about to inch away when Sammy glanced up and their eyes met over a sea of heads.

She gave him a quick smile of hello and took a step back.

"Ah, here's my lovely assistant, Ms. Shrinkola!" With a theatrical sweep of one hand, Sammy cleared an imaginary path through the crowd, his dark eyebrows raised in expectation.

Heads turned. People waited.

The Shrinkola rankled a bit, but nobody had ever called her a poor sport. She edged past the chairs and joined Sammy.

He was still grinning, his eyes shining with pure orneriness. Taking her by both shoulders, he turned her to face the crowd.

Now she could see that Mark Elliot was sitting front

row center. His arms were crossed, hands tucked in his armpits. Of course he was grinning too.

She'd seen her share of magic shows, and she knew what to do. She smiled and gave everyone a quick bob of her head. Mark was apparently the crowd leader, because when he applauded quite loudly, the others quickly followed suit.

At first glance she hadn't recognized most of the faces, and then she realized why they hadn't looked familiar. These faces had expressions. Even the borderline cata-tonics were showing signs of life. And if some of them didn't quite understand what was going on, it didn't matter. They were nonetheless caught up in the spirit of things.

"Are you ready, lovely assistant?" Sammy asked.

The liveliness in the room was infectious, and there was no way she was going to spoil the fun. No way she could keep a smile from touching her own mouth. "Ready."

He reached into the pocket of her lab coat and pulled out her red stethoscope.

Holding it high, he mused in a voice reminiscent of W. C. Fields, "Ah, a colorful little number."

He placed the eartips in his ears, then raised the round chest piece, holding it in the air for effect. "First, I must find your heart." He placed the end in the hollow between her breasts, then made an elaborate Charlie Chaplin mime act of trying to hear something.

When he pulled back, his face was a study in mock alarm. "No heartbeat. My dear, you can't be my assistant if you have no heart." He held up a forefinger. "We must operate! Please lie down." He indicated the long table in front of them.

"Sammy—"

"Dr. Cando."

"Dr. Cando, I don't think—"

"That's right. Don't think. Just do."

She played along. Sammy took her hand and helped her onto the table, then adjusted her skirt once she was on her back, staring up at the white ceiling.

With Sammy facing his rapt audience, he leaned over her, his brow creased with seriousness. He reached for the top button of her lab coat.

Rachel's hand flew up to stop him, her fingers wrapping around his wrist.

He patted her hand with his free one, making an intense study of her fingers. "Ah, what symmetrical digits you have, my dear."

She smiled, recognizing the classic W. C. Fields line.

She released his wrist and put her hand back down at her side.

"We can't have you running around without a heart, can we? We must get to the bottom of this." He leaned closer and winked. *Trust me,* the wink said. "Rachel?"

She blinked and gave him a tiny nod.

Starting below her chin, his nimble fingers undid her buttons, all the way to where the lab jacket ended just above her knees. Then he lifted the side nearest the patients, using it as a screen to hide his actions. He hunched over, ducking his head behind the jacket flap.

Like a hobo going through a trash bin, he began tossing things over his shoulder, muttering as he went. "Ah . . . mmm . . . ah . . ." He came up with a wrinkled tissue. Without looking at it, he pitched it over his shoulder, then pulled out a half-eaten candy bar.

He continued, verbally cataloging each item he found. "Pen. Gum. More tissue." Everything she had in her pockets.

The crowd's reaction began as a small hum, then grew into laughter and clapping, the noise increasing with each article he brought forth.

He pulled out something that hadn't been in any of her pockets—a frog fishing lure, the same lure she'd seen him and Mark drooling over a few days before in the bait and tackle section of the local discount store.

When he was done with his housecleaning, he straightened and held up both hands, his body language asking for silence. The room quieted. He hooked the stethoscope to his ears, then put the round end to her chest.

Once again he did his Charlie Chaplin impersonation.

Like a doctor who sees there is no solution but surgery, Sammy sighed and straightened, tugging the stethoscope from his ears. He rubbed his chin and cast a gaze ceilingward. "I don't understand," he muttered loudly enough for the crowd to hear. "Still no heartbeat." He pointed to the sky. "I must try one last time. Good assistants are hard to come by."

He lifted the flap of her jacket and disappeared behind it once more, voicing several ah-hahs and ah-hmms.

Rachel's attention was on Sammy, but she was remotely aware that the room had fallen silent, the audience waiting with rapt expectation.

Sammy didn't disappoint them.

"Ah-hah!" He popped up. Then, from the vicinity of Rachel's chest, and with the flourish of a dedicated magician, he drew forth a bouquet of real if slightly crumpled daisies.

The patients went wild. They laughed and clapped, their excitement reaching almost manic proportions.

When the din began to die down, Sammy once again listened to Rachel's chest, this time pronouncing her cured. Helping her from the table, he shouted, "Let's have a big round of applause for my lovely assistant, Ms. Shrinkola!"

The patients, along with Mark, clapped and yelled, apparently accepting the bouquet for proof of a heart.

After the applause ended, Rachel noticed that Sammy was facing her, toe to toe, buttoning her lab coat. As before, she put a hand up to stop him, but he only smiled, looked her in the eyes, and said, "It's my pleasure." When he finished with the buttons, he put everything back in her pockets, including the half-eaten candy bar. He straightened her name tag. "There you go, Dr. Rachel D. Collins. Good as new."

She tried to give the flowers back, but he wouldn't take them.

"You must have gotten them someplace. They must belong to somebody."

"Rachel . . ." He looked hurt. "Are you accusing me of taking flowers from some poor patient?"

No. Of course he wouldn't do that. As she clung to the bouquet with both hands, a soft daisy petal brushed her lip.

Her awareness blurred as she recalled the way his lips had felt on hers.

You have such a sensitive mouth, Rachel.

He was still watching her. Nothing escaped him. His eyes told her that he was remembering, too, and that he knew she was remembering. He smiled. And his smile was open and secretive at the same time, as if he were aware of something she wasn't.

"Thanks for being such a good sport," he said.

She was out the door and moving down the hall when she heard his voice echoing from behind her.

"Now, for my next trick. I will need a volunteer from the audience. . . ."

It wasn't until that afternoon, after the rumpled daisies had adorned her desk for several hours, that Rachel happened to overhear a conversation between two nurses. They were trying to figure out what had become of the daisies that belonged in the nurses' station.

• • •

Before it seemed possible, the warm days and warm-
nights of June slipped into the hot days and hot nights
of July, and the day they had all been working toward
arrived.

"Sammy's ready to leave," Dr. Fontana said from his
seat behind the desk. "You've done a good job."

Rachel stood before him, Sammy's thick file—a file
that had grown daily—in her hands. Even though she'd
braced herself for this moment, she couldn't control the
flutter of panic in her stomach.

"He's made remarkable progress these past weeks,"
she heard herself saying. Unconsciously, she clutched the
file tighter, her mind racing. "But we can't simply turn
him out. He has no means of support, no place to live.
His sister's house would be out of the question."

Dr. Fontana rubbed stubby fingers across the bald
spot on top of his head. "I thought about that. How do
you think he'd feel about a job here? As a recreational
director?"

The fluttering in her stomach began to subside.
"Recreational director?"

"He's got a way about him. He can really charm the
other patients."

Rachel's grip on the file relaxed.

"Of course, he still shows occasional signs of unpredictability. But I suspect that's simply a part of his
makeup. Still, like you, I don't think he's quite ready to
go solo." He pushed his seat back, hands braced on the
desk, prepared to rise. "Mark Elliot offered to let Sammy
move in with him. What do you think?"

Sammy and Mark sharing an apartment?

Dr. Fontana got to his feet. "Two peas in a pod."

For the first time since entering the office, Rachel
smiled. "What a perfectly alarming idea."

• • •

An hour later Rachel met Sammy in one of the private meeting rooms they had taken to using for their sessions. It was a smaller version of the living room, and more comfortable and private than the stark therapy room. And there were no cameras here.

Sammy immediately headed for the couch, sprawling on his back, hands behind his head.

"You look tired," Rachel said, sitting down at a table. There were shadows under his eyes. "Are you having trouble sleeping?"

"I stayed up reading most of the night."

"Oh? What were you reading?"

"The World According to Garp." He paused, thinking. "Funny stuff."

"Sad stuff."

"Very sad stuff."

He shifted his hips, getting more comfortable. Silence descended. Then Sammy's eyes drifted shut. His breathing became rhythmic. Within minutes he was asleep.

Without thinking about what she was doing, she found herself studying him. She'd heard of people having coal-black hair, or hair as black as a raven's wing. Sammy's was truly that black. Poetically black. And long. She'd never seen anybody's hair grow so fast. Maybe it had something to do with all that electricity surging through him.

Her center of focus widened, taking in his gently rising and falling chest, his lean hips and long legs in faded jeans that outlined muscles. With a feeling that was alarmingly like affection, she noted that over the past month he'd put on some much-needed pounds.

She couldn't help but recall the way he'd looked when he'd accidentally knocked her to the floor as he tried to escape. Painfully thin, with eyes like dark, sunken pools.

Or the first time he'd looked up at her with total defeat.

I'll be good.

He'd gotten to her that day.

Guiltily, she pulled her eyes away, forcing her gaze to the patient file in her hands. She opened it to the first entry.

He'd been with them almost three months. Not all that long. A very short time, actually. Some patients stayed for years before they were ready for discharge. She had always felt a great happiness in saying good-bye, knowing these people were whole again and able to live in the outside world.

Why did this time feel so different? Why did this time make her throat ache and her eyes burn?

Blindly, she flipped through the pages of typed notes, hardly seeing more than the pattern the paragraphs made on the crisp white pages.

If Sammy agreed to the hospital position, he would be there almost every day, she told herself. But there would be no daily sessions. No more trips downtown. No more drives. No more counting cricket chirps . . .

She closed the file and folded her hands on top of it. When she looked up, Sammy's eyes were open. Signs of tiredness were still there, but he was alert. Curious.

Finding him watching her so intently sent a reverberation through her.

Sammy unlocked his hands and sat up, all in one graceful motion. "What's wrong?"

So typically Sammy. He had an uncanny way of seeing right through her.

She clasped and unclasped her fingers. "Nothing."

"You're too quiet."

"I was just thinking, that's all. Actually"—she gave him a quick smile—"I have some good news."

He leaned closer, elbows on his knees, giving her his total attention.

She told him about the conversation she'd had with Dr. Fontana about Mark's suggestion and the position as recreational director. As she'd guessed, Sammy was eager to have the job. Before she knew it he was on his feet, moving toward the door, ready to find Mark and be gone.

She got to her feet more slowly. Then, with shaking fingers she pulled out her business card and quickly pressed it into Sammy's hand, lest he notice her trembling. "If you ever have a problem, I want you to call me, day or night. Even if it's three o'clock in the morning, I want you to call. Will you do that?"

The sparkle in his eyes dimmed. His smile faded.

She may be transparent to him, but he wasn't so easily read. She could only wonder if he was just now realizing that this was good-bye.

With his long, beautiful fingers, he slid the card into his T-shirt pocket. His knuckles still showed where the stitches had been. Then he surprised her by taking both her arms so he could look her square in the face. His eyes were dark and solemn. Once again she was struck by how far he'd come in so short a time.

"If I need you, I'll call," he said in a low, level voice. "If *you* promise to do the same. Will you do that, Rachel? Will you call if you need me?"

She didn't know what to say. Her mind stumbled along, searching for old standby words about doctor-patient relationships. But they sounded so false and insincere that she couldn't bring herself to voice them.

He made an exasperated sound. "Don't give me any more of that rules-of-ethics garbage."

For a brief, heartlifting second she wondered if this intimacy was what he'd been working so feverishly toward these past weeks. But the thought had barely formed when she saw the foolishness of it.

Silly, silly woman.

Her medical training had covered bedside manner. It had covered the handling of patient infatuation. But it had never prepared her for the opposite, for coping with a doctor's infatuation with her patient.

From the very beginning, even before their first session, Rachel had sensed a risk, a need to be cautious. A need to protect herself from danger. She had known that Sammy had the power to hurt her. So she had run from his brutal words, words that had zeroed in on the very center of her pain. She had hidden from him.

She just hadn't understood that it wasn't his coming that was going to hurt. It was his leaving.

She hadn't faced the fact that to make him well would mean to lose him.

EIGHTEEN

AUSTIN BENNET STOOD IN THE FRONT DOORWAY OF HIS house, pointing an accusing finger at Molly. "You've changed. Maybe your brother isn't the only one who needs to see a shrink." With that he left, slamming the door behind him.

Molly listened to the sound of the company car being backed from the garage—Austin's Mercedes was still in the shop—and all she could feel was guilty relief.

It seemed they were always fighting nowadays. The latest argument had started because of Molly's failure to have supper on the table the second Austin stepped in the door. She'd even magnified the offense by suggesting he find something to eat on his own. At first he'd simply looked stunned, his mouth moving as if he were a poor fish out of water. Then, when he realized she wasn't kidding, he'd exploded.

She found herself feeling a little sorry for Austin. She supposed her behavior *was* a shock to him. He was right. She *had* changed. She no longer moved through the day in a numb haze. She actually thought a little.

You've changed.

Coming from Austin, the words had been flattering. Sammy had spoken those very words to her, too, not verbally, but with his dark, expressive eyes.

You've changed.

How many times had she relived that awful moment of seeing Sammy's initial reaction? He'd quickly covered his shock and dismay, but she'd caught it. And it had dealt her a jarring blow.

Now, with Austin gone, Molly went outside to the toolshed, gathering what she would need: her spade and the round cardboard planters that could be set directly into the ground. Then she headed for the rose garden, toward the soothing scent of damp peat and rose petals. Not far away, from the direction of the house, gold-finches squabbled over one of several bird feeders.

Her birds.

It wasn't until that moment that she realized how much she would miss them. Several generations of birds had been coming to her feeders for years. There were many she could recognize, many she called by name.

But she knew when it came time for her to leave, they wouldn't go hungry. A lot of neighbors had begun putting out feeders, and her birds would be welcome. Still, that knowledge didn't make it any easier. It wouldn't make her miss them any less.

She set the tip of the spade in the ground, about twelve inches from the nearest bush. Foot to the blade's shoulder, she shoved it deeply into the mulched ground. This particular rosebush was the first variety she'd ever successfully grafted. It was the only rose of its type in existence.

But her roses were part of her past. An old dream. Sometimes people had to let go of old dreams.

And anyway, she reasoned, trying to make herself feel better about what she was doing, her dream had been sullied. She'd never wanted to raise flowers to hawk to local florists. She'd wanted to breed roses, to create new and exciting varieties. Somewhere along the way her dream had lost momentum. Her original vision had blurred.

She finished making a trench around the bush. Then, using the spade as a lever, she ripped the shrub's roots from the ground.

A few hours later Molly pulled her station wagon into Amy's driveway and turned off the engine.

She was dragging a potted rosebush across the tailgate when Amy slipped from the house, the screen door slamming behind her. Molly quickly inspected her daughter for signs of fatigue or ill health. Seeing none, she let out a relieved breath. Except for the lines of puzzlement across her brow, Amy looked radiant.

"I brought you and Chris something," Molly said, trying to sound cheerful, hoping she could get through this without breaking down. The last thing she wanted to do was worry her daughter.

Curious, Amy looked inside. The backseats were down and the car was loaded with rosebushes—dark green leaves and vivid blossoms in an array of colors. There was no way Molly could hide the fact that they were her roses. Her special breeds were simply too unique to pass off as anyone else's.

"Your roses?" Amy asked, looking up at her mother. "I don't understand. You can't possibly give me your roses. How can you part with them?"

It's hard.

"I'm tired of them," Molly said. "And I think they must be tired of me. They haven't been doing very well lately. They need a change of soil. A change of location. And I thought, what better place than your house." She nodded in the direction of the bare ground between the sidewalk and the wooden front porch. "You've been needing something there for a long time."

Amy's husband, Chris, made an appearance, scratching his head and yawning. He was temporarily working two jobs and had apparently been sleeping. Barefoot and in cutoffs, he picked his way across the yard and began carrying the rosebushes to the house.

For the next two hours they all worked together, getting the shrubs set in the ground. They finished with the last bush just before ten o'clock.

Chris and Amy asked her inside, but Molly declined. She needed to be alone now.

Amy hugged her mother. "I'll take good care of your roses. They'll always be yours."

Molly was grateful that Amy and Chris didn't press for an explanation. It would be hard to give one, and possibly harder to understand. All she knew was that she was gradually cutting her ties so that someday, when that jet trailed across the sky, maybe she'd be in it.

Molly drove home under a star-cluttered sky, the sweet scent of crushed petals and spilled peat lingering in the dark confines of the car.

Only a memory.

It was hard to leave old friends behind.

NINETEEN

SAMMY'S WORKDAY WAS OVER. HE WAVED TO A CLUSTER
of patients in the corner of the lounge, gave Bo Houston
a high five, then headed down the hallway to the
elevator.

Sammy was biding his time, playing it cool, trying
out an old adage, the one that said absence made the
heart grow fonder.

Problem was, it didn't seem to be working, and he
was worried that his absence had made Rachel completely forget about him.

Helluva deal.

He stepped into the empty elevator and punched the
fifth floor button.

Two weeks had passed since Rachel had released him
from her care, and he hadn't so much as caught a glimpse
of her blond head.

He'd wanted to prove to her that he could take care of
himself, that he could make it on his own. He'd wanted
to prove that he was a man, not a boy. And he'd wanted
her to miss him.

At first, as part of his strategy, he'd tried to avoid her.
But later, after too many days of no Rachel, he'd started
deliberately hanging around the very places he'd been
avoiding.

No luck.

He'd like to think that she was playing it cool too. But he knew better. Rachel wasn't the type to play games.

So this was it. D-day. He was going to stop by her office and see her. If that went okay, he was going to ask her if she'd like to go for coffee. He'd like to take her out to eat, or to a movie, or both, but he didn't have a car and he was a little short on cash. He hadn't gotten a paycheck yet. Actually coffee was more than he could afford.

When he got to her office it wasn't Rachel he found sitting behind her desk, but Sanderson, the jerk who'd doped him up and tossed him into solitary. Sammy didn't like seeing him at Rachel's desk with his pinky rings and stinking cologne.

"What are you doing here?" Sammy demanded, ready to toss the guy out on his ass. "Where's Rachel?"

Sanderson slid back the chair and stood, his movements calculated and self-absorbed. "She's gone. And since Mark Elliot left early for that convention in Chicago, I'm working overtime."

"Gone? What do you mean gone?"

Sanderson laughed his phony laugh. "Two days ago she just never showed up. Falling back into her old habits, I guess. She should have been canned a long time ago."

Sammy took a couple of steps closer and braced his hands on the desk. "What the hell are you talking about?"

"She was in the Impaired Physician Program for three years. Fontana's orders." Eyebrows quirked above a bland expression. "Don't tell me you didn't know?" he asked in mock surprise. "You were her baby, the first serious, long-term case she'd taken since quitting the program." He laughed again, slapping shut a file and lifting a whole stack in his arms. "Guess you were too much for her. But like I've been telling Fontana, Collins just can't cut it."

Sanderson should know better than to push him like this. Sammy could feel his thread-thin control slipping. But like the time at Molly's, he welcomed the release. He wanted to lose it.

Push me some more.

Sanderson's mouth curled into a pleased smirk. "Somebody said they saw her car at Taps. It's a bar on the rough side of town. A real dive." His expression grew thoughtful. "Who knows? Maybe I'll swing by there on my way home. If she's strung out on downers and booze, she might be in the mood for a quick lay in the backseat of my car."

Sammy lunged across the desk, files and papers scattering. He knocked Sanderson backward, following him to the floor.

"Don't hit me!" Sanderson screamed, raising an arm to deflect the blow. "I was just kidding. Kidding!"

Sammy grabbed two fistfuls of Sanderson's shirt, jerking him to attention. Two eyes, one blue, one practically colorless, twitched up at him. Somewhere in the tumble, Sanderson had lost a contact lens.

"You're the one who's impaired," Sammy said through gritted teeth. "You have about as much compassion as a damn snake. Less. Snakes feed only when they're hungry." Disgusted, Sammy shoved Sanderson's shoulders, then got to his feet.

He was almost to the elevator when Sanderson stuck his head out the doorway, shouting, "You better watch it, or I'll have you put away so long you'll never see daylight again!"

The threat had no impact. Sammy was thinking only about Rachel. He passed the elevator and headed straight for the stairwell. He threw open the door, metal clanging against cement block. Then he was taking the steps two and three at a time.

Rachel swayed, then straightened. She didn't want anybody to think there was something wrong with her. Even though there was.

She squinted her eyes against the murky glow of the corner streetlight, looking for her car, vaguely surprised to find herself back where she'd started. She'd rounded the block at least two times, maybe three. No sign of her car. She let out a weary sigh. She'd just have to walk home.

Home.

She didn't want to go home. She would have to think if she went home. Worse, she would have to confront herself if she went home.

No, she couldn't go there.

She swung around to face the building vibrating with life behind her. The pink neon lights on the front were supposed to say Taps, but part of the *a* was gone, so it said Tips instead, only there was no dot over the *i*. The letters gave off a low-pitched buzz, as if in warning.

Occasionally the door to the bar would open and a few twangs from a jukebox would float out before the door slammed shut.

She stood there, trying to decide what to do, trying to remember just how she'd gotten there. She seemed to recall another bar . . . some people . . . She'd given one of them her car keys. . . .

Her brain was too foggy. It was too hard to think, too hard to keep her thoughts running on the right track.

She suddenly realized how tired she was. A tidal wave of exhaustion almost knocked her to the ground. She was so tired she could almost lie down on the spit-stained cement and go to sleep. But that wouldn't do. Somehow she managed to alert enough undamaged brain matter to decide that sleeping on a sidewalk in front of a tavern was a bad idea.

She listed her problems, hoping to come up with a solution. One, she didn't have a car, and anyway, she shouldn't be driving. Two, she couldn't stay here.

A cab. She'd call a cab. When the cab came, she'd figure out where to go. One step at a time. That's what they were always saying in therapy. Take one problem, one day at a time. Don't ever think of the big picture. Don't ever think of the rest of your life.

That decision made, she headed for the bar. She shouldered open the door, the knob clammy in her hand. They should really wash that doorknob. A lot of germs were transferred by doorknobs. Maybe they should ban doorknobs. There you go.

Body heat, smoke, and noise blasted her in the face as she stepped inside. The toe of her shoe immediately snagged on the metal threshold strip. She caught herself and moved on.

Ought to ban those strips too.

Had she been here before? She vaguely recalled a phone booth on the other side of the room. Or had that been another bar? She couldn't remember.

There was more than one way for a person to lose her memory.

That insightful bit of wisdom filled her with awe. She should write it down for further reference. But she didn't have a pencil, and she didn't have any paper. And as suddenly as it had come, the thought drifted away and she could no longer remember it. Profound significance became tedious drivel. Dust in the wind.

Oh, well.

Turning sideways, she made her way through the crowd. Some of the buzzing conversation was directed at her. She heard a few Hey babys and Hel-lo mamas, but she didn't allow them to break her single-minded concentration. She had to get to the phone booth. Hands grabbed her. She didn't shrug them off. She simply kept moving, leaving the hands behind, until she finally gained the object of her quest.

Her next obstacle was the door. She hadn't seen a phone booth like it in years. It was made of wood, not metal, and the folding door weighed a ton. It almost seemed as if the wood had soaked up the humidity of the past twenty years.

She finally gained entry, feeling pleased with herself when she managed to get the door closed behind her.

At first she just stood there, staring at the pay phone.

Money. She needed money.

Her hand went to her shoulder. Her fingers touched a leather strap. Relief flooded her. She'd lost her car and her way, but she hadn't lost her purse.

Change. Pay phones took change.

She dug around in the side pocket of her purse, pulling out some coins and spreading them on the narrow wooden ledge under the phone. She couldn't distinguish one from the other. It was dark in the booth, but something told her that wasn't her only problem. Her hand flew to her face and she catalogued her newest loss: her glasses.

She was falling apart.

With another flash of insight, she realized that she didn't need a cab, she needed a friend.

Sammy.

She wouldn't have to explain what was wrong. Being Sammy, he would know. He would look at her with concern. Then he would talk to her in a low, soothing voice that would chase the confusion from her mind and make everything clear. Make everything better.

Suddenly she was frantic to put the call through.

She tucked the receiver between her neck and shoul-

der, trying to block out the cigar smell of the mouth-
piece. She grabbed a coin that looked like a dime and
tried to stick it in the slot. Too big. She tried another
coin, and another, until one of them finally fell with a
chink of metal against metal. She sobbed in relief. But
when she raised a finger to press the buttons, she
couldn't see the numbers.

Operator. She'd call the operator.

"That number can be direct-dialed," the operator
said. "And you don't have to put in any money until you
reach your party."

Rachel swallowed and clutched the receiver with both
hands. "I—I'm in a phone booth, and I can't see the
numbers. . . ."

"Are you vision-impaired?"

"Impaired?" Yes, yes, she was impaired. "No . . .
I'm . . . I just can't see."

The operator agreed to put the call through.

It rang again and again.

Answer. Please answer.

But the phone kept ringing.

The operator broke in. "Your party doesn't answer.
Would you like to try again later?"

It had been so hard for her to make it this far. She
hadn't considered the possibility of Sammy's not being
home.

One problem at a time . . .

"Yes . . . I don't know. Thank you. . . ."

She tried to hang up, missed, and let the receiver fall
from her hand. It clanged against the ledge.

Sammy felt closer to losing his mind than he had in all
the time since his accident.

Where the hell was Rachel?

He'd gone by her apartment, only to find it dark and her car gone.

On Mark's ten-speed, he'd pedaled up and down the hills of La Grange, checking out every bar. But there had been no sign of Rachel. And now it was almost one in the morning.

Where the hell was she?

He decided to make one more swing by Taps even though he'd already been there once with no luck.

He'd like to think that Sanderson was making the whole thing up just to cause trouble, but deep down Sammy knew better. From things Rachel had let drop, and the few answers he'd been able to pry from Mark, he knew that Rachel was still dealing with grief and guilt. And sometimes the world became too much for her.

Sometimes she fell apart.

Narrow bike wheels jarred across a street paved with red brick. Then Sammy was wheeling into the alley adjacent to the bar. He parked the bike near garbage cans and stacks of wooden crates.

Earlier he had felt strange stepping into a bar. He'd almost expected to get carded. Now he was fast becoming used to it.

The bar hadn't changed much over the past few hours. A lot of the same people were there, plus more. A lot more. The place still smelled of sweat, cheap perfume, and stale beer. Belly-rubbing music was still blaring from the corner jukebox. The air was still punctuated with the sound of clacking pool balls. Behind the bar was the same bartender with the same V-neck, membrane-thin T-shirt. Arms loaded with tattoos, a few unmistakably homemade, done with a pocket knife and ink from a ball-point pen. At least he loved his mother.

Sammy had always wondered about those Mom tattoos. How did a guy's mother react to something like that? Flattered? Or maybe worried that her son might never get married and she'd be baking apple pies for him for the rest of her life?

Sammy was aware of women checking him out as he worked his way through the crowd. He ignored their suggestive stares. He made two circuits of the room before heading for the dimly lit hall. She could be in one of the rest rooms, passed out.

He was cutting past the phone booth when something out of the corner of his eye caught his attention. He stopped and turned.

Rachel.

Through the nicotine-stained glass he could see her sitting on the edge of the seat, arms folded on the wooden ledge, head resting on her arms.

Feeling the need for caution, or rather the need to not startle her, he gently tapped on the glass with his knuckles.

No reaction.

He tapped again, louder this time.

Still no reaction.

He eased open the door, then squeezed himself inside, shutting the door behind him, partially shutting out the tinny blare of the jukebox and the roar of loud conversation.

"Rachel . . ."

She lifted her head, and his heart gave a small lurch. She wasn't wearing her glasses. Eyes that were slightly unfocused looked up at him.

She'd been crying.

"Sammy?"

She sounded as if she couldn't quite believe what she saw.

"What are you doing here?"

Her voice was slurred. Rachel—practical, logical, in-control Rachel.

"Looking for you."

The telephone receiver was dangling from the cord. He reached down and put it back in the cradle, briefly wondering who she'd been trying to call. "Come on. I'll take you home."

She shook her head, and he couldn't recall ever seeing such sadness on a person's face.

"I don't want to go home." She ran her fingers through her hair in a gesture that reflected frustration and confusion. She stared blankly ahead, focusing on something in her mind. "It's July 24th," she said bleakly.

Sammy knew for a fact that it was July 26. Somehow she'd lost two days. He took painful note of the circles under her eyes, the rumpled condition of her clothes. He'd never seen her look anything but fastidious. Had she been wandering the streets for the past two days? It hurt to think about it.

He felt angry with himself. All along, blind to what was happening, he'd looked to her for support and strength. While he was getting better, she was staying the same, maybe even regressing.

"Please go," she whispered. "I want to be alone."

"You've been alone too long."

She shook her head in tight jerks. Then, still not looking at him, she choked out, "I'm going to cry. Please leave." The words were forced through a tight throat, each syllable winding higher.

"Rachel—"

"I . . . don't . . . want . . . you . . . to . . . see. . . me . . . cry. . . ."

But then he proceeded to witness just that very thing. She buried her face in her crossed arms, her long-fought sobs breaking loose.

The sound of her anguish almost brought him to his knees. He lifted her from the seat and pulled her to him,

wrapping his arms around her, a hand cradling her head
while she pressed her face to his chest.

Not Rachel, of all people. It wasn't fair. She spent her
life healing people. But who healed her?

He wished to God he could help her, but he had no
answers. There had been a time in his life when he'd been
good with words. If he was still that person, then maybe
he'd know what to say to comfort her and ease her pain.
But he wasn't the person he used to be.

When her sobbing finally subsided, Sammy helped
her dry her tears and blow her nose.

"I didn't want you to see me like this." She sniffled,
head bent.

"Like what?" His voice was a million times lighter
than his heart. "In a phone booth?" Dumb line. His goal
had been to chase some of the sadness from her eyes, and
miraculously, she smiled a little.

Her purse had fallen to the floor, and she bent to pick
it up. She hit her head on the wooden ledge as she
straightened.

"Ow!" One hand flew to the tender spot. She frowned
and looked up at him. Then she surprised him with a
classic Sammy Thoreau line. "I hit my fucking head."

Then she laughed. With her head tilted back, she
laughed while tears still clung to her eyelashes.

Relief rushed through him. She was going to make it.
At least for tonight.

"Come on," he said. "Let's blow this joint."

She agreed.

They were stepping out the front door as the bartender announced last call for alcohol.

Outside, the air was heavy and damp, but after the
claustrophobic staleness of the bar, it felt great. It felt
like freedom.

Even though it was a Friday night, the streets were
hushed and dark. From a distance they heard the

occasional bark of a dog. Nearby came the sound of June
bugs dive-bombing the streetlight.

Rachel was clinging to Sammy's arm, the way people
do when they've had too much to drink. But he wasn't
complaining. "Where's your car?" he asked.

She looked up and down the street, past crumbling
curbs and blocked-up, stripped cars. "I don't
know. . . ." She frowned.

"Did you park it around here?"

She put a hand to her head. "I don't know. I can't
remember. I let somebody drive it. . . ."

God, Rachel.

A minute earlier he'd been feeling so sorry for her that
he ached inside. Now worry over her safety made him
feel impatient and angry. Now he felt like shaking her.
How could she do this to herself? Couldn't she see the
danger? She could have been picked up by anybody. She
could have been hurt, raped. But now wasn't the time to
come down on her.

"It's okay. Don't worry about the car." He'd call the
police when they got home. "It's a nice night for a walk."

"Yes. A walk. I like to walk."

Her voice was saying one thing, but her body
language was definitely saying another. It almost seemed
that the short bout of exuberance she'd displayed in the
phone booth had robbed her of all strength. She was dead
on her feet. Would she be able to make it the mile to his
place?

He hated to abandon Mark's bike, but he had no
choice. With a solemn, listing Rachel looking on, he
made sure the ten-speed wasn't visible from the sidewalk. He didn't want anybody ripping it off. He'd come
back for it early in the morning. Before the neighbor-
hood was awake.

Sammy took Rachel's purse, slung it over his shoulder, put an arm around her, and turned her in the direction of home.

It was still warm, the air so heavy it seemed to wrap around them, leaving their skin damp with dew. Rachel didn't have a whole lot to say, probably too tired, Sammy figured. When she did mutter something, it was just a word or two. More often than not, she merely sighed.

They stopped and sat down on a curb so she could rest, with Rachel leaning her head against Sammy's shoulder. Hardly a minute had gone by when she became dead weight and he realized she was asleep. He let her sleep for a little while, then woke her, afraid that if she slept too long, she'd be out for the night.

When they reached his apartment, he leaned her against the wall while he dug in the front pocket of his jeans for the key.

"I don't want to go home," she mumbled.

"You're not home. You're at my place."

He unlocked the door and pushed it open.

The apartment was actually a basement. He led her down the dark linoleum-covered steps to the bottom floor. Reaching around the corner, he flicked on the light to reveal a living room full of garage sale finds. Scratchy wool-covered furniture in forest green and maroon. Yellow lampshades with even yellower tassels. The painted cement floor was covered with a threadbare carpet of oriental design. Bookshelves were made of cement blocks and unvarnished pine. To top it off, one wall boasted a velvet painting of none other than the White House.

The interior designer wasn't home. Mark had taken his cat, Killer, along with a litter box and plastic scoop, to a weekend medical conference in Chicago.

"I'm sorry I'm so much trouble," Rachel whispered, eyes closed.

"You aren't any trouble."

He led her to a chair and made her sit down while he opened the foldout couch that he used for a bed. When he was done he turned to find her asleep again.

Now that the light was better, he could see just what kind of shape she was in. Her skirt and blouse were wrinkled and dirty, her nylons snagged, her face smudged. Even her fingernails were chipped.

Again that combination of anger and fear surged through him, along with a somewhat alarming and overwhelming urge to protect. He strode to the bathroom and came back with a wet washcloth. He used it to clean her face and hands. The coolness revived her a little, enough to get her going once more about being too much trouble.

"You're no trouble," he insisted. An understatement. He *wanted* her here.

"I'm sorry. . . ."

He rested his hands on his hips as he stood back and studied the situation. Briefly he toyed with the idea of letting her sleep in her clothes, but that would be uncomfortable for her and cruel and selfish of him. Just because he didn't want to torture himself by undressing her. . . .

Sammy dug through his drawer for clean clothes, debating on T-shirt color. White—too see-through. Green—too depressing. He ended up choosing blue.

Two days earlier she would have been out of luck. But since then he and Mark had been to the Laundromat down the street. Quite an interesting place, the Laundromat.

Trying to ignore the way his fingers trembled, he unbuttoned her blouse and slipped it from her shoulders.

Creamy skin.

White lace bra.

Softly swelling breasts with confined pink nipples.

He tugged the T-shirt over her head, letting out a

sigh of relief when it fell into place. Even though he'd been a gentleman and had quickly averted his eyes, the image of her nearly naked body would take up permanent residence in his brain. Like she'd told him, his storage and retrieval powers were way above average. And his brain was clicking away, definitely storing up her image to retrieve at a later date.

Even though he knew this wasn't the time to think about sex, there was only so much he could control. He'd been dreaming about Rachel for so long that it was impossible to be totally oblivious of her, regardless of the circumstances. But he would try. God, how he'd try.

He took off her skirt, then finished by removing her shoes and pantyhose.

Flat stomach. Tiny indented navel. Sweetly curved abdomen. Long, smooth legs.

He helped her into bed and covered her with a sheet.

He thought she was asleep when she opened her eyes and looked directly at him. "Do you know what July 24th is?" Her voice was stark, her eyes solemn, suddenly too sober, too rational.

They sentenced his madly humming hormones to solitary.

He had the feeling this was going to really hurt. He settled himself on the edge of the bed, his hip just touching hers. For the first time he actually felt older than Rachel. "No," he said, even though he had a fairly good idea of what she was about to say. He brushed her damp hair back from her forehead. "What's July 24th?"

"Jennifer's birthday."

They were the words he'd been expecting, along with the punch in the gut. Until that night he hadn't known someone else's pain could hurt so much. He was growing up fast. If he kept going at this pace, he'd be a hundred before long.

When he was sure she was asleep, he went to the

kitchen and called the police about her car. He found out
that it had been left in a no parking zone and towed
away. Fifty-dollar fine. She was lucky.

He figured he wouldn't be able to sleep, not with
Rachel so close. Not with Rachel so sad. He turned off
the lights, all except for the one in the bathroom. He
could have spent what was left of the night in Mark's
room, but he was afraid that if Rachel woke up, she
might be disoriented, so he sprawled out in the forest-
green chair near the couch. He kicked off his sneakers
and crossed his feet on the wool footstool.

His head was still buzzing with all that had happened, when he heard a clicking above his head.

He immediately recognized the sound. It was Mrs.
Davenport, the widow who owned the house and lived
upstairs.

She was an okay lady. She treated him and Mark like
grandsons, always baking cookies for them and leaving
table scraps for Killer. In return, Mark and Sammy spent
quite a bit of time perched among a clutter of dusty Avon
bottles and spindly philodendrons, balancing delicate
lipstick-stained teacups on their knees while playing gin
rummy.

Mrs. Davenport spent a lot of time telling them about
the old days and how she used to be a dancer. On nights
when Mrs. D. couldn't sleep, Sammy would wake up to
the sound of her tap shoes clicking across the ceiling
above his head as she relived her past.

Rachel awakened to feelings she'd almost forgotten,
feelings she'd hoped were in her past. The self-loathing
was bad enough, but it couldn't touch a despair so black
and so bottomless that it stole the very life from her
limbs, the very breath from her lungs. Stole her desire to
live.

She forced her eyes open and discovered that she wasn't in her apartment. It wasn't her ceiling looming above her head.

Her bleary, heartsick gaze trailed across the room, her mind registering old furniture . . . old yellow lampshades . . . a velvet painting. . . .

And Sammy.

As soon as her gaze touched on Sammy, some of the smothering darkness lifted.

He appeared terribly uncomfortable, sprawled as he was in a deep, scratchy-looking chair. His crossed feet were resting on a footstool, long legs stretched out in front of him, his head bent at what had to be an uncomfortable angle, his jaw shadowed with the passing night.

That was when the full impact of the situation hit her. Sammy had seen her when she was at her weakest, her most pathetic. He had witnessed the unsteadiness of her hands and heard the rasp on her ravaged vocal chords. And now she discovered that she couldn't face the disappointment in his eyes. He had believed in her, drawn strength from her. Now he would see her for what she really was—a fraud. A charlatan.

Who shrinks the shrink?

Who indeed.

Unable to face him, she dressed quickly and quietly and slipped away.

Sammy woke up with a stiff neck. Then, with a start, he remembered why he had a stiff neck.

Rachel.

His eyes flew to the couch.

Empty.

He shoved himself to his feet and tore through the tiny apartment to the kitchen, where he'd imagined fixing her breakfast, or at least a couple of aspirin and coffee.

No Rachel.

To the bathroom, where he'd imagined her splashing water on her face, maybe borrowing his toothbrush.

No Rachel.

Back to the living room.

He saw something he'd missed before. His blue T-shirt. It was lying in a careless heap on the floor near the foot of the bed. It looked as if the wearer had shed it in a hurry.

He noticed that her clothes weren't on the end table where he'd left them.

Rachel was gone. Checked out.

TWENTY

RACHEL MADE IT TO HER APARTMENT IN TIME TO stumble upstairs to the bathroom and throw up. When she was finished, she splashed water on her face, then, with shaking, sweating palms, braced herself against the porcelain sink to examine her reflection in the medicine cabinet mirror. Chalk-white skin, dark-rimmed eyes.

A total wreck.

I'm killing myself, she thought with almost clinical detachment. She was like a mouse in an exercise wheel, running and running, trying desperately to escape but getting nowhere.

She thought she'd managed to put days like yesterday behind her, days when she would lapse into a welcome oblivion. Days when she would wake up unable to recall anything of the past forty-eight hours of her life.

But they weren't behind her.

Painfully ashamed, she pulled away from the mirror, unable to face herself any longer. She crossed the hall to the bedroom, found her bed, and crawled into it.

Feeling hollow and brittle and bereft, she pulled the covers over her shoulder and curled to her side. Off in the distance, from the street below her two-story apartment, she heard the slamming of car doors, heard the sounds of laughter and conversation. People getting on with their lives.

• • •

Rachel had Saturday and Sunday to pull herself together. She didn't want to leave her apartment, but she somehow managed to retrieve her car complete with her missing glasses. Afterward, she drove straight home and hurried to the shelter of her apartment, quickly locking the door behind her, all the while aware of her pounding heart and dry mouth.

What are you so afraid of? she asked herself. What are you hiding from? But she knew the answer.

Sammy. She couldn't bear to face the disappointment in his eyes.

But she need not have worried, because Sammy didn't come.

Why didn't he come?

Thank God he didn't come.

Returning to work the following Monday wasn't easy. Twice she almost turned the car around, but in the end she couldn't allow herself to be that much of a coward.

When she got to the hospital, Dr. Fontana was waiting for her in his office.

"This is your last chance, Rachel." He pushed back his chair and rose to his feet. "I've got staff members breathing down my neck about you, and I can't blame them. When you don't show, they have to put in overtime. You left Sanderson with an afternoon of evaluations to complete." He paused and gave her such a hard look that she almost flinched.

"Either you get your personal problems straightened out, or I'll have to dismiss you."

Tough love.

Rachel was familiar with tough love. She'd used it herself on a few occasions. First you try understanding and patience. If that doesn't work, you bring out the big guns. Maybe that was her problem. She knew all the tricks. She was like a kid who had believed in magic until the magician showed her how it was done. Then it was no longer magic, but illusion. Smoke and mirrors.

She thought about how nice it would be to just give up. To admit defeat. To say, I can't cope with life anymore. But Rachel had too much stubbornness in her, too much foolish pride.

She straightened her shoulders, calling upon the façade she so often called upon, a façade many doctors used. They were taught very early on, while still in medical school, that a confident attitude was half of what being a doctor was all about, just as Sammy had said. Attitude. First you fool others, then you fool yourself.

"I'm fine," she lied.

"You might be fine now, but what about next July 24th? And the next? Or how about Mother's Day? Or Father's Day? Or what about the next time you see one of those sentimental commercials on television? Will you be fine then?"

She drew a deep breath. "Next time I'll be ready. I won't let it take me by surprise." She meant it. She only hoped she would somehow find the kind of strength she would need before the next time came along.

"Dammit, Rachel—" His expression lost some of its harshness. Now he looked more frustrated than anything else. "I don't want to lose you because of this. Look at the Thoreau case." He shook his head in amazement. "He has made remarkable progress. I honestly expected him to be bouncing off the walls for at least another six months, if not a year."

Rachel didn't agree. She was too messed up to have helped Sammy. He'd done it himself by strength of will, by love of life. "I can't take any of the credit. Sammy just decided he wanted out. And when he sets his mind to something, there's no stopping him."

"You're too modest. You're trivializing the part you played in his recovery."

She knew better. But she didn't want to talk about Sammy, not after what had happened. "I'll try to keep my nose clean," she said, hoping she could get away now.

"There are a couple of other things I want to talk to you about," Dr. Fontana said, stopping her as she turned to leave. "I see you've accumulated quite a bit of vacation time over the past several years. Why don't you take some of it? Maybe go on one of those ocean cruises my wife is always talking about."

No matter where she went, she would still be that mouse in that wheel; only the cage would be different. She shook her head. "It wouldn't do any good."

He shrugged. "I thought a change, a totally new setting might be beneficial for you. But suit yourself. There's just one more thing—I want you to re-enroll in the Impaired Physician Program."

She didn't belong in the program. Most of the doctors who attended were burnouts, drug addicts, strung out on downers and uppers. She wasn't like them. They had started on a downward spiral because of job stress and lack of sleep. They hadn't lost what she had lost.

"I once knew a cancer specialist," Dr. Fontana said, "who fell apart when he discovered he had lymphoma. He just gave up. And that wasn't the first time I'd seen such a thing happen. Why do doctors find it so hard to face their own illnesses? Especially if that illness happens to be in their line of expertise?" He looked her in the eye, his determination unrelenting. "I'm not giving you a choice about the program."

Maybe it was for the best. A person could remain shattered for only so long before permanent, irreparable damage set in. Nearly four years was too long to be consumed by grief.

"The meetings are still on Monday nights in the group encounter room."

"I'll be there."

She was scared. Before Sammy, she'd been better. At least she'd been coping. Now she seemed to be regressing. Somehow Sammy had brought her dormant emotions to the surface and made her feel and hurt again.

She didn't want to feel and hurt again.

Rachel was consumed with worry over what she was going to say when she eventually ran into Sammy. One minute she would decide to act as if nothing had happened, the next she would resolve to make some flip, offhand comment and hope he left it at that. But the work week passed without Rachel seeing Sammy at all. By Friday she decided he must be avoiding her—and that thought depressed her even more.

Saturday night Rachel lay in bed, staring into the darkness. It was late, past midnight she'd guess, but she couldn't sleep.

Even though the night was hot and humid, she hadn't turned on the air conditioner. She liked hot, humid nights. They reminded her that she was a living person. But since she worked all day in an air conditioned building, she never had much of a chance to feel the warm breath of summer. Sometimes the seasons came and went without her noticing at all. Sometimes she felt like a bystander in her own life, as if she were watching herself from a safe distance.

But there was no such thing as safe.

The days were beginning to get shorter. It was already August.

Dog days of summer . . . She'd always liked that phrase, but what did it mean? Did it mean it was too hot for dogs to do anything but lie around and sleep all day? Sounded like a good reason.

Dog days . . .

Her bedroom window was open and sounds from the outside floated in. An occasional car would cruise past, music from its radio blaring, then fading into the night as the car drove on.

Night sounds.

The whir of cicadas. The chirp of crickets . . . How many chirps would she count tonight if she tried? She guessed that the temperature was still close to ninety.

Off in the distance, from the west, came the low rumble of an approaching motorcycle.

It made her think of Sammy and the story he'd told her about riding his motorcycle on hot nights.

Her ears followed the sound. In her mind she could picture the motorcycle as it drew nearer, cresting the hilltop, passing the corner where a cement bench stood below a green street sign. Moving on . . . to stop just below her window.

She heard the rider rev the throttle a few times before cutting the engine. She couldn't recall ever seeing any of her neighbors on a motorcycle. The apartment complex housed a few staid singles like herself, plus several retired couples.

No pets.

No children.

But she could have missed the motorcycle. Just as she sometimes missed the changing seasons.

Footsteps sounded on the sidewalk. She waited, listening. Something small and hard struck her bedroom window, then rolled down the slanted roof to fall silently to the ground.

A pebble?

Not afraid—all Rachel's fears were intangible—she threw back the sheet and went to the window. There was enough light cast by the full moon for her to make out the silhouette of a man standing in the shadows of a sycamore tree.

Then a voice came out of those shadows, a deep whisper. "Rachel."

Sammy.

Her heart quickened. She pushed up the screen and leaned out, her hands braced on the wooden sill. Heavy night air stirred against her, pulling at her light cotton gown. "What are you doing here?"

"It's too hot to sleep. I got my motorcycle out of storage and thought I'd take it for a spin. I stopped to see if you'd like to come along."

She thought about the last time he'd seen her, drunk and incoherent. *I'm so ashamed.*

"I was in bed." The words sounded terribly lame, even to herself.

"Oh, sleep." The tone of his voice dismissed sleep as something entirely trivial. "You can do that anytime."

"Yes, but—"

"Come on, Rachel."

He was acting as if nothing had happened, as if that night had never occurred . . . and she silently thanked him.

Sammy spread his arms wide, his gesture seeming to take in the world. "It's a perfect night. A light dew, with just a touch of low-lying fog. What could be better?"

Darkness made people brave. It made Rachel brave. Maybe because there was something unreal about the night. Or the thick, sultry air. Or the full moon.

Or maybe, just maybe, it was because of Sammy.

Whatever it was, Rachel decided to go with him.

If there was a record for getting dressed, she must have broken it. Without bothering to turn on a light, she grabbed her clothes from the floor—an old T-shirt and a pair of cutoffs—and threw them on. Then she stuffed her feet into sneakers, put on her glasses, and hurried down the stairs.

The motorcycle had a kick start, so she waited on the curb while Sammy gave it a downward thrust of his booted heel. The engine roared to life as he settled himself on the long seat, giving it a couple of test bounces.

He flashed a grin in her direction. "All aboard."

Gingerly, she took her place on the seat behind him, careful to keep space between her stomach and his back. She'd never ridden on a motorcycle before, and now she searched for something to hang on to. She had latched her fingers on the leather seat beneath her when she felt Sammy's hands on hers. He worked her fingers loose, then drew them forward to wrap around his waist. "It's safer this way," he said over his shoulder.

Now the space between them was almost nonexistent. But to squirm away would mean she was physically aware of him—and Sammy never missed a trick. Her one concession was to lock her right hand around her left wrist instead of hanging on to him.

But it didn't matter. She was so close she could smell the fresh air trapped in his clothes. So close she could feel the curved bones of his rib cage on the sensitive skin of her inner arms.

"Ready?"

She nodded.

He toed the bike away from the curb, then eased the throttle open.

Sammy handled the bike with such confidence that it never occurred to Rachel to be nervous. They moved through the silent streets, through moonlight and dappled shadows, the warm night wind pulling at their clothes and hair. The blacktop beneath the rotating wheels still radiated heat from the sun's earlier intensity. They turned right, taking Highway One north, toward

Clear Lake. Once outside of town, the air turned cooler, carrying the enchanted night scents of green corn fields and freshly mown hay.

Riding behind Sammy with the wind whipping her hair was wonderful. Better than wonderful. Rachel hadn't felt this rush of exhilaration in years. She didn't know if she had *ever* felt it. Maybe as a child, just before a storm, when the sky glowed a hazy orange and dark clouds swirled above her head, the wind blowing strong and free, coming from some mysterious, unknown place.

Sammy said something over his shoulder, but the words were tossed behind them by the wind.

She leaned closer to ask him what he'd said, when the motorcycle's headlight went out, plunging them in darkness. Rachel tightened her hold on Sammy—she didn't know when she'd gone from clutching her own arm to clutching him—then she realized there was nothing wrong with the bike. Sammy had deliberately extinguished the light.

The moon cut a path along the black highway, which ribboned over gently sloping hills. Moonglow reflected off the bike's fenders and glinted against the silver spokes.

Magic.

A while later Sammy turned on the headlight and accelerated until they came to a one-lane road. He slowed enough to execute the turn. Then they were bumping along a dirt path, tree branches overhead, blocking out the stars and moon.

The path widened. Through the trees Rachel could see the shimmering lake. The heady scent of corn fields was replaced by the smell of pine needles and moss-covered wood.

Clear Lake. Even though it wasn't very far from La Grange, Rachel had never been here.

"Watch your head," Sammy told her.

They both ducked to avoid low-hanging branches. The motorcycle now moved on a narrow walking path that meandered along the edge of the lake. The head-lamp beam illuminated trees and dense shrubbery. In several spots the dirt path gave way to grass—evidence of their isolation.

They finally came to a small clearing, where Sammy pulled up near a picnic table and cut the engine. He took a deep breath. Beneath her hands, Rachel felt his stomach muscles contract and realized she was still clinging to him.

She let go.

"I came fishing here a few days ago. Careful of the exhaust pipe," he warned, steadying her as she got off. Then he pushed the bike backward and set the kickstand before swinging his leg over the seat.

Without hesitating, he strolled over pine needles and flat ground to stand at the edge of the lake.

Rachel went to stand beside him.

Hands deep in the back pockets of his jeans, he tilted his head and looked up at the starry sky. Off in the distance, from across the lake, an owl hooted. The sound echoed over the water and bounced off the trees lining the shore.

"Two months ago," Sammy began, "I wondered if I'd ever be standing here like this. I thought I might be spending the rest of my life in a padded room."

"You're too stubborn to have ever let that happen."

"I don't know if being stubborn had anything to do with it."

Water lapped gently against the bank, the sound hypnotic and soothing.

Sammy bent down and picked up a couple of rocks, testing them in his hand. "Ever skip stones?" he asked.

"I tried a few times when I was little, but I never got the hang of it."

"I used to make a few extra bucks skipping stones, betting on the number of skips. Fifteen's my record." Gracefully, he brought his right arm back, then forward. With a flick of his wrist he let go of the stone.

One, two, three, four, five . . .

Five skips. Each one left a pattern of rings that continued to ripple long after the stone had sunk to the bottom of the lake.

"I had a wasted youth," he said, explaining his talent. "I can remember every card trick I ever learned, every bit of sleight of hand." A frustration she hadn't heard in some time crept into his voice. "And skipping stones. All the important stuff."

Rachel didn't want him to be sad. She bent down and searched through the pebbles near her feet until she found a stone that was flat and smooth. Then, imitating Sammy as best as she could, she gave it a toss.

It plunked.

She waited, but it didn't jump out of the water.

"Here." Sammy handed her another rock. "Hold it this way." He wrapped her fingers around the rock. "With your thumb on top and your forefinger on the side. Your other three fingers support it from the bottom."

"Like this?"

"That's it."

She raised her arm.

"Don't throw it like a baseball. Throw it more like a Frisbee, but backward."

She'd never played Frisbee.

"And aim level, at the surface of the water."

She tossed. The rock plunked. Then plunked again! "I did it!" Immediately she began searching for more stones.

"Try this one."

She took the stone from Sammy. She was surprised to

find that instead of being round, it was almost triangular.

"Just before you release it, give your wrist a small flick."

She tried, and this time the stone hopped three times! The last one was a very puny hop, but a hop all the same.

For the next half hour they skipped stones. Sammy managed to skip one a total of nine times, Rachel four. Finally, tiring of the game, they walked back to the picnic table and sat on it, their feet resting on the seat, elbows on knees, staring out at the lake where the water still rippled in circular patterns. Bullfrogs croaked. Lightning bugs danced in and out of the trees.

Sammy was the first to break their companionable silence. "Why did you leave the other morning?"

His question took her completely by surprise, especially after the lighthearted rock skipping. She didn't want to think about that night. For the past hour she'd managed to put it from her mind.

"You didn't have to leave," he said.

"Yes. Yes, I did." She clasped and unclasped her hands. She swallowed at the sudden tightness in her throat. "I'm not who you think I am," she whispered, keeping her eyes carefully focused on the trees across the lake.

"I've always known who you were, Rachel."

She was mature enough to admit that there was a measure of truth in his words. Hadn't he frightened her with his all-seeing eyes?

"I don't have all the answers," she said.

"I never expected you to. Nobody has all the answers."

"I left because I was ashamed. I couldn't face you after you'd seen me like that."

"Rachel—"

She felt his fingers brush her cheek, gently turning

her face to his. Inside, she felt the same fear she'd felt that morning in his apartment. Now, just as then, she couldn't look into his eyes, couldn't bear to see them change. She didn't want him to see the real Rachel, the Rachel who was afraid. The Rachel who hurt.

She closed her eyes.

"Nobody expects you to be strong all the time," he said softly. "And nobody expects you to go it alone."

She opened her eyes and looked up at him. "There are some places where a person has to go alone," she said solemnly.

Her voice hadn't even trembled, but suddenly she felt like sobbing, like throwing herself into Sammy's arms and crying her eyes out. She blinked and turned away. She wouldn't cry. She wouldn't.

After a time, she managed to pull in a tight breath. "We better go back."

"There's something I'd like to do first."

He pushed away from the table and headed for the water. Before she was aware of his intentions, he'd peeled off his shirt and was working on his jeans. She quickly averted her eyes.

A few moments later she heard a splash and looked up in time to see Sammy's head break the surface of the water. He tossed back his hair, sending a sparkling shower through the air. "Come on in!" he shouted. "The water feels great!"

She sat there, hands locked between her knees. What to do, what to do?

"Wear my shirt if you want," he offered.

She was thirty-two and she'd never had a guy come to her window in the middle of the night before; she'd never sat on a minibike, let alone a motorcycle. And she'd never ridden down the middle of a country road with only the moon to light the way.

She'd missed a lot.

A few days before, when black despair had wrapped
its icy tentacles around her heart, she'd wondered how
she could possibly face another day, another week, another
month. . . .

Now she thought about how empty she had felt before
Sammy had come roaring into her life. Not only hours
ago, but months ago.

And it suddenly came to her that she hadn't been
coping at all. She'd been existing.

Slowly Rachel took off her glasses and set them beside
her on the picnic table. Then she got up and walked
down the gentle slope to the lake.

TWENTY-ONE

MOONLIGHT AND STARLIGHT.

A coyote howl carrying across the lake on the still night air.

Cool water gliding across hot bare skin.

There were different kinds of freedom. For Sammy, the motorcycle ride had been a heart-hammering shout-from-a-mountaintop kind of freedom. Now, swimming through cool lake water, Sammy was aware of a totally different kind of freedom. A freedom that was a little forbidden, while at the same time strangely spiritual. But there was one thing both freedoms had in common: an element of danger and unpredictability. Added to that was an element of sexuality.

Because Rachel was coming.

As soon as Sammy had seen her get up from the picnic table, he'd quickly taken a studied interest in swimming. No way did he want to chance frightening her. Not at this point.

One thing he knew about Rachel was that she needed a little fun in her life. She needed to see that there was still joy to be found in the world.

All week long he'd wanted to see her, but he knew she needed time to pull herself together. And when he finally did go by her apartment that night, he'd understood that he was taking a chance. He'd been prepared for her to tell him to get lost. He'd even been prepared for her to not answer the door at all—that's why he'd resorted to throwing pebbles at her window.

But she had surprised him by coming.

So far, the highlight of the evening had been when he'd turned off the motorcycle's headlamp. He could still feel the way Rachel had clung to him. He had heard her quick gasp and felt the hardness of her nipples pressed against his back. That's when he'd realized she wasn't wearing a bra. That's when his heart had hammered into overdrive and he'd run the risk of having the bike skid out from under him.

Later, she'd smiled at him and laughed and played, something he'd always known she was capable of.

But then he'd stepped over the line and gotten personal.

Mistake.

You weren't supposed to get personal with Rachel. But he wanted to get personal with her. Real personal.

When she suddenly told him it was time to leave he knew he couldn't let the night end with another slammed door. If he let her go, he had the feeling that this would be it. The end. *Adiós*, Sammy. *Arrivederci*. *Sayonara*. *Bon voyage*. Cheerio, old chap.

So he got it into his head that before he took her home he was going to do one thing: touch her. Not physically, although he wanted her that way, too, but emotionally.

To forge a bond with a person, you have to share experiences. Have to share a little bit of life, whether it's watching the same movie or eating the same pizza or going to the same concert. Or skinny dipping in a moonlit lake.

Behind him, he heard a gentle sloshing sound followed by a splash.

He turned and saw her moving through the water. Not a ripple disturbed the glassy surface.

He struck out in her direction. When he came up beside her she stopped and treaded water. He did the same, careful to leave a comfortable distance between them.

"What do you think?" he asked.

"You're right," she said a little breathlessly. "It's wonderful."

One thing he noticed right away was that she hadn't put on his shirt. As her hands stroked through the water, he could see her bare shoulders gleaming in the moonlight.

"Ever gone skinny dipping before?" he asked.

She tilted her head and gave him a look he could interpret only as sheepish. "One time I dove into the water and my top came off," she admitted. "Does that count?"

He laughed. "I don't think so."

She was actually joking around. He'd expected her to be nervous and a little uptight. Instead, she seemed more relaxed than he'd ever seen her. Then she really surprised him by doing something most unRachellike. She cupped one hand and shot a stream of water in his direction. She was a good shot. Got him right in the face.

With the heel of his hand, Sammy returned about a bucket of water, giving her a good dousing.

Boundaries disappeared.

They spent the next ten minutes splashing each other. They raced and laughed and goofed off like a couple of kids.

Until they accidentally collided.

Slick wet skin to slick wet skin. Thigh to thigh. Chest to chest—or breasts.

They sprang apart.

The laughter faded. They stood with their feet on the

rocky bottom, water barely covering the very breasts that had just pressed so erotically against his chest. They stared at each other, their breaths coming fast and hard while need for her clenched painfully inside him.

Without her glasses, Rachel looked even younger than usual—and a whole lot more vulnerable.

In control, he had to remind himself. That's what he was. *In control.* And anyway, tonight wasn't about his needs. It was about Rachel's. No matter how it might look, he hadn't brought her here to put the make on her. He'd brought her here because she needed a disruption in her life. She needed to be shaken out of the pattern she'd settled into over the past few years, since losing her daughter.

He was about to take a step back when he noticed something. It almost seemed as though Rachel had moved a little closer. Was it possible? He quickly decided it must have been an optical illusion caused by the shifting water.

"Sammy, I—" She stopped. The words seemed to lodge in her throat.

But he had a fairly good idea of what she was about to say. He had the childish urge to clap his hands over his ears and start humming loud enough to drown out all other sounds. It had worked when he was a kid, but he doubted it would work now. No, he was going to have to listen to her say it was time to go . . . or that she'd made a mistake and that she shouldn't have come, that she should have stayed home with her late night TV.

The next day she wouldn't answer his phone calls, or answer the door if he came by her apartment. A month from now she would hardly be able to remember his name. He would be just another case history in the old filing cabinet. In a year he wouldn't even be as much as a hazy memory.

Sammy who?

Oh, yeah. I think I remember him. Wasn't he the guy who gave me such a hard time?

But what scared him the most was that he would never know how it felt to hold her. Really hold her.

He was desperate. His hard-won maturity crumbled to be replaced by juvenile insecurity—and more than a little bit of all out panic.

He figured he had nothing to lose, so he closed the gap between them, grabbed her arms, and pulled her flat against him. His breath caught as her wet body slid against his.

They were stomach to stomach. Hip bone to hip bone. Knee to knee. Chest to soft, incredibly soft breasts . . .

Rachel.

He would have let her go in a second if she'd given the slightest indication that she wanted free, but she just stood, perfectly still, staring up at him, her eyes wide, her lips parted.

She raised her arms, and soon she was clinging to him, her fingers pressed into the slick flesh of his upper arms.

Stomach to stomach. Thigh to thigh . . .

He let go of her arms and slid a hand around her. With the other hand he touched her ribs, one at a time, until his fingers made contact with the swollen underside of her breast . . . until her nipple was settled in the center of his palm, until her soft flesh filled his spread fingers. . . .

He watched her face, trying to read her expression.

She closed her eyes and tilted her head back. Moonlight glistened off her neck and the delicate hollows beneath her collarbones. He bent his head, gently placing his lips on the graceful curve of her jaw, and trailed a moist path downward. She sighed, and sighed again, moving closer, pressing into him even more.

Then she further astonished him by lifting one leg and wrapping it around his hip.

Automatically, he slipped a hand beneath her bent knee and pulled her closer.

"Sammy . . ."

It could have been the wind, so softly did she breathe his name. But there was no mistaking the message she sent.

He needed to kiss her, needed to feel her mouth under his. As soon as his lips made contact with hers, she began returning his kisses with a feverish intensity.

Blood was roaring in his head, but through it came a voice he didn't want to hear from—the voice of logic, warning him that she was vulnerable, and that he shouldn't take advantage of that vulnerability. But he was vulnerable, too, he argued. Maybe he and Rachel would be good for each other. Didn't two negatives make a positive?

Yes.

His heart was thundering in his chest. His knees were weak and he felt as though he were going to explode. Yet he had enough clarity of mind to know that the first time with Rachel shouldn't happen like this. He wanted it to be soft, gentle.

He didn't want to hurt her.

But she was making small pleading sounds, driving him crazy. Suddenly her other leg came up and wrapped around him. He could feel her heels against the backs of his thighs, and before he could fully comprehend what was happening, she lifted her hips and he was buried deep inside her.

It was too much for him. He couldn't hold back, and about a half a minute later it was all over.

Her face was buried against his throat, her wet hair cold against his jaw. Her arms were like vises around his neck.

He was afraid to look at her. "Rachel . . . are you okay?"

She didn't respond; she only continued to cling to him. He tried to ease himself away, but as soon as he started to move she gripped him tighter. He was supporting her with his hands and arms, and everywhere he touched, he could feel the tension in her muscles.

Her stillness and silence frightened him. He didn't know what to do, or what to say. So he merely stroked her wet hair and asked her again if she was all right.

"I—I don't know."

Oh, God. He'd hurt her.

He had no idea what he was doing, but with murmured words and soothing hands he finally managed to get her to relax. She unlocked her legs and stood in front of him, her gaze focused on his chest.

"Rachel . . ." He cupped her cheeks and was surprised by the heat he felt. He scooped up some water and cooled her skin with it. Then he bent his head and kissed her softly on her sad mouth.

He'd seen Rachel shaken before, but this was different. Then it hit him. She probably thought he'd brought her here for sex and no other reason. Hadn't he been after her practically from day one?

"Rachel, look, I'm sorry. I know what you're probably thinking." He reached for her hand, lacing his fingers with hers. "But I never meant for this to happen. I never meant to hurt you, or make you sad—"

She shook her head. "You didn't hurt me. I *wanted* you."

He stared, stunned while his heart sung hosannas.

She drew in a shuddering breath and looked up at him. "I'm sorry."

He felt her embarrassment, felt her awkwardness and wanted to chase it away. She seemed frighteningly fragile, as if the wrong word, the wrong touch, might break her.

"I've never done anything like this before," she said. "It's been years since, well, I haven't— I don't— Not since my husband—"

He brought her hand to his mouth. "You don't have to explain."

In seeming fascination she watched as he kissed her fingertips. "I guess . . . we better go."

He smiled. "I don't think so. Not yet, anyway." He pulled her close. "There's something I want to do first, something I've wanted to do for a long time."

"What's that?"

A gentle breeze came up, rustling the leaves on the nearby trees.

"Make love to you."

TWENTY-TWO

HE OVERWHELMED HER. THAT'S WHY SHE HAD REACTED the way she had.

Far too often in the past years it seemed as if Rachel's life were over. Sometimes she wanted it to be over. Like one of the patients on C ward, she'd moved numbly through a haze of days and seasons, even years.

But then Sammy had come along. . . .

They left the water and now Sammy was lowering her on a bed of grass and sweet clover. Stars swirled overhead. A breeze skimmed her wet skin, raising goose bumps and hardening her nipples.

In the back of her mind, she knew it was important to remain true to herself, to cling to her own identity. That was her only strength, her only defense. But seeing the gentle promise in Sammy's dark eyes, she felt an immeasurable sense of peace and trust. It felt good to relax, to give herself to Sammy and his healing ways. . . .

He wrapped his arms around her and pulled her close, the length of him pressed against her, heavy and strong. "I remember how I would watch you, with your head bent, your neck so sweetly curved. I used to wonder what you would do if I put my mouth against your skin to taste you. I imagined taking off your clothes, one piece at a time. . . ." His mouth touched hers, and his tongue was warm as it gently coaxed her lips apart to slide deeply and intimately inside.

His hands explored her body, touching her everywhere. Fingertips moved reverently down her cheek. Knuckles gently stroked the pulse in her neck; an open palm caressed her breast. His touch warmed her blood until she felt hot all the way down to her toes.

He taught her something totally new: He taught her how to make love with wonder and joy. All of the emotional restraints she'd put on herself fell away for this one moment in time. She came to him with gentle gratitude, and a love so profound it took her breath away.

"Everyplace I feel a heartbeat, that's where I'm going to kiss you," he whispered, his breath grazing her tingling skin. He pressed his mouth to her temple, then her throat. He lifted her hand and placed his lips to the pulse beating so erratically at her wrist.

"Such tiny wrists," he marveled.

He was touching her—with his hands, his mouth, his body—but for Rachel it was more than physical. He was tapping into her, into her heart, her soul, her psyche. Touching her in ways she'd never been touched. Cherished ways. Wanting ways.

Beneath her hands she memorized the contours of his body. Taut muscles molded to strong bones. Skin both sandpaper rough and satiny smooth. Warm and cool.

With his tongue, he outlined her collarbone, then her breast, until he was pulling the entire tip into his mouth, wrapping her in a haze of erotic colors.

She lay open to him. Between her thighs she could feel his body pressing down.

He shifted his weight, slipping his hands beneath her, cupping her bottom, lifting her from the crushed and fragrant grass to him.

"And now . . . the last place to kiss," he murmured. "The last pulse beat."

"Sammy, I've never—"

"Hush. It's okay. Let me love you. I need to love you."

Then he kissed her where he'd promised to kiss her, stroking her gently with the tip of his tongue.

A blazing rush spiraled through her. She both melted and tensed while she clutched his shoulders and gasped his name in a voice that didn't sound like hers.

"I want to make it good for you." His voice was deep and husky. Bordering on out of control.

"It *is* good!"

"Swear?"

Her mind was in a frenzy. "I swear!" she sobbed out, needing him.

He shifted again, this time putting his hand on her knees, bending them so the soles of her feet were on the grass. Night air licked all the places his mouth had been. Her nerve endings were singing, her body screaming for him.

"Sammy, *I want you.*"

He positioned himself between her legs, not touching her at all, but he was so close she could feel the heat from his body shimmering above her.

And then he touched her.

"I've dreamed of this," he whispered raggedly as he lowered himself into her. "Sweet, sweet Rachel."

She couldn't take her eyes from his face. "Me too . . ."

Slowly, ever so slowly, he entered her until she surrounded his firm flesh. And as he made love to her, he wrapped her in his innocence and beauty, in the vibrant way he looked at life.

Everything that she'd experienced before had been nothing but a poor imitation of life. Sammy *was* life. And in some way, in his holding her, his touching her, she was suffused with his electricity. She could feel it humming through her veins.

The world was no longer a dark and frightening place. A lonely place. It was sun-kissed daffodils dancing in wide-open valleys. It was mountains and clear blue sky. In her blood flowed wonder and awe. While she lay in his embrace, she was whole. She was brand new.

Sammy took a deep, shuddering breath that sounded like a sob. His eyes, beneath love-heavy lids, were bright with passion.

One hand stroked her neck, where her pulse was fluttering, then trailed to her rapidly rising and falling rib cage, across her muscle-taut abdomen. . . . She drew in a sharp breath as his hand went lower to where they were joined. He stroked her until her legs began to tremble. Deep in her womb, she felt something that was like a painless contraction. Tighter and tighter it wound. . . .

She clung to Sammy's sweat-slick shoulders. She heard him say her name in a soothing yet hoarse voice. She felt his hand against her perspiring temple, as if to calm her, heard his broken words. And then she felt herself falling . . . and felt Sammy catching her. . . .

Gradually she returned from the wonderful place Sammy had taken her, once again becoming aware of the smell of his damp skin and the crushed sweet clover beneath her. Of the stars swirling above while the comforting weight of his body pressed into hers.

He wrapped his arms around her, hugging her tightly, and he whispered her name over and over, his face buried against her neck, his warm, uneven breath against her ear.

When his breathing steadied, when his heartbeat no longer slammed against his chest and her chest, he raised himself enough to plant a gentle kiss on her swollen lips.

She felt so vulnerable, so fragile. *Now he knows me better than I know myself,* she thought, suddenly afraid. *If he touches me just so, or if he doesn't quit looking at me with such exquisite tenderness, I will surely shatter into a million pieces.*

Rachel thought she knew all about sex. But she had never experienced anything like what she'd felt with Sammy. At one time she'd actually come to the snobbish conclusion that sex must be a lower-class sport. Sex with David had always been mechanical, unexciting. A slightly unpleasant duty to get out of the way, like going to the grocery store or cleaning the house. In fact, she'd always wondered what all the fuss was about.

Now she knew.

With a trembling hand Sammy stroked damp hair from her forehead. "Oh, God, Rachel, I—" He stopped, his voice cracking with emotion.

She touched her fingers to his lips. "Don't say you're sorry," she whispered. "Please don't say you're sorry."

"I'm not sorry. Sorry's not the word for what I'm feeling." He closed his eyes, took a deep, trembling breath, then opened them. "I don't think what just happened was ordinary. Do you? I mean . . . wow."

She laid her head on his shoulder. "Yeah," she murmured. "Wow." The understatement of the century.

It was difficult gathering all their clothes and putting them on. Not because they couldn't find them— although that was a problem too—but because they had to stop several times to laugh, and kiss, and hold each other.

They did finally manage to dress and look respectable once more, although their hair had dried pretty strangely. Most of Sammy's stuck straight up, but Rachel's was plastered to her head and slicked back, making her look like somebody from the twenties. Sammy teased her, saying she should be wearing a pencil-thin ankle-length skirt and white mink boa and walking a sheared poodle. She told him he needed a tattoo on his arm and a pack of Luckies rolled up in his sleeve.

Soon after, they were on the motorcycle, taking the bumpy road back. By the time they hit La Grange the sky was beginning to lighten and birds were singing like crazy.

Sammy pulled up to the curb in front of Rachel's apartment, cut the engine, then walked her to the door.

This was the part he'd been dreading. Back to reality. He could already see a slight doubt settling into Rachel's green eyes.

She dug into the back pocket of her cutoffs, pulled out her keys, and unlocked the door. "Would you like to come in for coffee?" she asked, swinging open the door.

He'd like to see her place. He'd like to spend the rest of the morning with her, the rest of the day and that night. But he recognized her invitation as strictly obligatory. And even though he thought he understood where she was coming from, he couldn't help but feel hurt.

He wanted her to be head over heels in love with him. But he figured she was feeling major guilt over having sex with an ex-patient, or, as she had explained, once a patient, always a patient.

"No thanks." He shoved his hands into the front pockets of his jeans, then tossed a glance over his shoulder to his bike. "I'm kinda tired . . . and you probably want to catch some sleep . . . ?"

He deliberately made his statement into a question. To make it easy for her to go either way.

"Yes, you're right." She was already inside, already

closing the door, as if eager to be done with this after-sex scene.

He jumped toward her, placing one foot across the threshold and a hand on the door. "Rachel—"

At the lake he'd almost blown it. He'd almost told her he loved her, even though he knew she wasn't ready to hear something like that from him. Maybe she'd never be ready. . . .

"Maybe I'll see you tonight?" he asked instead.

It was a relief to see her relax a little.

"That would be nice," she said.

He wanted to barge into her home, lock the door behind him, and take her to bed. Instead, he gave her a quick kiss. "See you later."

He was hardly aware of walking from her door to his motorcycle, but suddenly he was straddling the bike, with the motor purring under him. With his left foot he engaged the clutch. Then, with a flick of his wrist, he opened the throttle and went roaring down the empty street.

Molly held the box of warm chocolate chip cookies in one hand and knocked on Sammy's apartment door with the other. From inside she heard a crash, followed by a curse. Then the door was flung wide open.

She'd never met Sammy's roommate, but she decided this must be Mark. His curly hair was a little flat on one side, as if his head had just left a pillow. And his eyes were a little puffy.

Oh, dear. Coming here had been a spur-of-the-moment thing. She hadn't thought about the time. Just because she'd been up since five A.M. didn't mean everybody else had.

Her early morning rudeness didn't seem to daunt the man in front of her. He swung the door even wider, inviting her inside—an exceedingly friendly gesture considering that he probably had no idea who she was. As far as he was concerned, she could be selling cookies door-to-door.

Molly introduced herself and explained about the cookies.

"You just missed Sammy," Mark told her. "He's making a milk-and-juice run. But come on in."

She wanted to leave the cookies with him and be on her way. She wasn't very good with strangers. But not wanting to be impolite, she stepped inside, intending to stay but a few minutes.

The place was full of old wool-covered furniture that gave off the smell of dust and mold. In one corner, on a bookcase made of cement blocks, stood a red lava lamp. She hadn't seen one of those in years.

She held out the box of cookies, saying they were still warm.

Mark pounced on them. He had the lid off and a cookie in his mouth in about a half a second.

"I have to ask you something," he said around a mouthful of cookie. "I've been doing this thing with anybody new. It's what I call my initial reaction survey. I want you to tell me in one word your first impression of me."

His total lack of inhibition left her without words. "I'm not sure . . . I . . . ."

He finished the cookie and pulled out another. "I'll help you. You thought nerd, right?"

"No!"

"Okay, then ugly."

"No! Of course not!" Actually, she thought he was kind of cute in an unusual sort of way. Maybe a puppyish sort of way, but she doubted he would want to hear that. And anyway, it was more than one word.

"Fat, then."

Her eyes flitted down his baggy Hawaiian shirt, loose jeans and bare feet, then back up. It was hard to say, but he didn't appear overweight to her.

He grabbed a palm leaf and a macaw to get to the flesh beneath the fabric. "I can pinch more than an inch," he said, almost as a dare.

"Cute," she said quickly, out of desperation. "When I first saw you, I thought cute."

"Oh, come on."

She could tell he didn't believe her.

He turned his head this way and that, chin held high. "My features aren't chiseled. They're more like puttied. My face is round, my hair is round, my head is round." His eyes zeroed in on hers, intense and serious. "Did you really think cute?"

She laughed. "Really."

He smiled, and she noticed he had a dimple in one cheek. Cute.

Five minutes later they were sitting at a wobbly kitchen table, drinking coffee. Mark sat across from her, a calico cat curled up on his lap.

The kitchen was much brighter than the living room—all yellow and white, with sunlight spilling in through high windows. In the center of the table was a bouquet of zinnias stuck in a peanut butter jar. Mark explained that the landlady always brought them flowers.

It was rare for Molly to feel so totally relaxed with someone she'd only just met. It usually took months, sometimes years before she reached such a stage in a relationship.

After her marriage she'd lost contact with most of her friends. It was hard to explain Austin to them, and even harder to invite people over with Austin's disapproving presence always lurking in the background. Now it occurred to her that she had missed friendly companionship.

She had missed times like these, when quiet conversation was shared over coffee.

They made small talk and discussed how Sammy was getting along. Great, in Mark's opinion.

Pretty soon Mark was telling her about his job and about the hospital medical training psychiatrists were required to put in.

"It was Christmas, and a few of us decided to do something special for the kids on the pediatric floor. We dressed up as clowns and went around to all the rooms. There was this one little kid I'd gotten to know pretty well because he'd been there a year." Mark paused, sipped his coffee, then went on without looking up from his mug. "On Christmas Day he flatlined. And there I was, in that stupid clown suit."

By the time Sammy returned, Molly and Mark were on their third cup of coffee. It wasn't until she heard the front door slam shut that Molly realized she'd forgotten about coming to see her brother.

Footfalls sounded across the living room floor, then there was Sammy, standing in the kitchen doorway.

Molly looked at him with dismay. His clothes were wrinkled and smudged. His hair was wild. He needed a shave, and his eyes were bloodshot.

Fear shot through her. *He's gotten his memory back* was her first thought. And he'd picked up where he'd left off before the accident. Drinking all night, hung over all day.

"Molly-o! Great to see you!" He set his bag of groceries on the counter, then came over to give her a hug and kiss the part in her hair.

"He stayed up all night," Mark explained. "I tried to get him to hit the sack, but he was too wound up."

Molly relaxed a little. Sammy didn't smell like stale

whiskey, and he didn't act hung over. In fact, he seemed almost buoyant.

From long ago she recalled a similar sense of euphoria. Now she knew he hadn't gotten his memory back. Instead, he was acting like someone in love.

Who? Who had he met that she didn't know about? Then she recalled the almost telepathic communication he and Rachel Collins seemed to share. Could it be Rachel?

She wouldn't ask now, not in front of Mark. But later, as Sammy walked her to the door, she voiced her question. "Is it Rachel?"

Sammy knew exactly what she was talking about. There was no hesitation in his answer. "Yes."

"Sammy, is that wise? She's your doctor. And she has problems of her own to resolve. She told me about her daughter, and I've seen the way she acts whenever children are mentioned."

"It doesn't matter. I want to help her. I love her," he said simply.

Molly was scared for him. When Sammy loved somebody, he loved them unconditionally. With heart, mind, and soul. Was Rachel capable of accepting that kind of unconditional love? Was she worthy of it?

TWENTY-THREE

RACHEL PACED BACK AND FORTH IN HER BEDROOM, THE wood floor cool and a little tacky under her bare feet. For the past two hours, ever since Sammy had dropped her off, she'd vacillated between euphoria and agony, with agony steadily winning.

She'd tried to sleep—a total impossibility. It was like trying to sleep during a tornado, an earthquake, an electrical storm.

She couldn't quit thinking about the previous night. What had she done?

She'd had sex. With a patient.

No, with Sammy. And it had been more than sex. Much more.

It didn't matter what words she used. There was no excuse for what had happened.

If only she hadn't answered when he came to her window . . . If only she had told him no, she couldn't go with him on his motorcycle ride . . . If only she hadn't gone swimming . . .

It wasn't Sammy's fault. He'd tried to be a gentleman. After all, *she* had made the first move. That thought made her feel even more guilty.

Sometimes between the bouts of anguish, her mind would wander in a different direction, a pleasant direction. She would think about the freedom she'd felt while riding on Sammy's motorcycle, the wonder of their lovemaking, and before she knew it, a slight smile would touch her face, and she'd catch herself looking forward to seeing him again.

See you later.

Once she even went so far as to imagine throwing herself into his arms. He would smile his breezy smile. Then he would kiss her and pretty soon, pretty soon . . .

No.

There could be no next time.

Even if he weren't her patient, the last thing she could handle was any kind of relationship. It wouldn't be fair to Sammy. He expected and deserved more from her than she could give. And when he was gone, what would she do then?

She would miss him.

By four o'clock that afternoon Sammy couldn't wait any longer. He hopped on his motorcycle and headed for Rachel's. He hadn't even tried to sleep, knowing it would be impossible, and except for a couple of Molly's cookies, he hadn't even tried to eat. He was too keyed up.

He parked his Harley in front of Rachel's apartment, cut the engine, pocketed the keys, and got off the bike.

On the way to Rachel's door, he couldn't help but notice that the curtains were pulled shut.

Already picking up bad vibes, he knocked and waited, then knocked again. This was what he got for giving her time to herself, for trying to be a sensitive, nineties guy. She wasn't going to answer.

He hadn't wanted to crowd her or push her into a corner, but now he could see that he shouldn't have let her out of his sight. He shoudn't have left her alone to think. Thinking could get a person into trouble.

He was getting ready to knock again, wondering how hard her apartment would be to break into, when—surprise of surprises—the door opened.

And there was Rachel.

Her hair wasn't slicked back anymore, and she smelled like soap. She was wearing a pair of khaki shorts and a black T-shirt—just right for a ride along Cliff Road, the perfect place to check out the sunset.

His first inclination was to hold her and kiss her, but something about her body language made him hesitate.

"Sammy, I—"

He didn't know what she was thinking, but he wasn't going to let her turn him away. He slipped inside and shut the door behind him.

"Sammy—"

"Get some shoes on and we'll go cruise Cliff Road."

He wanted to touch her, hold her, taste her. He took a step closer.

She took a step back.

Her immediate reaction stunned and hurt him at the same time. He thought about how worked up he'd been all day, about how he couldn't wait to see her again.

And here she was, backing away from him!

"I think you should go," she said.

"Go!" Her rejection stung, and his thoughts became a painful blur. He grappled with the sudden urge to make her feel what he was feeling, to hurt her the way she was hurting him.

"I'm not going anywhere until you talk to me. What's the matter, Rachel?"

He watched as she swallowed and blinked, then made a helpless gesture with one hand. "What happened last night was wrong. . . ."

"Wrong!" The word came out louder than he'd intended. "Lying is wrong. Cheating at cards is wrong. Stealing is wrong. But what happened between us wasn't wrong!"

"You have to go. I can't see you anymore."

Just like that. Without a twinge of regret, without a single explanation. It staggered him. He'd expected her to feel guilty or confused, which he could have handled. But rejection . . . He hadn't been prepared for her to tell him to get lost.

How could she do this?

How could she just shove him away? He knew he wasn't the right guy for her, knew she could do a thousand times better than him, but dammit, he loved her.

His hurt and anger increased.

"Here I was, afraid you'd think I took you out to the lake to put the moves on you." He let out a harsh laugh. "*I'm* the one who was used. I was the one who was the damn piece of ass!"

She flinched. "Sammy, please—"

He couldn't listen, couldn't look at her anymore. It hurt too damn much.

He turned to go, his gaze taking in the tiny apartment, noting its sparseness. There wasn't as much as a single knicknack, or a photograph, or even one of those dime-store paintings. It reminded him of the fake living room at the hospital, but this was worse, because somebody actually *lived* here.

Rachel lived here.

"Look at this place!" He swung around and strode to the kitchen. "Does anybody live here?" He jerked open the refrigerator and looked inside. Practically empty. "Is this just a stage set?" He slammed the door. "Are these just props?"

He turned and headed upstairs, taking the steps two at a time. "How about up here?" he shouted over his shoulder, his voice echoing off the walls. "Does anybody live up here?"

Upstairs he saw the same thing. More of nothing. Bare walls, bare floor, bare dressers. She hadn't followed him, so he shouted down the stairwell. "Don't you have any pictures?"

When she didn't answer, he continued. "I have an idea. Why don't you get yourself some picture frames, but don't take the people out that come with them. Just leave them in. How does that sound, Rachel? Instant family and friends."

He cocked his head and waited for a reply.

Silence.

His anger began to fade, disappearing as quickly as it had come. With a shaking hand he raked his hair, then leaned against the doorjamb, forehead on his arm. He blew out a long breath.

Get a grip, Thoreau.

You don't own her. If she doesn't want you in her life, there's nothing you can do about it. It's not going to do any good to run through her house like a crazy man. That wouldn't get him any points in the old etiquette department.

And anyway, what did he have to give Rachel?

Nothing. Not a damn thing.

He was a nobody. A guy with no future and no past. Maybe it had been his way of coping, but all along he'd fooled himself into thinking he would eventually get well. He'd seen his X rays. He'd read the medical journals. It was time to face the music. He wasn't going to get his memory back. You can't remember something that isn't there.

Why had he ever thought Rachel would be interested in somebody like him? Now he could see that he'd mistaken sympathy for something more. He'd mistaken it for attraction. Maybe he'd even mistaken it for love.

For the first time since his accident, Sammy felt all of thirty-eight years old. Older than thirty-eight. A lot older.

Slowly he made his way downstairs. When he reached the bottom step, he looked around.

No Rachel.

He checked the kitchen.

No Rachel.

She must have left while he was upstairs throwing his fit. Not that he could blame her. Hell, she was probably next door calling the cops. Or the funny farm.

Exit, stage left.

He was halfway out the door when he heard a muffled sound from somewhere behind him.

He stopped and listened.

Beside the stairs was a closet. With his heart doing double time, Sammy crossed to it and opened the door.

Sitting on the floor, amid scattered shoes and dust, her arms hugging bent legs, her face buried against bare knees, was Rachel.

And she was crying.

For a second his heart stopped beating. For a second he forgot to breathe. He stood while he let the shock waves roll over him.

"Rachel . . ." His voice came out a hoarse croak.

There was no reaction from her.

With almost robotic stiffness, he made himself move, made his knees bend. Not thinking about what he was doing—he was too confused and anguished to think—he managed to coax Rachel to her feet.

Not looking up, she threw herself at him, burying her face against his chest.

God, her skin was so cold.

He held her tightly, trying to warm her, alarmed at the violent shaking of her shoulders, at the violence of her weeping.

"You're . . . mean!"

His heart stopped again, the truth of her words hurting like hell. "I know." He hugged her to him, the way he had after they'd made love. He hadn't wanted to let her go then, and he didn't want to let her go now.

"I'm sorry," he whispered, his lips moving against her ear.

"No, y-you were right about my a . . . part . . . ment." She forced out the words between shuddering sobs. "But you're wrong . . . about my . . . my feelings for you—"

She looked up, her eyes streaming with tears, her nose red. "You're the best"—she hiccuped—"the most w-wonderful thing . . . that's happened . . . t-to me for a long, long t-time. . . ."

He grabbed a tissue from a nearby end table and wiped the tears from her cheeks.

She took the tissue from him. "Thanks," she muttered. Head bent, she blew her nose. When she was finished, she took a deep breath, then let out a trembling sigh.

"Would you like a drink of water?" he said.

She nodded and followed him to the kitchen. He rummaged around and found a clean glass, filled it with tap water, and handed it to her.

She took a drink, sniffled, then pressed the back of her hand to her nose.

She was breaking his heart.

"When I was little," she began, "my grandmother used to make me drink water whenever I cried. You can't cry when you're drinking."

She offered him the glass, then pulled herself up to sit on the countertop.

Sammy took a drink, put down the glass, and went over to stand in front of her. His own throat felt tight and his eyes burned. "I'm sorry," he choked out, leaning his forehead against hers. "I thought I could help you. I thought I was strong enough for you to lean on, but all I've managed to do is hurt you more."

She raised her hands to his shoulders, then wrapped her legs around him. "Don't be sorry for making me feel alive," she whispered, eyes half closed. Her nose was still a little red, her lips swollen.

He leaned closer and pressed his mouth to hers. Her soft lips, cool from the water, salty from her tears, parted under his. Around his waist, her legs tightened. He could feel her breasts pressing against his chest, feel his body heat seeping into her.

He slid his hands up her thighs until he was supporting her bottom. Then he scooped her from the counter, astonished by love. Fifteen minutes earlier he was never going to see her again.

Now he was going to make love to her.

They untangled themselves long enough to make it upstairs to the bedroom. Once there, Rachel lifted her arms while Sammy eased her T-shirt over her head. Then he removed his own, kicking off his boots at the same time.

"You're sunburned," Rachel said, watching him. Everything suddenly seemed a little unreal. She felt dazed and emotionally drained.

Sammy cast a dismissing glance at shoulders that were more tan than red. "That's what I get for riding my bike without a shirt."

She was standing beside the unmade bed, the backs of her legs pressed against the side of the mattress. He stepped close, reached around her back, and unhooked her bra. He slipped it from her shoulders, freeing her breasts.

"Promise you won't scare me this time." Dark eyes regarded her while thumbs circled her nipples. She felt a potent sensation of pleasurable pain.

"I'll try not to."

He unbuttoned her shorts, then eased the zipper down. "Does it make you sad when I make love to you?"

"No. Well, maybe a little sad. But only because it's so nice."

It was the closest she could come to admitting the truth. She couldn't tell him that having him touch her was so wondrous, so pure, so spiritual, she almost cried from the sheer beauty of it.

He eased her shorts down over her hips. Her underpants followed, and then she stepped free.

"I've wanted to see you in the light."

She suddenly wanted to cover herself. "I have stretch marks," she stammered, feeling incredibly shy.

"Where? I don't see any."

"Here." She touched a faint line that ran across her hipbone. Before she fully comprehended what he was doing, he knelt in front of her and kissed the spot she indicated.

"Any more?" he asked huskily.

"Here." She pointed to the other side.

His hands were suddenly splayed across the back of her thighs. She felt his warm breath on her skin as he shifted his lips to her other hip, placing them against another tiny silver mark.

She could hardly stand. To steady herself, she reached out for his shoulders. Feeling the heat of his skin under her palms, she instantly let go.

"It's okay." He put her hands back where they had been. Then he stroked her bottom while he continued to press feather-soft kisses on her stomach.

Her knees were trembling. She collapsed against the bed.

Sammy stood up and removed his jeans and briefs at the same time. Then he was beside her, pulling her to him.

He covered her mouth with his, stroking deeply with his tongue while his hand caressed her.

She felt drowsy and aroused at the same time—a powerfully erotic combination. It made her stretch and curl against Sammy's lean body, made her kiss him back in the most langorous way.

He was between her legs, ready to enter her when he paused. "Please don't cry anymore," he said, his voice tight and husky. "I can't handle it when you cry."

Something deep within her womb clenched again and again. She couldn't speak. For an answer, she arched her hips and took him inside her.

TWENTY-FOUR

RACHEL OPENED HER EYES TO FIND THE BEDROOM FILLED with the hazy orange glow of early evening. Beside her, Sammy was asleep.

He was sprawled on his back, a white sheet tangled around him from waist to calves. The low light cast shadows over his chest and arms, making him seem made of bronze.

Once again she marveled at how fast his hair had grown. Right then, one recalcitrant lock lay rakishly across his smooth forehead.

Rachel's hand moved to brush it back. But before she could touch him she stopped herself, letting her hand fall back to the bed. She didn't want to wake him. She wanted the freedom to watch him awhile longer.

Most people looked more vulnerable with their eyes closed. With Sammy, it was just the opposite. Because his eyes, his magical, poetic eyes reflected a sensitivity that was so uniquely Sammy.

What had she done?

What was she going to do?

Don't think about tomorrow.

But she wasn't the type of person to take life lightly, and distress managed to edge its way into her thoughts.

Maybe she should slip out of bed and get dressed

before Sammy woke up. And then what? Run? She'd done it before. She could do it again.

But she was tired of running. And it was too late. Beside her, Sammy shifted . . . and she found herself being regarded by sleep-blurred, solemn eyes.

Her heart gave a lurch. And she had the strangest notion that he had somehow felt her regrets and doubts and had been awakened by them.

"What are you afraid of, Rachel?" he asked quietly, his voice rough, sexy, and intimate.

How Sammy. How like him to go directly to the most guarded part of her heart, a place she didn't want anyone, especially Sammy, to see.

You. I'm afraid of you. I'm afraid of the day when you will leave me behind. Because I'm not very good at saying good-bye to the people I love.

But she couldn't speak the words. She couldn't tell him she loved him. She knew all about guilt, and the last thing she wanted was to chain Sammy with her love.

There was fire in him, a passion for living. She knew he wouldn't be content to stay in La Grange and entertain patients for the rest of his life. These past few months had simply been a phase in a long healing process, a time when he could pick up the pieces and put himself back together before returning to the world. Soon he would discover who he wanted to be and he would fly away.

At first he would probably miss her a little, the way someone might miss a favorite teacher. But little by little he would become caught up in his new life and his memories of their short time together would dim as his new world brightened. Maybe he would even stop by to see her sometime. And he would be shocked at how old she looked. He would be sad and maybe a little irritated to see that she still wore her grief like a black arm band. . . .

But for now . . .

"Isn't it okay to just be happy?" he asked.

It was already too late; she could see that now. If he left immediately, right that second, it couldn't hurt any less than if he left in a week, or a month, or a year.

She smiled, coming to a decision. And if her smile was a little bittersweet, well, that was fine too. Because she wasn't a young girl rushing innocently into love, thinking it would be forever. She knew the pain of love, but she also knew of the wonder of love. And she was ready. Ready for both.

They decided they were starving, with neither one able to remember when they'd last eaten a meal. They thought about going to the grocery story, but quickly dismissed that idea. It would take too long. Their stomachs couldn't wait through all the stages involved in buying foodstuff and preparing a meal. They needed something fast.

Dinner ended up being a drive through McDonald's.

On the back of the motorcycle, Rachel braced two bags of food and drinks between her legs while clinging to Sammy as they headed north, out of town.

At the highest point of Cliff Road was a roadside stop with a picnic table. It overlooked a hazy valley of corn and a rapidly setting sun. With the scenic spot to themselves, they sat at the table, eating and watching a huge red sun dip below the horizon.

Rachel took a bite of French fry. "My daughter loved to go to McDonald's," she said, surprised at her words. It was very possibly the first time she'd spoken of Jennifer so casually. It hurt, but not as much as she'd expected. Because it felt right to make Jennifer a part of today.

Sammy was watching her, the setting sun reflecting in

his eyes. He nodded and smiled. "Kids and McDonald's. They go together."

Rachel nodded and pulled out another fry. "She loved McDonald's, but she was scared to death of Ronald."

"You know who scares the absolute hell out of me?"

She shook her head and waited for his solemn confession.

"Woodsy Owl."

They both laughed. And Rachel felt lighter than she had in years.

When they were done eating they continued to talk, with their conversation gradually getting more nonsensical by the minute. Rachel dimly understood that their silliness was probably due to lack of sleep, but she wasn't ready to go home.

Darkness came quickly. Sammy gathered all the wrappers and threw them in the trash can. "Work tomorrow." It was a reluctant statement. A reminder of the adult world.

Rachel sat on the tabletop, fingers gripping the edge, legs swinging. She didn't want to think of leaving. She didn't want to think of the magic ending, of saying good-bye to Sammy, even for a night.

He came and stood in front of her, working his legs between hers, his hands braced on her bare knees, his thumbs rubbing small circles. "I hate to think of taking you back," he told her. "I'm afraid of the cool reception I might get next time I see you."

She was distracted by his hands, which were now moving up her legs to her hips, her waist, her ribs, then around her shoulders. He urged her backward. She let go of the table to cling to his hard-muscled arms as he lowered himself on top of her. Through the layers of their clothing she could feel his arousal between her spread legs.

"I'm afraid you'll tell me to get lost," he whispered.

His mouth, cool from the ice he'd been chewing, came down on hers. One hand slid under her T-shirt to cup her breast, his thumb stroking her hardening nipple.

"I'm glad you aren't wearing a bra," he told her.

She couldn't believe the effect he was having on her. It was stronger than it had been before they'd made love that first time. She'd never thought she had much of a sex drive, but suddenly she couldn't get enough of Sammy.

She wished they were naked. She wished they weren't so close to the road.

Sammy pressed his straining zipper against the seam of her shorts, a reminder of just how he could make her melt and sigh. At the same time, his cool tongue filled her mouth, moving with the rhythm of his hips.

She finally pulled her mouth away and gulped for air. They both struggled to subdue their ragged breathing as their chests rose and fell. "You could come home with me," she gasped.

He pressed an open-mouthed kiss to her throat, then she felt him smile. "I was hoping you'd say that."

They knew they couldn't continue like this, not when they both had to work. And since spending the night together had little to do with sleep, they decided it might be best if they didn't see each other during the week. But by Tuesday Sammy couldn't stand it any longer. He had to see Rachel. Even though it was eleven P.M., he got on his Harley and headed for her apartment.

Once there, he wasn't surprised to find her windows dark. He picked up a small pebble and tossed it, careful to aim at the screen and not the glass. He hit his target, the stone rolling off the first-story roof to fall to the ground. He thought he caught a flicker of movement in the window. A few moments later the front door opened.

It seemed as though it had been two weeks, not two days, since he'd last seen her. He slipped inside, closed the door behind him, and pulled Rachel into his arms. God, she felt good, and smelled good—clean, like soap and fresh air. Beneath her thin gown he could tell that she wasn't wearing anything. He could feel the warmth of her sweet body, calling to him.

They didn't wait to go upstairs. They shed their clothes and tumbled to the floor.

The remainder of the week passed in much the same way. Nights spent making love and losing sleep, days spent anticipating those sleepless nights.

Saturday finally came around. They cruised the backroads on Sammy's motorcycle, stopping at all the historical markers and roadside curiosities.

Earlier, while going through some of his things, Sammy had come across an old 35-millimeter camera. He spent a large part of the day taking pictures of scenery and winding roads . . . and Rachel. A couple of times he set the automatic timer so they could both be in the shot.

Rachel begged to take one of him, so he posed in front of his Harley, one hip resting on the seat, booted feet crossed at the ankles, arms crossed at his chest. Rachel laughed and told him she'd be scared if she didn't know him.

By the end of the day they were both sunburned and tired, a good kind of tired. At Rachel's they showered, ate, then tumbled into bed and made slow, sweet love.

Sunday morning they woke to the sound of rain pattering softly against the windows, so they spent the day curled up on the couch, eating popcorn and watching old movies on the VCR. Later they talked quietly, sharing stories—some happy, some sad. At one point Rachel became quiet and Sammy became concerned.

She got up, went to the closet, and came back with a small box. When she sat down next to him, Sammy saw that the box was full of photographs.

Pictures of Jennifer.

There were probably at least a hundred, taken at all of the stages little kids go through. He saw Jennifer as a red-faced newborn, as an infant and a toddler, and finally as a kindergartner.

Sammy lifted out a five-by-seven picture in an ornate gold frame. A beautiful child laughed up at him from a swing, her hair lighter than Rachel's, her eyes a vivid blue. Small, chubby hands clutched the chain links on either side of her radiant face. He felt a knife-thrust of pain at the thought of what Rachel had suffered.

"That was taken on Easter," Rachel told him. "At Scarborough Park. We used to go there a lot. They have a slide that's a spiral. Jennifer and I loved to go on that slide." Her eyes were unfocused as she relived the scene from her past. Then she sighed and began putting the pictures away. When she came to the one of Jennifer on the swing, she paused, then stood it on the end table near the couch.

Molly was in the kitchen when she heard the front doorbell ring. Since Amy had moved out, the only people who ever came by were salesmen, children selling candy, the paper boy, and, on rare occasions, a neighbor.

She opened the door to find Mark Elliot standing before her. His crooked smile seemed to say, Bet you never thought you'd see me here. Under his arm was a thermos. From a bent finger dangled two cups.

"Ready for coffee?" he asked.

"Mark . . ."

She hadn't seen him since the morning she'd delivered cookies to his apartment. Since then she'd deliberately visited Sammy when she was sure Mark wouldn't be there. She didn't know why. It wasn't that she hadn't liked him, because she had. Now she ran a nervous hand through her hair.

"Aren't you going to ask me in?"

Even though Austin was at work, she couldn't keep from casting a glance over her shoulder. Habits die hard. "I don't know. I don't think I should." *Let you come into Austin's house,* she added silently.

"Sammy told me you probably wouldn't be game, but I thought I'd take the chance. I'm not asking you for a date or anything. I know you're married. I just like talking to you, and thought you may have liked talking to me."

"Oh, I did, but . . ." She looked down at her chewed nails, then back at Mark. "Before you come in I think I should tell you that I'm not the kind of person who . . . who . . ." *Who has affairs.* She couldn't say it, but she didn't have to.

"I know. That's what Sammy said. In fact, he told me to leave you alone. *Leave my sister alone.* Those were his exact words. But I thought it was rather prejudiced of him. He wouldn't say that if I were a female friend of yours." He dangled the cups a little higher. "Coffee. That's all. And somebody to talk to. I have a brother and sister, but I can't always talk to them. Sometimes I need someone from outside the family."

She knew what he was telling her. He was telling her this was purely a friendly visit, but she wasn't sure. . . . He couldn't find her attractive, of course not. He was so young . . . and she was so old. All those gray hairs. He'd surely seen all those gray hairs. Of course he wasn't attracted to her. And that was good, she told herself. Because if he *did* like her, she would have to tell him he couldn't come in.

When she left for good, when she was finally free of Austin's censure and disapproval, she wanted that freedom to be total. The last thing she planned to do was run straight into the arms of another man. Maybe someday when she could hold up her head again, when she no longer cast nervous glances over her shoulder, when she was her own person once more, maybe then she might be interested in somebody. Maybe someone warm and funny. Someone very much like Mark.

But not now.

"Just coffee," she stated, stepping back to open the door a little wider.

Mark didn't hesitate. He was inside the house in half a second. "And cream," he said, heading straight for the kitchen. "If you don't have cream, milk will be fine."

TWENTY-FIVE

SATURDAY.

And not a damn thing to do.

Rachel was at a medical conference, and Mark was nowhere around. That left good old Sammy climbing the cement block walls of Mark's apartment.

Being alone with time on his hands was not one of Sammy's favorite things. When he was alone, he thought too much. And over the past couple of weeks Sammy had become aware of a restlessness growing inside him. No matter what he did, no matter how physically tired he became, he couldn't seem to unwind. At night he had a hard time sleeping. And whenever he did finally fall asleep, it never lasted long. He would jerk awake, his hands clenched, jaw stiff, heart hammering.

If he was with Rachel when it happened, he would turn to her, his first instinct being to wake her and hold her tightly. But then he would remember the dark smudges under her eyes, and he would let her sleep.

If he was at Mark's, he would get up and pace, or sometimes he'd go for a walk, even if it was the middle of the night. Sometimes, if Mrs. Davenport was up, too, he'd join her on her front porch for tea.

He knew what his problem was. For months he'd held himself together by pretense. A pretense of being able to get his memory back. But now that he'd faced the truth, there was a void inside him that even Rachel, as much as he loved her, couldn't fill.

He scanned the apartment. Mark's apartment. Each lampshade, each piece of furniture was Mark's. There was nothing of Sammy Thoreau there. And it was the same at Rachel's. Even though they had picked up a few things at antique stores and auctions, the decor reflected Rachel, not Sammy.

He was a shadow, a man with no real substance.

He didn't want to be a crybaby, wallowing in self-pity, but he sure as hell felt sorry for himself.

He paced from the front door to the kitchen. He stopped and restlessly picked up a newspaper, quickly thumbing through it, his mind not registering a single word. He tossed down the paper.

This hollow feeling, he hated it. He felt that if he only knew more about his past, then maybe the emptiness would go away. He'd questioned Molly lots of times, enough to drive a saint crazy, but suddenly he felt the need to talk to her again. Maybe during the conversation they would stumble onto something that would make him feel less obscure.

He found Molly sitting on her backyard deck, watching the birds.

"I left some bird feeders up over the summer," she said as Sammy dropped into a chair beside her. "I can't imagine a world without birds, but sometimes it makes me sad to watch them. They spend their lives ready to fly away, constantly watching for predators. What an existence for creatures who give so much and ask so little."

"It doesn't seem fair, does it?" Sammy wondered if Molly ever consciously thought about the similarity between herself and the birds she loved. "They deserve a sanctuary where they can be safe without worry."

"Yes." She turned to look at him. "Yes, that would be nice."

They talked quietly for a while, then, the ever-perceptive Molly asked, "Sammy, what's wrong?"

"Oh, hell." He rubbed a hand across his forehead . . . and he began to tell her how confused he was, how useless and empty he felt. "Have you ever had one of those dreams where you're running and running, searching frantically for something, but you don't know what it is? And all the while there's this god-awful sense of urgency inside you. This feeling that if only you could find whatever it is you need, then everything would be okay. But you never find that mysterious something. It's always just another arm's reach away."

Molly was watching him with compassion in her eyes. An older Molly. A wiser Molly. A more together Molly.

So many years lost. So much time gone by. He felt cheated. He wanted to get that time back.

"When you were little, you used to whistle," she said. "So much that it sometimes drove me crazy. Do you remember that?"

He nodded.

"Sammy . . . why don't you whistle anymore?"

He thought about it. "I don't know," he said quietly, thoughtfully. "I don't know."

Molly got up from her chair. "I think you should come with me. I have some things in the attic you might want to take a look at."

Since Austin didn't seem to be around, Sammy followed Molly into the house and up the narrow stairs into the attic. Musty, undisturbed air greeted them.

"You left the older boxes here quite a few years ago," Molly explained. "The new ones are everything I packed up from your apartment."

Against one wall was a stack of boxes, maybe twelve

in all. Three of them were well-used, the kind where the softly worn sides were covered with scribbled-over labels and the edges were rounded instead of squared. The other boxes were new, carefully identified with Molly's neat printing. They didn't say *Sammy's things*, they just said *Sammy*. And maybe that was appropriate. After all, the boxes were him.

Sammy didn't ask Molly why she hadn't mentioned the boxes before. Like him, she'd probably been afraid. She'd probably known he wouldn't have been ready. "Thanks, Molly. Thanks for everything."

She left him alone in the dimly lit attic with its wooden rafters and single bare bulb.

He was just getting his life together. Did he want to risk screwing it up again?

Yes, because he couldn't continue the way he was, not with this thing gnawing away at him.

He started on the old boxes. He had no memory of packing them, but he hoped to find the contents at least partially familiar, because that would be easier to deal with than going through the belongings of a stranger.

He lifted the top box—it had a solid feel—and carried it to the center of the attic, under the dangling bulb. He settled himself on the floor beside it, legs crossed. Then, his heart racing with dread and anticipation, he opened the lid, releasing a musty smell of years gone by.

The first thing Sammy saw was the folder for his high school diploma from River Bend High. He opened it and a photograph fell out. It was of his graduating class, taken on the football field bleachers. The girl next to him was Lisa Grafton. Months earlier, he'd asked Mary Dawn to stand beside him, but by graduation they'd split up, not that they had really ever gone together. He'd never been the kind to give a girl a ring, or ask her to go steady. He'd just taken it for granted that he and Mary Dawn would always be together.

In the picture he also spotted Luke and Harper.

Crazy Harper. The guy had been nuts about music and had spent a lot of time bragging about becoming a big rock star. Sammy had believed him, because Harper was good. At school dances Harper would play guitar and sing so sweetly that his mother, who usually signed up to be a chaperone, would break down and cry, embarrassing the hell out of her son.

Sammy hoped Harper's dream had come true.

He set aside the diploma and reached back in the box.

As he sifted through the memories, the past few months fell away, along with the forgotten years. . . .

He dug out old black and white photos of his mother, a person who had seemed more like a distant aunt than a parent. He knew he wouldn't find any pictures of his father. There weren't any. Sammy had been born after his parent's divorce, and any pictures of his father had been destroyed. But there were lots of pictures of Sammy and Molly together. Birthday shots, and Easter shots, and just plain goofing-around shots.

Halfway through the box he came upon a stack of newspapers, yellow with age. He immediately recognized the underground paper he and some of his high school friends had put together. The official school paper had been called *The River*, the underground was the *Undercurrent*. Sammy had wanted to name it *Undertow*, but Mary Dawn had thought it sounded too dark and dismal. Too negative.

"*Undertow* makes it sound like we have no choice in the course we take," she'd argued. "That we're pulled against our will. And anyway, I like the double meaning of *Undercurrent*. It says we aren't afraid to take on controversial, *current* issues."

Mary Dawn's social seriousness was sometimes a pain. But for the most part, Sammy liked it. It was one of the things that had attracted him to her in the first place.

So, even though Sammy secretly preferred *Undertow* because he had a weird sense of humor, he didn't make a big deal out of it. He was too laid back to sweat the little things.

As the heat in the attic intensified with the day, Sammy read through copies of *Undercurrent*, seeing familiar bylines and familiar faces. He smiled at the usual surreptitious finger-throwing poses, along with the fake mug shots of Harper and Luke, who'd helped out with the paper.

The memories were still there. That was good. But at the same time it was depressing to think that people like Harper were getting gray hairs and putting money into retirement accounts.

There were spiral notebooks stuffed with stories he'd started but never finished, evidence of his long-ago dream of becoming a science fiction writer. He'd even come up with a bumbling character named Drake the Flake who had somehow become a regular in *Undercurrent*.

Together he and Mary Dawn would take a popular topic and satirize it. She would sketch the cartoon and Sammy would write the story. He could remember laughing his ass off over their effort, only to be embarrassed as hell a week later when the paper came out.

How could something that seemed so damn witty seem so stupid a few days later? But that's how it was in high school. Things changed fast. People changed fast.

Adolescence was like being on a runaway train, catching fleeting glimpses of the scenery as the train hurtled on, never stopping, never slowing down. There had been times when he'd wanted to jump off and catch his breath.

Sammy and Mary Dawn had met during their sophomore year in high school. They were in the same driver's ed class. She was aloof and sexy with her short skirt and long brown hair that hung straight on both sides of her face. In class they'd never said more than hi and bye until the day of actual behind-the-wheel driving.

They'd been taken to an open field so they could practice backing. There was only one tree within a mile radius, but Mary Dawn had somehow managed to plant the car's back bumper against the poor, unsuspecting sapling.

Sammy had sprawled in the backseat, clutching his stomach and laughing until tears streamed down his cheeks.

Without waiting to shift from reverse to park, Mary Dawn had jumped out, leaving the door wide open. She'd hurried across the field, her long bare legs flashing in the sunlight.

The instructor had looked behind him at Sammy and raised both eyebrows as if to say, Women, who can figure them out?

Sammy managed to catch his breath long enough to dive from the car and run after Mary Dawn. Stepping beside her, he said, "Hey, look, I'm sorry!" He was still a little short on air.

She stopped and swung around. "I don't like to be laughed at!"

Sammy could see that her face was tear-streaked, too, not with laughter like his, but with anger and humiliation. He stared, fascinated, while glistening drops caught the sunlight and reflected it like a perfect poem. The most peculiar sensation filled Sammy's chest, as if somebody had knocked the wind out of him, or he'd just caught his first glimpse of the Northern Lights.

Girls had fallen into three fairly distinct categories for Sammy. The goody-goodies who were so phony they made him sick. The girls he found interesting but only if they kept their mouths shut. And then there were the ones he liked to talk to but wouldn't want to kiss. Now, suddenly, here was a girl he would like to talk to *and* kiss.

"I'm sorry," he said. "Come on back to the car. You still have ten minutes of driving time left."

Head bent, hair brushing one cheek, she looked up at him. "You won't laugh at me even if I mess up?"

"Cross my heart. I'll even lie on the ground and let you use me for a speed bump."

She smiled through her tears. "You're really kind of nice, you know that?"

From that moment on he was a goner.

Mary Dawn . . . They were inseparable through the remainder of their sophomore year and all through their junior year. But then he told her he loved her, and she told him good-bye.

Sammy finished with the old boxes, and moved on to the new. He was prepared for these to be different, more disturbing because they wouldn't hold as many memories.

But as he went through them, he could see that a lot of it was the same kind of stuff. Spiral notebooks filled with half-formed ideas and stream-of-consciousness pieces.

From his college days he found a legalize marijuana poster. It showed a longhair watering his potted marijuana plant on the front porch of his home. Underneath the poster were pictures of Jay and pictures of Molly, along with pictures of Jay and Molly together.

Good ol' Jay.

If he were here right now, wouldn't he get a buzz out of this memory-loss bull? He'd laugh and joke, and pretty soon Sammy would be laughing and joking, and it wouldn't seem so bad. But Jay wasn't there. . . . And Sammy wasn't laughing. . . .

He wanted to stop digging through the boxes. He wanted to leave everything where it was and get out. Run.

But he couldn't stop. He'd come this far. He wasn't going to back down now.

Soon he was into the post-Vietnam era. That's where things really began to change, really began to get strange. He dug out concert ticket stubs, along with a handful of parking tickets. There were overdraft notices from the bank, overdue bills . . . a ticket for driving under the influence. He'd even had his license revoked for six months and had put in a year of community service work. And those weren't the only offenses. He'd been arrested more than once for starting a fight. He'd been evicted from his apartment for disturbing the peace.

Certainly not the level-headed adult he'd expected to find.

He came upon some ragged-edged magazines and found that they contained a few of his articles. One, for a magazine called *Cheap Travel*, was a brief, semihumorous story about flying coach class. Even though it made Sammy smile a couple of times, he recognized it for what it was: filler.

He picked up the next magazine and found another article. And another. As he read them, he didn't find it hard to see that they'd been plunked out for the sake of quick cash. The stories were all mildly entertaining. One on the plight of the whales even bordered on moving. But what had happened to the passion of the Vietnam story he was supposedly so famous for? What had happened to the energy and freshness? Drake the Flake had more life in him than these flat stories.

He found a manila envelope. Inside were twenty or so pages held together by a rusty paper clip. Sammy straightened a curled corner.

A manuscript, or the start of one. *The Edge*.

At first he thought the piece was science fiction, but after the first couple of lines he could see it was more New Wave. The Edge wasn't a world, or a place, but the central character's state of mind, and that state of mind was one of bleak despair.

Five pages into the manuscript, Sammy knew the author had been writing about himself, about something that made him crave death rather than live another day.

What the hell . . . ?

He continued to read, unable to shake the feeling that he was intruding in someone's personal life, spying on that person's deepest and darkest secrets. He had to keep reminding himself that this was *his* life—and that hurt him. For the first time since his accident, he wondered if he really wanted to fill in all the blanks.

He'd opened the boxes though he'd been afraid to confront himself, partially because he'd expected to feel inferior to the person he once was—a folk hero, someone who seemed bigger than life. Instead, he found testimony to a life gone wrong. Instead of finding a hotshot journalist, he'd found a man consumed by darkness.

And he couldn't help but wonder if his car accident had been an accident at all.

Had it been attempted suicide?

Soft footfalls sounded on the stairs. And then Molly was there, checking on him.

"How are you doing? I thought you might like some iced tea."

Molly. Good ol' Molly. He wanted to jump up and hug her. He wanted to tell her he was finished so he could get the hell out. He wanted the smothering sensation in his chest to go away.

He tossed down the manuscript. He couldn't read any more of it. Then, forcing some control into his voice, he asked, "Molly, what happened to me?" His heart was hammering so loudly, he could hardly hear his own words. "I'd expected to come across things I didn't remember, but I didn't expect to find a totally different person."

Molly sighed a little sadly, a little resigned. "Vietnam. Vietnam happened. It changed a lot of people." She sat down on the top step. "This is why I wasn't eager for you to open these boxes. I wish you could accept what has happened to you and get on with your life."

"It's not that easy. Something is missing. A part of *me* is missing." He raised both hands and raked his hair back from his forehead, trying to make sense of it all. Nobody knew what it was like to have nineteen years disappear from your memory. Nobody understood.

"When I was in high school," he began, "I came up with this plot for a science fiction book. It was about a planet where scientists implanted tiny moths into the brains of troublemakers. It took about an hour for the moth to steal the victim's soul—his essence." He pressed a hand to his chest. "I feel like that sometimes. As if somebody has stolen my soul."

Molly was watching him with sad, solemn eyes. "You have to believe me when I say that you are more yourself today than you were a year ago. *That* Sammy was somebody I didn't know. He was a stranger who had locked himself away from everybody he cared about. You're back now. Try to accept that. Let go of the past."

Why did he get the feeling she was hiding something? "Molly, if there was something I should know, you'd tell me, wouldn't you? You wouldn't keep it from me?"

"I've told you everything I can possibly think of." Her gaze was direct. Unblinking.

He believed her. Molly would never lie to him.

He went back to work. Later, he ate a sandwich Molly brought, but he couldn't have said if it was peanut butter or bologna.

Hours passed. The light filtering in the tiny attic window changed from the pure white of midday to the red-orange of early evening. He had almost reached the bottom of the last box when he pulled out an envelope—a letter. It was soft to the touch, as if someone had folded and unfolded it a million times, maybe carried it in a pocket or wallet.

Sammy settled back against a wooden ceiling brace and opened the envelope.

A letter from Mary Dawn, dated six years earlier.

Dear Sammy:

Even though we haven't kept in touch, I want you to know that I think about you often. I think about the good times we had, and I sometimes wonder if we made the right choices in our lives. If I made the right choice.

That's what it's all about, isn't it? Choices. And timing.

Sometimes I wonder if we'd met later in life, when we were more mature, more ready for whatever it was that was happening between us, then maybe it would have worked. Then maybe I would have been ready. Maybe I could have handled it.

But I wasn't ready. And now I can admit that I was scared. I had my whole life ahead of me. It was too early to make any kind of commitment to anyone, not even you.

I was too inexperienced to know that what we had was something special. Too self-centered to realize how rare it is to find a person you can be totally one with, someone who shares your interests and dreams. Someone who is a true friend. In my ignorance, I assumed there were lots of people out there like you. How wrong I was.

Whenever I read an article you've written, I remember those days at *Undercurrent,* and I'm filled with pride over what you've done with your life. I'm so glad I knew you. I only wonder how different things might have been if I'd made a different choice, if I hadn't run away when you told me you loved me.

Mary Dawn

Sammy sat in silence for a long time, staring blankly into space. Then he examined the envelope, looking for a return address. The ink was faded, but he could make out a faint postmark from somewhere in Nevada.

He went through the rest of the box, looking for more letters from Mary Dawn, but the only thing he found was a fifteen-year class reunion invitation with a listing of schoolmates and addresses. Mary Dawn was included.

Had he gone to the reunion?

Had he answered her letter?

Until today, Sammy hadn't thought about his memory loss affecting anybody but himself. But maybe it had. Maybe it had affected Mary Dawn. Maybe he was in some way tied to her without even knowing it. She could be waiting somewhere right now, wondering why he'd dropped out of her life.

Mary Dawn.

Rachel.

Oh God, Rachel. His love for her was a sweet ache in his soul. She had brought him back from a dark place, a bad place. She had saved his life.

But Mary Dawn had been a *part* of him. She had been his first love. He could remember times when they had both burst into the same song, or started talking about the same thing at the same time. Halves of a whole. To see her would be a little like seeing the old Sammy.

Maybe Mary Dawn was what he needed to make himself complete.

But Rachel. Oh God, Rachel.

Slowly, methodically, he repacked the boxes. By the time he made his way downstairs, total darkness had fallen.

TWENTY-SIX

WHEN RACHEL HAD GOTTEN HOME FROM THE MEDICAL conference the previous night, she'd half expected to find Sammy waiting for her. But there had been no sign of him.

Now, as she was slipping on her shoes, getting ready to leave for work, she heard the low drone of an approaching motorcycle. She reached the bedroom window in time to see Sammy pulling up in front of her apartment. A sleeping bag was strapped to the back of his motorcycle.

He was going away.

It shouldn't have been such a shock. Lately he'd been so quiet, so thoughtful. She'd known a change was coming. But that knowledge hadn't prepared her for the overwhelming panic she now felt.

Standing to one side of the window, Rachel watched. Instead of jumping off the bike the way he usually did, Sammy sat there a few moments, as if bolstering himself to come inside. When he did finally start toward her apartment, his movements were slow and reluctant.

He didn't knock. He'd quit knocking weeks ago. She listened while he opened the door and came inside, listened while he called her name. His voice sounded different. Strained.

A change was coming.

She gripped the windowpane, unable to move. "Up here!"

Footfalls sounded on the carpeted stairs as she continued to stare out at the motorcycle on the street below. Behind her, she heard him pause just inside the bedroom door.

"Rachel?"

She couldn't make herself turn around. "See that sycamore tree?" she asked. "Last year it was struck by lightning. I didn't think it was going to make it, but this summer it managed to produce a few scraggly leaves." She couldn't stop rambling. "I don't think it will make it another year—"

"Rachel, I have to tell you something."

The pain and desperation in his voice gave her the strength to turn.

He stood there, his face showing the emotions battling within him. It made her think of another time, at the beginning, when he'd accidentally knocked her to the hospital floor. He'd stood in the doorway then, too, wanting to run, while his conscience told him to stop and see if he'd hurt her. Except for a couple of bruises that had quickly healed, he hadn't hurt her. But now . . .

She could see that this was hard for him, but she could make it easier.

"You're leaving," she whispered.

"Yes." Relief appeared in his eyes. He wouldn't have to say the words. She'd spared him that.

Memories of the joy he'd brought her flooded her mind. He was so spontaneous, so open. He had somehow managed to cling to childlike artlessness as he'd grown into a sensitive man.

But he hadn't always been that way. Molly had told her that before the accident Sammy had been a troubled recluse. Would he become that way again? Would the harshness of the world knock him down?

"Once," she began quietly, turning back to stare out the window, "when I was in the first grade, I went on a field trip to the zoo with my class. The zoo had polar bears. All of them looked about the same, but while most of the bears just lay around, one particular bear played and tossed a ball and did wild crazy bellyflops in the water that made all of us double up with laughter. He was wonderful."

She took a deep, stabilizing breath, then continued. "About a year later I went back to the zoo, but this time all the bears just sat around. I thought the funny bear must have died, and I asked a zookeeper about him. He told me he was still there, and he pointed. I looked, but all I saw was a sad, pathetic, tired bear. I asked if he was sick, but the keeper shook his head and told me no, he'd just grown up. I went home and cried until I made myself sick."

She turned toward him. "So . . ." She made a hopeless gesture with both hands. "Wherever you go, whatever you do, don't change," she begged. "Please, don't change."

The pain she felt was mirrored in his eyes, his beautiful, soulful eyes. She understood that it hurt him to see her pain and know he was the cause. A person could hide only so much from the ones she loved. And that made her love him all the more. Made her hurt all the more.

"I love you, Rachel. I never wanted to hurt you. But there are things I have to do. People I have to see. I have to find myself. I have to be somebody."

Gently, she reached up and touched his face. "You've always been somebody. Somebody very special. But I understand why you have to go. Please don't let what has happened between us affect your life. I'm a big girl. I went into this with my eyes open. I knew there would come a time when you'd go."

But not so soon.

Oh, God, he was crying. She couldn't handle this. She had to be brave for him. Strong for him. "Sammy, don't take it so hard. It's not your fault. Did you think I expected you to stay forever?"

Surprise showed in his expression. "Yes."

"I never wanted to imprison you. I never wanted you to feel obligated to me. That's not what love is about."

Quickly, as if he couldn't stand not touching her anymore, he closed the distance between them. Then he was holding her and kissing her with all the pain and passion of a thousand men, bruising her all the way to her soul.

His lips left hers, but his fingers remained threaded through her hair. "I want you to promise me something," he said, his dark, glittering gaze burning into her. "I can't leave unless I know you'll be okay."

"I'll be okay."

"No drinking. I've got to know that. You've got to promise."

Cut him free. Cut him free. "No drinking. I swear."

"Good." That relief again. Oh, how that relief hurt.

He let her go, the way she'd always known he would. Then he reached into his pocket and pulled out an envelope, the kind photographs come in. "Here." He pressed the package into her hand, then turned to go.

She followed him down the stairs and stood in the doorway as he mounted his motorcycle, watched as he braced his arms on the handlebars and kick-started the engine.

She took a step closer. "Wait!"

His head came up.

"Do you need anything? Money?"

He smiled a little crookedly and shook his head.

"There you go. Always looking out for me. It's about time I learned to take care of myself."

And then he was gone, roaring out of her life.

She stood in the doorway a long time, staring at nothing. Finally some children walked by and she heard their nervous giggles and saw them whispering behind their hands. She stepped back and closed the door.

She was still holding the photographs. With hands that didn't tremble, she opened the package.

Memories.

Warm, wonderful memories. Of winding roads and hazy sunsets. Of her and Sammy, laughing, their hair tangled by the wind, noses sunburned.

There was one picture she stared at for a long time. The one of Sammy leaning against his motorcycle.

It captured him perfectly. There was a teasing gentleness in his eyes that belied the wildness of his hair and the belligerence of his pose.

She had loved him so much. So very, very much.

Moving as though she were sick, or very old, she crossed the room and leaned Sammy's picture next to the gold-framed one of Jennifer.

TWENTY-SEVEN

IN THE SOLITUDE OF HER APARTMENT, RACHEL ATE HER supper—not a TV dinner but a meal she'd actually prepared herself—then washed the dishes. Outside, there was a mellow tang to the air that whispered of fall. Bittersweet fall.

Rachel wanted to hang on to summer as long as she could. All her memories of Sammy were sweet summer memories. In a few months, snow would cover the ground and everything would be frozen. She didn't know if she could face another long Iowa winter. Maybe she should take that cruise Dr. Fontana was always trying to talk her into.

She walked into the living room and stared at the videocassette on her coffee table. Mark had dropped it off earlier, explaining that he'd just finished the rough edit, and Sammy had wanted him to make sure Rachel got a copy.

It was a visual case history. Sammy's case history. It was standard practice to compile a record of unusual cases such as Sammy's for use in student education. She'd viewed several in the past few years. But never one of Sammy.

Was she up to it?

So far she'd done fairly well. It would have been easy for her to have fallen back into her old ways of drug and alcohol abuse, but to do so would have been the same as saying that Sammy had never existed for her. And she couldn't do that. Instead, she had to be brave.

He had taught her that there was still joy to be found in the world, even after great loss.

She crossed the living room, slipped the tape into the VCR, then backed to the couch and sat down.

Fade in. . . .

There was a musical intro, then a shot of the hospital and its grounds. An obviously hand-held camera bobbed closer to someone standing on the hospital steps—Mark.

"Sammy Thoreau came to us in an almost catatonic state," Mark began in a sober, theatrical voice.

This was going to hurt. This was going to hurt a lot.

Her instinct screamed at her to shut off the player. But she couldn't make herself stop the tape any more than she could have kept herself from falling in love with Sammy. Even though her heart was hammering in her ears and panic-filled thoughts were racing through her head, she forced her attention on the screen.

This was different from other tapes she'd viewed, more flamboyant thanks to Mark's unusual method of presentation. She could see that Mark had given up his floral print shirt for a white lab coat. His hands were buried deep in the roomy pockets.

"At a previous hospital, Sammy Thoreau had already been diagnosed as chronically debilitated," Mark stated. "Which in plain English means that he was expected to remain a vegetable for the rest of his life."

Mark walked toward the double doors at the top of the steps. "Come on inside and see what happened to that chronically debilitated patient."

The picture cut to a wide shot of Sammy. Rachel

immediately recognized the scene—it was their first
session. Mark had obviously spliced it from one of the
progress tapes, which she hadn't yet had the courage to
watch.

Mark continued to narrate, but his words were just a
hum in Rachel's head. Her attention was on Sammy.

Sammy was slouched in a chair, feet sticking out, one
arm draped over the chair back. A very studied pose.
Very deliberate.

Very scared.

She hadn't been able to see it that day. She hadn't
known him well enough, but she could see it now. His
fear.

He's come so far.

She watched as he got up and paced the room, his
actions, his body language that of a teenager.

The dispassionate eye of the camera kept recording.
At one point Sammy approached the camera, made a
face, mouthed some words, and stuck his hand up to the
lens. For the sake of young viewers—or possibly as an
example of Mark's strange sense of humor—his extended
middle finger was blacked out. She smiled, but it didn't
feel like her usual smile. There was a sadness to it. She
felt old . . . and wiser than she wanted to be.

"A difficult patient," came Mark's dry voice-over.

Of course they couldn't show everything, but the
scenes they did show were in sequence. And seeing the
sessions at a rapid pace gave Rachel a fresh perspective.
She'd always known that Sammy had made amazing
progress, but until now she hadn't realized just how
amazing.

She was with Sammy in most of the frames, and she
was surprised at how in control, how professional she
appeared, even in scenes where she knew she'd been
falling apart.

Fool the patient, fool yourself.

She was just beginning to get over her initial shock when she got another. Sammy suddenly took over the narration.

To hear his voice sent waves of pain through her. But she couldn't look away, couldn't miss a single gesture, a single word.

The story moved on, the narration changing from third person to first.

Sammy had progressed past the session room. The filming became a little more varied and original. There were wide shots and close-ups. Of Sammy and Mark playing Frisbee on the hospital lawn, then a game of baseball with the patients, some of whom were wearing their hospital pajamas. Shots of Sammy working as entertainment director. The camera panned the crowd, pausing briefly on animated faces and clapping hands. In the voice-over, Sammy explained that everybody needed to feel a part of something.

The next scene—the finale?—took place where the program had begun: on the hospital's front steps.

The double doors opened and Sammy, dressed in a shirt and tie and faded jeans, stepped into the sunlight.

His hands were shoved deep into the front pockets of his jeans; his eyes reflected the sun as he focused on the distant horizon.

Two words appeared on the screen: The beginning.

Credits—unusual for a university tape—began to roll. Rachel almost missed them, her eyes were so blurred by tears.

The screen became blank, then a new set of words appeared against a background of solid black.

Dedicated to Dr. Rachel Danielle Collins, without whom this happy ending wouldn't have been possible.

Sammy

A good-bye.

The most wonderful, the most painful good-bye she'd ever had.

When she'd recovered enough to talk, she called Mark.

"What did you think?" he asked, the phone line practically vibrating with his excitement. "Did you like it?"

She prayed she could get through this without breaking down. She gripped the receiver with both hands. "I loved it."

"Sammy and I had been working on it off and on, putting it together for the university. It still needs some polishing—you probably noticed some of the rough spots. But the dedication, Sammy put that in right away."

"It was wonderful. Thank you."

After hanging up, she rewound the tape, then pressed the play button and curled up in a corner of the couch to watch it again. When it was over, she sat in the dark, emotions rolling over her.

She hurt.

She'd lost the two people she loved most in the world. And now it was going to be so hard, so abominably hard to get through the rest of her life. She'd been trying to heal, but now, seeing Sammy again, hearing his voice again, made the pain come hurtling back with all its jagged edges. Pain tore at her throat, at her insides, sharp and insistent and not to be ignored.

She remembered something an instructor had once told her.

In order to heal people, we must sometimes take their pain into ourselves.

At the time she'd thought his words a bit melodramatic. She didn't think so anymore.

TWENTY-EIGHT

SAMMY PULLED INTO PARIS, NEVADA, POPULATION 1,325. Following the directions given by the gas station attendant, he turned his bike onto Main Street, his eyes searching the row of buildings until he found the sign that read PARIS WEEKLY. Taller than it was wide, the office was squeezed between a ma and pa grocery store and an insurance company.

Things hadn't changed all that much. Mary Dawn was still staining her fingers with printer's ink.

During the past few weeks Sammy had covered a lot of ground. He'd even stopped in Wyoming and Montana to see Harper and Luke. Thinking back over his travels was a little like watching one of those old movies where the character runs in place while the background moves behind him.

At night he tossed his sleeping bag on the ground. During the day, whenever he got tired of the wind beating him raw, he'd pull into a truck stop and ask a semi driver to draft him. Not a very safe way to travel, riding a few yards behind a big rig, but it was a change of pace.

But the moths were still at work. Instead of fading away, the emptiness in Sammy seemed to be spreading.

He inched the bike along the crumbled curb and cut

the engine. Heat radiated from the machine. His palms
tingled from too many hours spent wrapped around the
hand grips.

But he was here. And now that he was, he hesitated,
unsure of the reception he'd get. He stood, legs straddling the bike, and rocked it onto the kickstand. Then
he dismounted and headed for the building.

When he opened the screen door a bell jangled above
his head and a woman's voice yelled from somewhere
behind the chipped counter and the maze of stacked and
tied newspapers. "I'm back here!"

Mary Dawn?

"I can't let go of this thing, or water will go
everywhere!"

Sammy edged around the counter, heading in the
direction of the voice and a narrow open doorway. Inside,
he found a woman bent over a toilet, hand in the tank,
a curtain of straight brown hair hiding her face.

Hearing his footsteps, she looked up and her mouth
dropped open in shocked disbelief.

Mary Dawn.

"Speedbump!"

He'd almost forgotten the goofy nickname he'd earned
that day of the driver's ed disaster.

Her hair was still the same color, but now it was
shoulder length. There were a few fine character lines at
the corners of her eyes and mouth, but she was Mary
Dawn. He would have recognized her anywhere.

"I thought you were the plumber!" Apparently she
forgot about her immediate problem. She straightened,
her hand coming out of the tank. Water shot into the air
like a geyser, hitting the ceiling and ricocheting around
the small room.

Mary Dawn screamed, stuck her hand back in the
tank, and stopped the eruption.

"You always did have the worst timing," she said, water dripping from her face onto her T-shirt.

Sammy had avoided most of the downpour by jumping back. Now he stepped into the tiny bathroom, nudged past her, and reached down beside the toilet, near the floor, to close the shutoff valve. That master-plumber move accomplished, he straightened. "You never could keep your cool during a crisis."

"You're still rescuing maidens in distress."

"Wait till you get my bill."

She made a face and shook water from her hands. "Ugh."

"And here I always thought toilet water was something that was supposed to make you smell good."

She laughed. He laughed.

Amazingly, there was no strain between them. It didn't seem that any time at all had passed since he'd last seen her. There were none of those awkward, What's it been, close to twenty years? questions that had been asked when he'd stopped to see Harper and Luke.

He helped her wipe up the water. Then, while she towel-dried her hair, he walked into the front room to stare through the fly-specked window. There was hardly any traffic. No lane markings on the narrow street. He'd seen only one streetlight on the way into town. Nice. Quiet.

"Not exactly the fast track," Mary Dawn said, coming up beside him.

He turned. She'd brushed back her damp hair and changed into a dry shirt.

"But we don't have muggings or murders," she added.

"How long have you been here?"

"Over six years. At first the townspeople didn't like the idea of an outsider taking over the local wipe—that's their definition, not mine. But I think they're beginning to warm up to me."

"Looks like a nice place."

"It grows on you." She let out a tired breath. "It's been a helluva day. My feature writer quit last week, just up and left without any notice, so I've had to pull double duty. I could use a drink. Want to join me?"

He hadn't come over a thousand miles to leave after five minutes.

The drink ended up being a can of tepid Coke, with Sammy seated on a broken swivel chair and Mary Dawn on a turned-over milk crate. Mary Dawn took a couple of swallows of Coke, topped it off with Jim Beam, then offered the bottle of whiskey to Sammy.

He shook his head. The last thing he wanted was to become reacquainted with alcohol.

"Ah." She nodded. "On the wagon. I remember reading about the trouble you were having with booze. It surprised me. I never thought you'd let anything take hold of you."

"I've pretty much got a handle on it now."

"That's good to hear. It's tough. My first husband was an alcoholic."

"Husband?"

"I've been married and divorced twice."

Mary Dawn stared, smiled, and stared some more. Then she leaned close and gave his forearm a squeeze. "It's *so* good to see you. I mean it."

"It's good to see you." He meant it too.

They talked about high school, and about some of the funny things that had happened during those years. A couple of times Mary Dawn laughed so hard she almost fell off her milk crate.

It wasn't until later that the tone of their conversation changed. Mary Dawn, fidgeting with her soda can, said, "I, ah, wrote you a few years ago. Did you ever get my letter?"

So, there had been no contact between them. Why

hadn't he answered her letter when it had obviously meant so much to him?

"If you got it, you never answered. I really didn't expect you to." She was suddenly rambling like a nervous teenager. "I've never known a writer who liked to answer letters."

"I got the letter."

"Oh. Well . . . . I wrote it right after my second divorce. I was really down, really—"

"I'm sorry I didn't answer. I guess I just didn't know what to say."

"That's okay. It was kind of strange to write you after so many years."

"No stranger than having me show up here."

She smiled, thanking him with her eyes. Then she pushed a stray strand of hair behind her ear—a familiar gesture, with one difference.

When she brought her hand down, Sammy caught it. "What's this?" he asked teasingly. "No ink under these nails?"

"I've gotten lazy. The *Paris Weekly* isn't printed here. It's done in Hildalgo for less than I could possibly do it. And anyway, you were always the one with ink in your veins, not me. You loved to tell the story. I just loved the excitement."

Her smile faded. Once again her eyes became serious. "Sammy, what are you doing here?"

Trying to keep the moths away.

He let go of her hand. "I'm kind of on a nostalgia tour, looking up old friends. So far I've seen Harper and Luke. And now you."

"You're kidding. Luke was at the class reunion, but I haven't seen Harper in years. What's he doing?"

"Factory work."

"He's not a musician?"

"Guess not."

"What about you? I haven't seen anything by you in a while. Are you in a slump?"

"I guess you could say that."

"Don't take this as an insult. I know you're way too good to be putting in time at the *Paris Weekly*, but if you're looking for a diversion, I could sure use a feature writer."

The moths hesitated. Feature writer?

"It might get you over your slump. Sometimes it's good to just dive into something totally new. Helps a person recharge."

He rubbed his hand across the back of his head, feeling the small scar beneath his hair, a scar he would always carry. He would tell her about his accident, but not today. Today he wanted to be just like everybody else. "I haven't written in a while. I might be pretty rusty."

"That's okay. I'll edit everything. Come on, it'll be just like old times."

Old times. He liked the sound of that.

TWENTY-NINE

A MONTH PASSED, AND ANOTHER. RACHEL'S DAYS FELL into a pattern, and she was careful to never let that pattern vary, finding an odd comfort in routine. She continued to attend the Impaired Physicians meetings. A couple of times she felt herself slipping. When that happened, when she began to crave a drug-blurred reality, she would head for the nearest door and walk out her depression.

She was going to make it. She wasn't going to be one of those women who moped through the days, whining about the men who'd left them. This time around, she was old enough to know that love didn't always mean security. It wasn't a promise of a lifetime together. Sometimes love had more to do with letting go than with hanging on.

Winter came and she survived it. On several occasions, she even enjoyed it. Mark talked her into joining a group of staff members who organized social events. They put on fund-raisers and hospital parties. They went Christmas caroling.

The last time Rachel had gone caroling, Jennifer had been with her. It had started to snow—huge flakes that had fallen from the night sky to melt on Jennifer's red cheeks.

It snowed this time too. And even though the flakes were small and the night wasn't as hushed, it was nice. A little like coming home after a long absence and finding that things hadn't changed all that much while you'd been away.

One evening Rachel decided to phone her mother.

It was hard to lift the receiver. Even harder to dial the number. And when her mother's voice came over the line, Rachel almost hung up. A year ago she would have. But now she didn't.

"It's me . . . Rachel."

She gripped the phone, listening to the silence at the other end.

Then she heard, "Rachel . . . h-how are you?"

They didn't talk about Jennifer. Instead, they discussed safe subjects, like work at the hospital and some of the people Rachel had gone to school with.

"Sara Grant," her mother said. "You remember her. She just joined the Peace Corps. I'll bet her suitcase was full of makeup and hairspray. I don't know what she'll do when she can't find an electrical outlet for her hot rollers. And Angela Sebastian—she quit her job at the courthouse to become a lifeguard somewhere in Arizona. Can you imagine what the sun will do to that freckled skin?"

Rachel smiled. "She'll have to wear lots of sun block."

It wasn't the same. Too much had passed between Rachel and her mother for their relationship to ever be the way it had been before. And there could be no starting over, no undoing what had happened. But Rachel was able to accept the fact that the cruel words her mother had spoken the day of Jennifer's funeral had been spoken out of grief. And Rachel, more than anyone, knew what grief could do to a person.

"I better let you go," Rachel said after a while.

"You'll call again?"

"Yes. I'll call again."

•   •   •

Spring came. The grass turned green. Lilacs bloomed and birds returned to build nests. Time passed. . . .

One night, as Rachel reached to turn off the light, her gaze was drawn to the *Des Moines Register* on her nightstand.

She'd had it only three days and already it was falling apart. She couldn't stop reading a certain article. By Sammy. Even though she practically had it memorized, she picked it up and read it again.

It had caused quite a stir at the hospital, with staff and patients alike. It seemed the feature story had first appeared in a small-town paper in Nevada, but after being spotted by the editor of the *Las Vegas Times*, it had been picked up and run by larger newspapers throughout the country.

It wasn't a political piece, or a controversial one. It was about everyday life and everyday people—special people. Sammy's writing sang. It was funny and sad, touching and honest, reflecting a warmth and deep respect for humanity.

He had truly come full circle . . . and then some.

She was so proud, so incredibly proud. . . . The ache of her love and pride lay like a weight in her chest and throat. Her blurred gaze fell to the bottom right-hand corner, to the author's bio.

Sammy Thoreau is the nationally renowned award-winning author of *Through the Looking Glass, A Soldier's View.* A former resident of La Grange, Iowa, he now resides in Paris, Nevada.

She folded the newspaper and turned off the light, then lay back to stare up into the darkness, waiting for sleep. Reading the article had brought Sammy near. If only she could let go . . . She must let go.

It seemed hours later when she finally began to drift off. She was almost asleep when something—a sound?—jerked her to full wakefulness. She listened intently, unable to decide what, if anything, had roused her. A rattle? Had she heard a rattle? It must have been a dream, her longing simply playing tricks on her.

Since Sammy had left, there had been times when Rachel had heard his laugh, or heard him shout her name. She would turn to look, a smile forming on her lips, and then she would remember that he was gone. At night she dreamed about him, and the dreams were so real that when she awoke she carried his presence in her heart and thoughts all through the day.

Even though she knew the sound she'd heard wasn't Sammy, she couldn't stop herself from looking.

She threw back the covers. Her bare feet made contact with the cool floor. Slowly, step by step, she made her way to the window. Standing to one side, she looked out, her eyes straining.

Nothing. Only the echo of her own yearning.

It was hard to believe that spring was almost over. Another Mother's Day had come and gone—and Rachel had survived it. No drinking, no oblivion, no days spent stumbling around in a sorrow-filled stupor.

She'd kept busy making plans for the upcoming fund-raising costume party to be held in the university gym. Jennifer had been in her thoughts, but instead of the memories being jagged-edged, they were bittersweet and cherished. The final acceptance of her loss gentled Rachel, making her feel both infinitely wise and infinitely fragile.

The day of the costume party eventually rolled around, leaving Rachel with only one problem. Mark. He refused to wear the clown suit she'd rented. Why was he being so obstinate? she wondered. He would make a wonderful clown, and he certainly was never one to pass up a party.

There were several hours left before the dance started. All she could do was hope he would change his mind.

The sun was going down when Sammy pulled into town, tired and smelling of exhaust fumes and grease. His bike had broken down on Interstate 80 somewhere between Lincoln and Omaha, Nebraska. He'd had to hitchhike to the nearest town, buy a new clutch, then hitchhike back. He'd lost eight hours in the process, but he'd kept on the road, spending the last 150 miles fighting highway hypnosis.

He needed a shower. He needed sleep, but more than that, he needed to see Rachel.

But when he got to her apartment, there was no answer to his knock.

He would have thought he was too tired for his heart rate to increase, but it did. Panic thumped in his chest. Where was she? Had she moved? Had she met and married some rich doctor?

Was she all right?

What should he do? Wait on the step until she came home? Stop by the hospital?

Was he too late?

Was this one of those situations where you could never go back home?

He'd gone without sleep too long, he decided. His thoughts were a confused jumble. He ended up hopping back on his bike and driving to Mark's. Thank God *he* was home.

"I can't wear this damn thing," Mark said after they'd finished with their back-pounding greetings. "Rachel had this notion that I'd make a great clown," he explained. "But I don't do clowns. I tried to talk her into trading me her Peter Pan outfit, but she wouldn't do it."

It was the first time Sammy had ever seen Mark look scared. He had always thought of Mark as fearless. Funny, the things that upset people.

Sammy snatched the bundle of red, white, and blue material. "I'll wear it." If Rachel wanted a clown, she'd get a clown.

It took him ten minutes to shower and dress, another ten to master the costume with its ruffled collar and red pompoms that ran from chin to crotch. He checked the mirror. His hair was too long, his eyes bloodshot, and he hadn't shaved for five days.

He pulled on the curly orange wig and stuck on the rubber nose. Not much of an improvement. He seemed like a cross between a hung-over Emmett Kelly and a homicidal maniac.

"You look great!" Mark said. "Much better than I would have."

"I look the same as you would have looked, only taller."

"No, *no*. You give the whole thing a certain, I don't know, call it flair."

"Thanks," Sammy said wryly. Until now, he hadn't realized how much he'd missed Mark's high energy.

Killer ambled in, took one look at Sammy, hissed, and ricocheted out of the room, breaking the speed of light as he went.

"That's one weird cat," Sammy said.

"They say pets often take on their masters' characteristics. I'm hoping that will eventually happen and he'll calm down."

After a cup of Mark's thick coffee, Sammy was back on his bike. He was having a little trouble. The ruffle on his sleeve snagged on the brake lever, and his floppy shoes got caught under the gearshift mechanism. Since he was wearing sneakers, too, he finally ended up kicking off the clown shoes and handing them to Mark.

Pretty soon he was tooling down Broadway and doing fine until he had to stop at a red light. He looked to his left and found the elderly couple in the car next to him staring.

The passenger window was open. Sammy revved the bike, bounced a little on the seat, and said, "Underneath this I'm naked."

They turned away. Some people had no sense of humor.

In five minutes he was rolling into the parking lot of the university gym. The deep reverberation of rock music shook the air. He could see people strolling in and out of the main entrance; a square of light illuminated the sidewalk each time the door opened and closed.

When he stepped inside, the overwhelming combination of heat, noise, and wall-to-wall people hit him all at once.

How was he going to find Rachel in this mess?

He made the mistake of looking for her among the nondancers. He should have gone directly to the dance floor, because that's where he finally spotted her. And when he did, his heart did a flipflop.

She made a perfect Peter Pan with her short cap of blond hair and tiny figure. And she was dancing and laughing and having a good time.

Without him.

Was he too late?

He waited until the band played a slow song, then he

cut through the crowd. Off to his left, a guy dressed like one of the Blues Brothers was moving directly toward Rachel. Sammy increased his pace, garnering some well-earned dirty looks in the process.

"Excuse me," he said, coming up behind her and speaking in her ear. He was certain his heart was going to explode, it was pumping so fast. "I couldn't get a polar bear suit. How would you feel about dancing with a clown?"

She turned—very, very slowly.

The deafening noise in the gym faded. It was one of those suspended moments in time, when nothing else and nobody else existed.

"Clowns are okay. It's Woodsy Owl I always try to avoid." She made a choking sound. "*Sammy*—"

And then he was holding her to him, and it was the most wonderful feeling in the world. He didn't care if the room was loud and crowded and hot. He didn't care if he'd always hated the song that was playing. Suddenly it was the best song in the world. Suddenly the words had a whole new meaning, a whole new depth.

Over the months he'd learned that his obsession with the past wasn't all that unique. Even without memory loss, others felt its pull just as strongly. But for Sammy, the pull of the present had proven stronger. Maybe if he'd never met Rachel, things would have been different. Maybe things would have worked for him and Mary Dawn. But he *had* met Rachel. She was a part of his life. His *present* life.

The time he'd spent in Nevada with Mary Dawn had been a revelation. He was the same person he used to be, and yet he wasn't. His accident and everything that had happened to him since had changed him in subtle ways he'd never be able to understand.

But he knew he needed Rachel. And he prayed that she still needed him.

The slow dance was over, and the music changed to a heavy metal number. "We have to talk," he shouted.

She nodded.

He took her hand and cut a path through the crowd, moving toward a side door marked exit.

Once outside, night air cooled hot skin. The closed door muffled the party sounds. Rachel watched as Sammy pulled off his wig and nose, then stuffed them into his pocket.

The temperature was hovering near the seventies, but suddenly she was cold. What was Sammy doing here? She didn't want to get hurt again.

"Rachel, I—"

Behind them the door opened, letting out a blast of rock music and a crowd of laughing people.

Sammy cast a glance over his shoulder. "Let's go for a walk."

They headed down the sidewalk to a street lined with maple trees and two-story brick houses.

They moved in silence for a while, and Rachel had the feeling that Sammy was using the time to get his thoughts together. He pulled in a deep breath. "While I was gone, I looked up some old buddies of mine," he said. "I found them in a bar, half lit at three in the afternoon. All they could talk about was the good old days, as if their lives had ended after high school. The memories of their past were weighing them down."

He stopped, and Rachel stopped. "The past is the past," he said. "A person can't go back because everything that has happened in between changes the whole picture."

What was he saying?

He put a trembling hand to her cheek. "I thought I was empty before, but it was nothing compared to living day after day without you."

Her throat tightened. She could feel tears coming. "You broke my heart."

"I'm sorry, Rachel. I wish I could take away the pain I've caused you. And I'm sorry I left, but it was something I had to do."

He had done so much for her. He had healed her. His love had made her strong—but not strong enough. "I was getting better," she said. "I was getting over you." She'd been pretending. She would never get over him. As long as she lived, she would never get over him.

"Should I go? If you want me to go, I will." His voice cracked. "It will hurt like hell, but I'll leave . . . if that's what you want."

He was standing there in his clown outfit, his hair sticking out and hanging over his ruffled collar, his eyes red, his face unshaven. He looked half angel, half rebel. Love for him flowed over her and through her, frightening in its intensity.

"I know something now that I didn't know last summer," he said. "My love for you isn't the love of a boy. It's not a quick-growing, infatuated love. It's an adult love. A grow-old-together love. A perfect love."

Perfect love? Was there such a thing? Was there really such a thing? She couldn't go through his leaving a second time. She knew she couldn't handle learning to live without him again.

"Rachel . . ."

He cradled her face in his hands, the brilliance of his soulful eyes burning into hers. In his face she saw a gentle wisdom she'd never seen there before.

"This time's for keeps."

She closed her eyes while a silent prayer of thanks flowed around her.

A child's voice drifted clear and sweet from the upstairs window of a nearby house. "Look, Mommy. There's a clown on our sidewalk."

"Get back in bed. What would a clown be doing out this time of night?"

"Maybe he lost something."

"Well, now he found it, so go to bed."

Rachel opened her eyes and smiled at Sammy.

He was back. And Rachel would believe he was here to stay because he'd said so . . . because she'd seen the depth of his love in his eyes . . . because the voice of a mother reassuring her child had echoed that promise.

A warm breeze stirred, and off in the distance a cricket chirped. Sammy took her hand, and side by side they walked.

And then he did something she'd never heard him do before. He began to whistle.

THIRTY

MOLLY STOOD IN THE KITCHEN WHILE A SOFT CONTENT-
ment wrapped itself around her.

It was almost time.

She'd just come from visiting Amy and Chris and
six-month-old Melinda, one of the sweetest, most beautiful babies Molly had ever seen, every bit as beautiful a
baby as Amy had been.

They were a family.

And Sammy was back—with Rachel, where he belonged.

Everything was complete.

Years ago Molly had quit thinking very deeply about
life. Because thinking deeply only caused sorrow. But
lately she'd been making up for all the time she'd spent
in limbo. Lately she'd been doing a lot of thinking and
she'd come to the conclusion that Sammy's accident had
been his salvation. It had given him a second chance,
something not many people got.

Molly was the only one who knew how Jay had died.
The old Sammy's tragic memory would be safe with her.
She would keep it locked deep in a secret place in her
heart, along with her lost dreams and lost love.

A second chance . . .

She looked out of the kitchen window and saw blue
sky beckoning to her through green leaves.

And she wondered what the weather was like in
Florida.

If you enjoyed *Forever,* be sure to watch for Theresa Weir's next heart-grabbing contemporary romance, *Last Summer,* on sale in August 1992 from FANFARE.

Set amid the glittering lights of Hollywood and the desert heat of Hope, Texas, *Last Summer* is the emotionally powerful tale of a bad-boy actor and the beautiful widow who tames his heart. Johnnie Irish has a wild reputation. Driven out of his hometown, Hope, he finds instant success in the movies and makes headlines with his outlandish behavior. But no one knows of his devastating illness—diabetes—and the daily insulin shots he must give himself. When circumstances force him to return to Hope, he has revenge in mind. But then he meets local resident Maggie Mayfield, and all thoughts of getting even disappear with the awakening of desire. . . .

In the following excerpt, Johnnie sets foot in Hope for the first time in fifteen years, and Maggie gets her first glimpse of the man she's sure she won't like.

Johnnie Irish adjusted his dark, wire-rimmed sunglasses, gave a nod to the pilot, then paused in the doorway of the charter plane.

Something had definitely been lost arriving by air, he decided. To get the full effect of Hope, Texas, a guy had to approach it by land. He had to cross miles and miles of desolate desert, tumbleweeds, and broken-down shanties. He had to see all the billboards bragging two-headed snakes and five-legged lambs.

As a teenager, Johnnie and some buddies had wandered into one of those roadside shacks. They'd plunked down a buck fifty only to discover that the snake was pickled and the lamb was stuffed. From the highly visible black stitches, they'd quickly decided that the freak appendage had been added by some myopic seamstress. Doubled up with laughter, tears streaming from their eyes, they'd been kicked out of the joint—which only made them laugh all the harder.

Johnnie had been kicked out of a lot of places since then. Bars, hotels. Restaurants.

Towns.

Hope, Texas, in particular.

Three months ago, when he'd gotten the phone call asking him to be the main attraction in Hope's homecoming parade, he'd laughed out loud, right into the receiver. But he'd been harboring a bitterness toward his hometown for a long time, and wouldn't revenge be sweet? So, fifteen years after being tossed out on his ass, he'd decided to come back.

Desert wind, not yet heated by the day, felt good against his skin. He'd forgotten how clear and un-tainted the air was here. He took a moment to pull it deep into his lungs.

He could see the promised car waiting for him—the parade convertible. Standing beside it, shading her eyes with one hand, was a dark-haired woman. For a second panic thumped in his chest while his mind spun backward to his childhood and all its horrors. For a second, he thought the woman was his mother; then his head cleared and he remembered she was dead. He let out his breath in relief.

Maggie Mayfield watched as Johnnie Irish stepped from the plane. They had agreed to meet here, at the private airstrip in order to keep his arrival place secret.

Even from a distance she could see that his hair was too long, his jeans too faded. They weren't the kind of jeans that had been made to look old. These *were* old. They'd most likely been purchased dark blue, but through the years they had conformed and faded to the contours of his body until they were a part of him. Besides the decrepit jeans, he was wearing a red and white baseball jacket and leather high top sneakers.

She thought of all the ruffles and patent leather waiting along the parade route and felt a stab of irritation. He could have at least dressed up a little.

Right from the start, she'd been against inviting Johnnie Irish to their community. Hope was surrounded by mile after mile of desert. To the south, the nearest town was forty-five miles away. It boasted a movie theater and a Piggly Wiggly. To the north was Chester, some sixty miles away. Its only building was a combined tavern and gas station.

There was no fast lane in Hope, Texas. Sure, the kids drank, and Maggie knew that drugs had filtered their way into town. That kind of thing was everywhere. But she'd like to think it wasn't nearly as bad here as other places.

So why had they rolled out the red carpet to welcome the very type of person they prided themselves in being without? Why had they invited Johnnie Irish into their midst when he was the embodiment of everything they didn't want in their town? The man stood for drugs and sex and alcohol. He was known for his loud, drunken parties and his flagrant disregard for the law and other people's property. In short, he was a bad example—the *worst* example for their young people—and she'd told the town council so.

"It isn't every town that can brag that they helped raise a movie star," George Bailey had argued.

"And think of the money he'll bring in," Mabel

French had added. "Think of the excitement, the life! We need some excitement and life in Hope."

In the end they'd taken a vote and Maggie had lost six to one. And since she was the head of the parade committee, she now had the dubious honor of escorting their guest into town.

She watched as he bounded down the steps toward her, watched as a lizard skittered in front of him, across the cracked cement to disappear behind a tumbleweed.

Maggie had never had the desire to see a Johnnie Irish movie. Screwball comedies didn't appeal to her. Not that she was against silliness. She just preferred deeper, more meaningful stories. But she'd seen a lot of magazine photos of him, plus interviews on a couple of morning shows. Enough to be prepared for Johnnie Irish's celebrity arrogance and celebrity good looks. She was even prepared in case he decided to turn his lady-killer charm in her direction—not that she thought he would. She wasn't his type. She was too flat, too straight up and down. Too plain.

From interviews she knew his voice would be deep and bluesy, with just a hint of a drawl left from his Hope, Texas, days. She knew that his body and face would be fascinatingly perfect.

Well, not mannequin perfect, or classically perfect. No, not classical. But then classical didn't make a woman's pulse quicken. Dangerous. Dangerous was what made a woman's pulse quicken.

From a certain angle, his nose appeared a little crooked, most likely broken in a fight. He was always getting into fights. Beneath dark, slashing brows his eyes were as blue as the Texas sky, but not as clear. There was something in them . . . something secretive. Maybe a holding back . . . or maybe a seductive promise. . . .

But she'd always figured that the camera was kind to him. Some people just photographed well. Nobody could really *look* like that.

But now, as the distance between them closed, she discovered that the camera hadn't done him justice. And with dismay, she found herself falling victim to his looks just like one of her starstruck high school students. For the first time in years, she actually regretted the flatness of her chest.

He was a few yards away when her brain went comatose. She could feel her knees begin to tremble, her heart begin to pound in her ears.

And then he was there, standing in front of her, the rounded toes of his sneakers lined up opposite her leather taupe pumps. She looked up. She couldn't see his eyes. She hated talking to someone who was wearing dark glasses. Worse yet were glasses with mirrors where all you saw was a distorted image of yourself.

As she fumbled in her mind, trying to dredge up her practiced words of greeting, her hair whipped across her mouth. She pulled back the lank strands, holding them at her neck with one hand. "I'm Maggie Mayfield. Welcome to Hope!" How eloquent. And it really wasn't Hope at all. They were ten miles from Hope.

"Hope." He braced his hands on his hips and cast a leisurely glance around at the stark, desert landscape.

Nothing but sand and sky, scrub pine and yucca . . . and goatheads that stuck to the soles of your shoes. He rocked on his heels. "A nothing town in the middle of one giant litterbox."

This wasn't going at all like she'd imagined. What a perfectly horrid thing to say. Not exactly the words she'd expected. Certainly not the words she'd relay to the *Hope Chronicle* when they interviewed her tomorrow. But his opening comment had been good for one thing. Her knees stopped knocking and the roaring in her head ceased. Her brief, starstruck moment was over. And now that her eyes were no longer clouded, she could see that Johnnie Irish was a little lax in the grooming department. What she had at first mistaken as carefully cultivated *Miami Vice* stubble, was actually no more than wino neglect. And sure it was windy, but his hair looked as if he'd raked his fingers through it about a million times. And was that alcohol she smelled? Was the star of their homecoming parade drunk?

Maggie wasn't a native of Hope. She and her husband, Steven, had moved here for his health, but Maggie had quickly grown fond of the little town. Even after Steven's death she had stayed on. And now she couldn't help but jump to Hope's defense. "How can you talk that way about a town that helped shape who you are now?"

He shoved his hands in the front pockets of his jeans and looked down the highway that led to Hope, Texas. "That's why I *can* talk that way," he mumbled, more to himself than to her . . . or maybe he was speaking to the town itself. "I've got a right."

She didn't understand. Once again she thought about all the excited, expectant people waiting along Main Street. She thought about their months of preparation and how the whole town had gotten into the spirit of things. She thought about the huge banners draped across the street:

HOPE WELCOMES JOHNNIE IRISH.
JOHNNIE IRISH DAY.
WELCOME HOME, JOHNNIE IRISH.

What a slap in the face.

People had come hours early just to get a good spot. At this very moment they were standing near curbs, waiting, a camera in one hand, the colorful confetti they'd spent latenight hours shredding and cutting in the other.

They were waiting to welcome home a hero, not some overgrown brat hurling out insults instead of smiles.

"This whole thing will take an hour, tops," she told him, her voice loud and clear. "All you have to do is wave and smile. When the parade is over, we'll put you in a car and whisk you back to your plane."

He moved past her, reaching for the driver's door. "Okay then. Let's go do it."

"Oh no you don't." She cut in front of him, guarding Cora Stevenson's classic Caddy. "I drive," she said, her gaze never wavering from his dark glasses.

She had the feeling that the eyes behind them were scanning her quite thoroughly. She didn't like the sensation. Now she was glad she hadn't given in to the urge to conceal her nose freckles with makeup or have her hair done. She certainly didn't want him to get the wrong idea and think she'd taken any extra care over her appearance for him.

"I don't remember you," he said with bluntness. "You from Hope?"

"No. I moved here a few years ago. But even if I'd always lived here, I doubt you would have remembered me. I'm sure we would have run in different circles."

One side of his sensual mouth turned up and he nodded slightly, as if agreeing. He took off his glasses, and now she could see why he'd chosen to wear the dark lenses in the first place. To hide the condition of his eyes—which a generous dose of red-chasing eyedrops wouldn't begin to cure. She thought of an apt description for the *Chronicle. The bright red of his jacket perfectly matched his eyes.*

And yet her sarcasm was tempered with something else—irritation, possibly. What made a person so self-destructive? Did he think so little of himself? Or was he just too caught up in the fast lane to stop?

"I know how we can settle this," he said. "We'll do the rock, paper, scissor thing. You win—you drive. I win—I drive. Ready? One, two—"

She just stood there, staring at him.

"Come on," he coaxed, a fist held out between them. "You know how to play, don't you?"

"Of course I do!" This was too ridiculous.

"One—"

Grudgingly she put her fist beside his.

He smiled. "Two. Three!"

His fist remained closed, hers open. He was rock, she was paper.

He flashed her another ornery grin and shrugged. "That crazy paper."

"Yeah," she agreed a little feebly, feeling somewhat bemused. "That crazy paper."

She wasn't really conscious of movement, but suddenly she was sliding behind the Cadillac's huge steering wheel. She started the engine, then maneuvered the boat of a car onto the deserted highway, cringing when the tires squealed as she took off. It wasn't her fault. She wasn't used to driving anything with power.

Her passenger let out a taunting laugh. "Sure you don't want me to drive?"

"No thanks. I want to live long enough to spot Elivs working at the local A&W."

He laughed again. Who was the comedian here, anyway? And what had gotten into her? She was never sarcastic.

He leaned forward and flipped on the radio, spinning the dial through several stations until he came to one he was apparently searching for. Then he settled back in the seat while rock music vibrated in the dash and the wild wind whipped their hair about their heads.

"Who took the horny toad queen this year?" he yelled over the noise of the wind and the radio.

She had no answer for that, so she pretended not to hear him.

"Becky May was so honored, last I knew. It was actually a toss-up between her and Selma Johnson.

They both spent quite a bit of their senior year on their backs."

He was as incorrigible as some of her students.

"Phil Ferguson still live around here?"

"He's a car salesman at the Chevrolet dealership."

"No kidding? I always figured he'd end up discovering a cure for the common cold or something. Don't get me wrong. Phil was an okay guy. Kind of a pencil neck, but okay. Now his old man was another story altogether. Kicked me out of Hope High."

"What a surprise," Maggie drawled.

"He still principal?"

"Yes."

"The world keeps turning, but old Hopeless just stays the same."

"Sometimes it's all right to stay the same. Why change a good thing?"

He shut off the radio, then turned toward her, his left arm draped across the back of the seat. "Humans need variety or else their brains stagnate. What do you do for excitement? For a buzz?"

She could tell him that she liked to watch sunrises and sunsets and the stars at night. She liked to play piano in a big empty room, but those were joys, not the thrill seeking he was talking about. "I don't feel the need for a buzz. I'm content."

"You're stagnant."

It was pointless. He was too mixed up to understand, and that made her feel a little sorry for him.

They stopped at the edge of town so he could take his place on the back of the car, his feet in the seat.

"Smile and wave," Maggie told him. "That's all you have to do."

He smiled and waved, demonstrating his remarkable skill. At that moment, she could easily understand how he'd managed to charm the pants off so many women. Lucky for her, she was immune to that sort of thing.

She put the car in gear. In another hour, she promised herself, this would all be over.

They had decided to put their town star near the middle of the parade, behind the Hope High marching band and directly in front of cute as a button Susie Mapes and her twirling baton.

Getting into place was only a matter of edging into the opening that had been left for them. Maggie had the Cadillac in line just minutes before the police siren wailed, announcing the start of the parade.

She let out a pent-up breath. Everything was going like clockwork.

The band, comprised of horns and drums, played a most peculiar rendition of *Hey Jude*, then went on to *You Are the Sunshine of My Life*. The band instructor was new to Hope High, and it was her belief that the kids were happier playing top forty tunes. The problem was that top forty didn't translate well to horns and drums.

The parade went smoothly, with waves of clapping and much confetti tossing. Occasionally Maggie would glance over her shoulder to find her passenger behaving. He'd put his sunglasses back on and he was smiling and waving, just like he'd promised.

They were almost to the half-way point—Clark's Drugstore—when from the vicinity of the backseat and very near her ear, came the metallic sound of a pop-top being opened, followed by a hissing fizz.

She looked over her shoulder. Johnnie Irish had his head tilted back, elbow high, guzzling down a beer.

What happened next was strictly reflex. Maggie forgot all about the manual transmission while she slammed on the brakes. The car shuddered and bucked and died. Johnnie Irish let out a curse. His hands flailed. Beer sloshed. Then he disappeared over the trunk.

Time seemed to crawl and fly all at once. Maggie fumbled for the latch, shouldered open the door, then realized the car was rolling backward. She slammed down her foot on the brake pedal, at the same time remembering to turn off the ignition and pull out the emergency brake . . . all the while praying that she hadn't run over Johnnie Irish.

She found him sprawled on his back, half under the car's huge chrome bumper, mouth open, eyes closed.

Out cold.

Susie Mapes was standing nearby, clutching her baton, her eyes huge, the tassles on her white boots trembling.

In the distance, a few wobbly notes of *Take A Letter, Maria,* could be heard drifting on the air. As the solo performer most likely realized something was amiss, the notes died.

Maggie crouched down at Johnnie's side. "Don't try to move," she told him.

The words had barely left her mouth when he tried to lever himself up on both elbows, winced, put a hand to the back of his head, then sank to the ground, his face pale. "You're one helluva driver, Maggie May," he gasped.

Just when she was feeling major guilt, when she was feeling that this fiasco was all her fault, something beside him caught her eye.

A syringe.

Luckily her back was to the crowd that was rapidly gathering behind them. She scooped up the syringe, hiding it against her palm and wrist—not for Johnnie's sake, but the town's.

"I think you lost something." She pressed the capped and loaded syringe against his hand—which curled around it with familiarity.

"My fix," he mumbled, relief in his voice. "Thanks."

He could hardly move, but somehow—most likely from habit—he managed to effectively pocket the needle inside his jacket.

Up until that point, in spite of everything Maggie knew about Johnnie Irish, in spite of everything he'd said and done, she had kind of liked him. But now she felt a keen sense of disappointment, and more than a little sorrow.

All her life, she'd been guilty of giving people false nobilities. There was a danger in that, because she'd fooled herself many times. She'd imagined people the way she'd wanted them to be, not the way they really were. And she had started to do the same with Johnnie. Because he was so good-looking, because he had charmed her with his ornery smile, she had begun to hope he was more than what he seemed. But she should have known better. Celebrities weren't like real people. Aside from the booze and drugs, acting messed them up somehow. It made them so they couldn't tell the difference between what was real and what wasn't.

Behind her, Maggie could hear Susie—who before today had been one of Johnnie Irish's biggest fans—trying to explain what had happened. Her voice was teary and breathless and full of shocked disbelief. "He splashed beer in my hair, and he said the F word. . . ."

Maggie sat back on her heels. "I think we better have the ambulance swing by."

Above her, the welcome banner billowed and filled with air, the enlarged letters mocking her and the town.

WELCOME HOME, JOHNNIE IRISH.

Welcome home, indeed.

On the ground, Johnnie Irish moaned and said, "I think I'm gonna puke."